ROSIE HENDRY

SECRETS AND PROMISES

Complete and Unabridged

MAGNA
Leicester

First published in Great Britain in 2021

First Ulverscroft Edition
published 2022

*A catalogue record for this book is available
from the British Library.*

ISBN 978–0–7505–4983–7

1

Norfolk — July, 1944

Bessie Rushbrook pressed harder on her bicycle pedals, riding up and over the steep railway bridge, then steered sharp right into the station yard. She braked and jumped off, then leaned her bike against a wall near a row of tomato plants. The splash of red ripening tomatoes replaced the colourful flowers that had once flourished there before the days of Dig for Victory.

Catching her breath, Bessie smoothed down her silver threaded blonde hair, tucking away a few strands which had escaped the roll at the nape of her neck, and checked her hat was straight.

'Evening, Bessie.' The voice startled her. She turned and saw the stationmaster standing in the booking hall doorway. 'You here to meet the Norwich train?'

'That's right.'

She walked towards him. 'Is it running late?'

'A few minutes, could be worse.' He pulled out a fob watch from his waistcoat pocket and checked the time.

Bessie knew he'd happily talk until the train arrived, but she wasn't in the mood for idle chatter tonight. 'I'll go through and wait for it.' She gave him a quick smile and walked in, through the booking hall, and out onto the platform.

Pacing up and down, Bessie's thoughts turned to Grace's letter. Its arrival last week had been a shock.

1

She hadn't heard from her for ten years and knew nothing about Grace's life in London, her marriage, or even that she had an eight-year-old daughter, Marigold. Then, out of the blue, Grace had asked for her help, hoping she'd give her child a home away from the latest danger terrorising London. Bessie and her husband, Harry, had said yes. There'd been no hesitation. Bessie hoped that looking after Marigold would be a chance to close the wide gulf between herself and Grace.

The sound of an approaching train could be heard in the still evening air. By the time it slid under the railway bridge and came to a halt alongside the platform with a hiss of steam, Bessie's heart was thudding hard. She watched, dry-mouthed, as several doors opened, and a handful of passengers spilled out. There were some GIs returning to the nearby base, their exotic voices contrasting with those of the locals.

She spotted a young woman and a small girl climbing out of a carriage near the far end of the train, and knew it was them. The child looked so much like Grace had at that age, with the same long blonde hair worn in two plaits. Bessie stood unable to move, tears filling her eyes. But then she gathered herself together and hurried along the platform towards them.

'You must be Bessie?' The young woman held out her hand, smiling. 'I'm Helen MacDonald. I work with Grace.'

'Hello.' Bessie shook her hand.

'And this wee lass is Marigold.'

Bessie wished she could throw her arms around Marigold, hug her, and tell her who she was. It would help the child if she understood that she hadn't come to live with strangers, but with family. But Bessie couldn't do that, Grace had asked her not to reveal who she was, and she would stick to her promise, as she always did. Instead, she crouched down so that her eyes were level with the little girl's and smiled at her. 'Hello.'

Marigold eyed her cautiously, fiddling with the red ribbon on the end of one of her plaits. Bessie noticed her striking blue eyes, the colour of cornflowers, exactly like Grace's.

'Hello,' Marigold whispered.

The train's guard was shouting for passengers to get on board, slamming carriage doors shut as he made his way towards them.

'Have you got all your things? Suitcase? Gas mask?' Helen checked everything was there, and then put her arm around Marigold. 'I'm sure you'll be fine here with Bessie, it's much safer for you than in London.'

'It was good of you to bring her,' Bessie said. 'Thank you.'

'I was glad I could help. Right, I must get on board. It's nice to have met you.' Helen climbed into the carriage, closed the door behind her and stuck her head out of the open window. 'Grace sends you her best wishes and said to tell you she knows Marigold will be safe with you.'

'We'll take good care of her.'

The guard touched his hand to the front of his cap as he passed them. Reaching the end of the train, he raised his green flag and blew loudly on his whistle.

'Goodbye.' Helen waved as the train pulled out of the station, the engine belching out grey chuffs of smoke as it picked up speed.

Bessie waved back, watching until the train had rounded the bend and disappeared, leaving a sooty trace in the air and the platform empty except for the pair of them. Marigold stood quite still, staring down the line where the train had gone, and with it, Bessie thought, her last link with home. What must she be thinking and feeling? She didn't know Bessie, or who she was, only that she'd been left in a new place with a strange woman, miles from her mother and home. A wave of protectiveness surged through her.

'You must be tired,' Bessie said, gently. 'Let's get you home.' She picked up the suitcase and held out her hand.

Marigold hesitated for a moment before slipping her hand into Bessie's.

'I've brought my bicycle to carry your suitcase in,' Bessie explained, leading Marigold out through the booking hall. 'It's a trade-bike, so your case can go in the basket.'

With the suitcase stowed in the large wicker basket at the front of her bicycle, Bessie pushed it along with one hand and held on to Marigold's hand with her other.

'Have you been out of London before?' Bessie asked as they dawdled past the row of village shops.

Marigold shook her head.

'I expect it will seem strange to begin with, much quieter, but I'm sure you'll soon get used to it. I hope you'll enjoy living on our farm, we've got lots of animals. A calf was born just last week.'

Marigold didn't reply but appeared to be listening. If she'd rather not say anything for now, that was fine, Bessie thought; she could carry on doing the talking for both of them. It seemed better to talk than walk in silence, more friendly, but going at Marigold's slow pace, it was going to take a long time to get back.

'How about a ride in the bicycle basket along with your case?' Bessie suggested. 'It will give your legs a rest.' Marigold looked at the basket doubtfully. 'It's plenty big enough for you.'

Marigold considered for a few moments, then nodded in agreement.

Bessie leaned her bicycle against a wall. 'I'll lift you in.'

As she went to pick Marigold up, the sight of the child standing with her arms held out ready, made her catch her breath. It was as if the years had peeled back and she was about to lift a young Grace again. Only this wasn't Grace, Bessie reminded herself, but Marigold, Grace's daughter. Swallowing down the wave of emotion threatening to overwhelm her, she scooped the little girl up and placed her in the basket. 'There you are.'

Marigold gingerly settled herself down, sitting on top of her case so only her head and shoulders could be seen above the high-sided basket.

'Is that all right?'

Marigold nodded, her hands gripping the sides.

'Off we go then.' Bessie took the weight of the bike and pushed it along, taking care to keep it level and give Marigold a smooth ride back to Orchard Farm.

As they rounded the last bend in the lane leading down to the farm, Bessie spotted twelve-year-old Peter, who lived with them, sitting on top of the gate. His chestnut brown hair gleamed in the evening sunshine.

'Look! Peter's waiting for us.'

Bessie had told Marigold about him and everyone else who lived at the farm as she'd wheeled her along.

Peter jumped down and ran over to meet them,

skidding to a halt beside the bike.

'Hello, Marigold.' He smiled at her, his grey eyes warm and friendly. 'I'm Peter, welcome to Orchard Farm. I hope you'll be happy living here, it's a good place to live.'

'Hello,' Marigold mumbled.

'Shall I open the gate for you, Bessie?' he asked.

'Yes, please.'

She watched him hurry off, thinking how thoughtful it was of him to come out and wait for them. But then Peter knew what it was like to go and live somewhere new where you didn't know anyone.

2

Marigold stared at the house; she'd never seen anything like it before. It was nothing like her own home in a terrace, one of a line of identical houses in the street. She lived at number sixteen with her mother in the upstairs half, while Mrs Fox, their landlady, had the downstairs. This house was low, like a bungalow, with lots of windows along the side and was painted a bottle green colour.

'It's made from two old railway carriages.' Bessie pointed to the different parts. 'With an extension built on at the back to make it bigger.'

Marigold could see the shape of the carriages, lined up end to end, like the ones she'd travelled here from London in. There was still the outline of the doors along the side, but instead of seeing seats and compartments through the windows, there were curtains and glimpses of rooms inside. They had built a wide roof over the carriages, extending out further like the brim of a hat. It was a funny house, but cosy looking.

Bessie led her up a short flight of wooden steps, then in through a door at the end of the extension part and into a small porch. Here, there were coats hung up on a row of hooks and boots lined up underneath. Peter came behind them, carrying her case.

'Everyone's looking forward to meeting you.' Bessie opened an inner door and walked inside. 'Here we are, then.'

Marigold followed her but halted at the sight of three more strangers. She reached out and slipped her hand into Bessie's, who squeezed it back.

'This is my husband, Harry.'

The man sitting in the armchair by the stove got to his feet and limped over to them.

'Hello, there.' He smiled at her, making the corners of his blue eyes crinkle up. 'Welcome to Orchard Farm.'

'Hello,' Marigold said.

'And this is Dottie and Prune.' Peter introduced the two young women over by the sink, washing up. 'Dottie's the shortest with blonde hair and Prune's the tall, dark-haired one. They're Timber Jills working up in the woods.'

'Hello.' They both smiled at her.

Marigold did her best to smile back. 'Hello.'

'Come and sit down.' Bessie led Marigold over to the table. 'I'll get you something to eat. Peter, will you put Marigold's case in her room, please?'

Sitting at the table, Marigold watched as Bessie cut slices off a loaf of bread, buttered them, then spread raspberry jam on top; she hadn't seen this much butter being put on bread for a long time. At home, they just had a scrape of margarine.

'Is there any spare for me?' Peter sat down opposite Marigold, smiling at Bessie, his grey eyes hopeful.

Bessie laughed and handed them each a plate of bread and jam and a cup of creamy milk. 'I knew you'd be hungry too.'

'What, again? Peter is always hungry, Marigold!' Dottie dried her hands and came over to the table, where she wrapped her arms around his shoulders and kissed his cheek. 'It's lucky for him he lives on a farm where food's not in such short supply, otherwise, he'd eat an entire week's rations in one go!'

Peter grinned at Dottie and tucked in.

Marigold stared down at her own slice of bread and jam. It was different from what she'd eat at home, richer and more colourful. She picked it up and as she raised it to her lips, the smell of rich yeasty bread hit her, and her mouth watered. When she bit into it, the tang of sweet raspberries combined with creamy butter mingled on her tongue. She chewed slowly, savouring every delicious morsel.

'I'm going to check on the cows.' Harry took his cap off a peg by the door. 'You'll be able to meet them tomorrow, Marigold. You can have a go at milking if you like.'

She stopped chewing and stared at Harry. Before today, she'd never even seen a cow, but earlier, they'd passed some on the train. They looked scary with their pointy horns. Marigold wasn't sure she wanted to go anywhere near a cow, let alone milk one.

'Have you ever milked a cow?' Prune asked.

Marigold shook her head. Did they expect her to milk a cow?

Peter put down the cup he'd drained. 'The cows are lovely and very gentle. Beautiful Jerseys with big brown eyes and toffee-coloured fur.'

Bessie laid a hand on Marigold's shoulder. 'Don't you worry, it can all wait until tomorrow. You must be tired, so eat up and then we'll get you to bed.'

* * *

Half an hour later, Marigold lay snuggled up with Blue, her toy rabbit, hugged in her arms. She breathed in the faint smell of home on his soft fur. Closing her eyes, she pretended she was back there in her own bed, with her mother nearby in the living room after returning from her work at the hospital. Everything was normal and as it should be.

Marigold's eyes snapped open. She wasn't at home — that was miles and miles away. Her throat tightened and she started to cry. She didn't want to come here and had told her mother so many times, but she wouldn't listen.

Why couldn't she stay at home? she'd kept asking. They had lived through the Blitz when the bombs had rained down, night after night, while they'd slept deep down in the Underground. Her mother didn't send her away then. Marigold could have been evacuated at the start of the war. Lots of her friends from school had gone, but she'd stayed at home.

So why did she have to leave now? Her mother had explained that it was because of Hitler's doodlebugs. The rockets which came buzzing through the air like angry wasps. They made everyone stop and hold their breaths, listening for the engine to cut out. Then you waited. Hoping and praying it would miss you, waiting for the roar and flash to come from somewhere else. Then you knew you'd survived. That time. But no one knew when they'd come next or where they'd fall. After what had happened to Daddy, her mother said she couldn't risk losing Marigold. It was too dangerous for her to stay in London now.

So then shouldn't her mother leave too? What if a rocket fell on her? Marigold shuddered at the thought and hugged Blue tighter. She could have left with Marigold, but she'd said she had to stay in London and do her job because they needed nurses now more than ever. Her mother couldn't even take time off work to bring Marigold to Norfolk herself. She'd had to travel with her mother's friend, Mrs MacDonald, who was coming here to visit her husband in the RAF.

Marigold's tears soaked into Blue's fur as she clung to him. She'd never been this far from home before, or even stayed with anyone else except her parents and Mrs Fox, but now she was here with strangers. Her mother knew them and said they were good, kind people who'd look after her well, but they weren't her mother and where they lived, wasn't her home. And it never would be.

★ ★ ★

'She's fast asleep, curled up with her toy rabbit.' Bessie slipped into bed beside Harry. 'She's worn out, poor little mite.'

'Being evacuated is hard,' Harry said.

'I hope she'll soon settle in and feel like it's her home.' Bessie paused for a moment. 'What do you think of her?'

'She's just like her mother to look at . . . when I first saw her . . .' Harry's eyes met Bessie's.

'I knew what you were thinking from the look on your face. I thought the same thing when I saw her at the station.' Tears filled her eyes. 'I wanted to hug her . . . but I couldn't.'

Harry opened his arms, and Bessie snuggled up to him, resting her head on his chest. 'We've got to respect Grace's wishes and not tell Marigold who we are, even if it's not what we'd want. At least Marigold's safe here with us, and now we've got the chance to get to know her.'

Bessie sighed. 'But it's not the same though, is it? Her not knowing about us.'

'It's not as it should be, Bess, it's as it is. Try not to worry about it and hopefully she'll know one day.' He stroked her arm. 'Marigold's got the chance to get to know us for ourselves and that will count for something, make it easier for her if Grace ever tells her the truth.'

'I'm glad Grace turned to us again. It can't have been easy for her to send her daughter away. Things must be bad in London.'

Harry sighed. 'We never thought we'd have to go through it again, not after last time, and here we are again, the world torn up with fighting.'

'And George is out there somewhere in France.' Bessie shuddered. 'Please God, he makes it through and comes back.'

'He will, Bess, he will. Wouldn't it be grand if we had them all home again? George, Grace and Marigold too. We've got to hope it will happen one day.'

3

London

Grace hesitated on the front step. Now she was home, it would hit her that Marigold had gone, leaving a gaping hole where she used to be. Her daughter wouldn't be tucked up in bed asleep as she usually was when Grace got home from a late shift. There'd be no warm arms around her neck in the morning because Marigold was now miles away from here . . . but in a safer place.

'Is that you, dear? Come on through and I'll make you some tea.'

Grace was glad to hear her landlady's voice and closed the door behind her.

Ada Fox had already poured the tea by the time Grace had taken off her coat and gone through into the old lady's cosy living room.

'Thanks, Ada.' Grace sat down at the table and warmed her hands around her cup.

'I thought you could do with it after a long shift at the hospital, and then coming home to the . . .' She waved her hand in the air. 'The silence. I can feel Marigold's not here. The old house seems empty without her, and I'm going to miss looking after her while you're at work. She's been a right little ray of sunshine in my life.'

Grace reached out and patted Ada's veiny hand. 'I know. I've kept myself extra busy at work, so I didn't have to think about it, but coming back here . . .' She

13

sighed. 'I had no choice, but to send her away. If she was hurt, or . . .' Her voice caught and she paused to compose herself, 'killed by a doodlebug, I'd never have forgiven myself. She's all I've got left after losing John.'

She chewed her bottom lip. This war had already robbed her of her husband, leaving her a widow at twenty-nine. She would not risk her daughter's life now Hitler was aiming these new weapons at London.

'You did the right thing.' Ada clasped Grace's hand. 'What's a bit of us missing her . . . compared with knowing she's safe and out of harm's way? She'll come home when it's all over, you wait and see.'

Grace nodded. 'Marigold will be safe in Norfolk with Bessie and Harry. I know they'll look after her well.'

'You're lucky you knew them to send her there. It's better than her going away to live with complete strangers like most children have to.'

'Marigold's never met them, though.'

'But *you* know them and are sure she'll be fine with them. That security is a lot more than most mothers have; they've had to send their children off into the unknown, not knowing where they'd end up or who with.'

'I know, you're right, Ada, but she sobbed so hard this morning at the station. I nearly said she didn't have to go, but I *had* to send her.' Her voice wobbled again. 'I had no choice. I'm going to miss her so much.'

'I know, ducks, but you can go to see her when you get a bit of leave.'

'One day.' Grace smiled tearfully. 'Not for a while though, she'll need time to get used to being away. If

I go too soon, it might unsettle her.'

But it wasn't only the risk of unsettling Marigold that would stop her going, Grace thought. It was far more complicated than that. If she went to see Marigold, it would mean returning to the place she'd ran from, the place she'd been too ashamed to go back to when things went wrong.

Bessie and Harry were welcoming Marigold to their home, but would they be happy to have Grace back in their lives again after what she did?

'I'll write to her often, it will make her feel closer and I'm sure it will please Marigold to get letters.'

Ada smiled. 'Remember, she'll be missing you, too. Send her my love and tell her I'll write to her soon.' She nodded towards Grace's cup. 'Come on, drink your tea before it goes cold.'

4

Norfolk

The thrumming of engines seeped into Marigold's dreams and through the fog of sleepiness, she wasn't sure if they were only in her mind . . . or real. Then her instinct kicked in. They were definitely real. Marigold woke with a start, her heart racing as the air above the house throbbed with the noise of planes. They were about to be bombed. She shrieked and leapt out of bed, yanking the curtain aside and darting out into the living room.

'Bessie!' Marigold rushed over to the sink where she was drying the dishes. 'The bombers have come. We must get to the shelter.'

'It's all right.' Bessie laid her hands on Marigold's shoulders. 'You're shaking!'

'We need to go. Now!' She grabbed Bessie's hand and started tugging her towards the door.

'Hold on! It's only the American planes taking off, not enemy bombers. They're late leaving this morning.'

Marigold's body sagged with relief, and tears flooded her eyes and trickled down her cheeks.

'You're safe here.' Bessie drew her into her arms and hugged her.

Marigold rested her head against Bessie's flowery apron. 'I thought we were going to be bombed — like we are at home.'

'Enemy bombers rarely come here, that's why your

16

mother knows it's safer for you.' Bessie gently brushed strands of hair out of Marigold's face. 'We're all glad you're here. Peter was saying so at breakfast.'

Marigold looked around the room. She'd been in such a panic; she hadn't noticed only Bessie was here. 'Where is he?'

'Gone to school. You were exhausted last night, so I left you to sleep in. Dottie and Prune are off working in the woods and Harry's outside somewhere. You'll see them all later. Are you hungry?'

She nodded.

'I'll make you some porridge. You can have some honey in it, from Harry's bees, if you like. Sit yourself down, it won't take long.'

'Thank you.' Marigold sat down at the table, glad to be off her legs, which were shaky with relief that it hadn't been enemy bombers.

The honey tasted of sunshine and flowers. Marigold scooped up another spoonful, dipped it into the golden pool in the middle of her porridge, then popped it into her mouth. It was warm, sweet and delicious.

'Do you like it?' Bessie asked as she kneaded dough at the other end of the table.

'It's lovely.'

They fell into a comfortable silence as she ate her breakfast and Bessie worked on the dough, stretching and pulling it, folding and kneading.

Marigold looked around the room as she ate, thinking how different this was to her home in London. It had no upstairs, the only steps being the ones leading up to the front and back doors. She'd been down the back ones when Bessie had taken her to the lavatory last night. There was no indoor bathroom here, only an outside lavatory in a little brick hut, where there was a wooden seat with a hole in it and a bucket underneath, and no chain to pull. She'd been frightened she was going to fall in.

'When you've finished your porridge, go and get dressed and then I'll show you around.' Bessie divided the dough and gently laid the portions in two loaf tins. 'I need to put these to rise and clear up, and then I'll be ready.'

Back in her room, Marigold dressed and did her hair, brushing it out carefully. As she wove it into two long plaits, tying the ends off with ribbons, she wondered what her mother would think of this strange house.

Marigold liked her room. It led off the large living room through an arched doorway which could be closed off with a curtain. There were two sets of windows, one looked outside and the other back into the living room, all hung with cream-coloured muslin curtains. Underneath the outside facing windows, there was a table on which stood a sewing machine. Her bed, with its pretty patchwork cover, was opposite, tucked in under the windows, facing inwards.

'Are you ready?' Bessie called from the other side of the door curtain.

'Yes.' Marigold pulled the curtain aside.

'Good girl.' Bessie smiled at her. 'Do you think you'll be comfy in here?'

'Yes, thank you. Was this Dottie or Prune's room?'

'No, this was my sewing room. I work as a seamstress as well as working on the farm. I used to have a bigger table in here, but we swapped it around with the spare bed in Peter's room. I didn't think you'd want to share with him as it's nicer to have

18

somewhere of your own.'

'Thank you.' Peter seemed nice, but Marigold was glad she didn't have to share a room with him. Having a room on her own was much better.

'Right, I'll show you the other bedrooms.' Bessie led the way across the living room and opened what looked like an ordinary carriage door, except it was painted butter yellow. 'This is Dottie and Prune's.'

When Marigold peered in, she expected to see the familiar inside of a compartment, like the ones she'd sat in yesterday. To her surprise the seats and luggage racks were gone, and the room was light and airy with white walls and a curved ceiling. Two beds, covered with patchwork quilts, stood either side of a chest of drawers. All the windows, both inside and outside facing, were covered with cream muslin curtains, like in her own room.

'Peter's room's next door.' Bessie closed the door and moved on to the next one.

Marigold followed her into the room, where there was one bed, a chest of drawers and a large table with a map of Europe spread out on it. Small flags were positioned in different spots across the map.

'Peter follows what's happening with the war.' Bessie gently touched one of the small Union Jack flags. 'He and Harry listen to the news on the wireless then move the flags about, going by what they hear is happening.'

Next, Bessie led Marigold into her and Harry's room where there was a double bed, a set of drawers and a wardrobe. Two pictures hanging on the wall caught the little girl's eye.

'That's Harry, taken in the last war.' Bessie pointed to the older-looking picture. 'The other is our son,

George. He's somewhere in France.'

'Is he a soldier?'

'Yes, but not a fighting one, he's in the Army Medical Corps, looking after wounded soldiers. There's a bit more to see, then we'll go outside.'

Marigold followed Bessie across the large main room where everyone lived and ate, at the heart of which was a black cooking stove built into a brick fireplace. There was a kitchen area in one corner, with a sink and cupboards and to the side of it another door.

'This is the pantry.' Bessie opened the door and stepped aside.

Marigold gasped when she saw the well-stocked shelves; there was a lot more food here than they had in their kitchen cupboards back at home. There were jars of jam and honey, bottled fruits, pickled onions and beetroot, a metal meat safe and stone bread crock, and a cold slab with butter and milk on it.

'We don't do badly for food here. It's much easier living on a farm than in London.'

Marigold would have loved to show Bessie's pantry to Mrs Fox, who spent hours queuing up to buy food.

'Let's go outside.' Bessie picked up a basket from behind the pantry door and held out her hand.

Marigold slipped her hand into Bessie's and followed her outside.

★ ★ ★

As Bessie led Marigold into the cool, dim interior of the shed, two swallows swooped out of the open doorway.

'Look, up there.' Bessie pointed to a mud nest moulded onto a beam under the roof. 'You can see

20

the swallow chicks' yellow beaks resting on the edge.'

Marigold craned her neck, staring upwards. 'Won't they fall out?'

'No, they're usually fine. If you come and have a peep in here every day, you'll see how quickly they grow. They'll be out of the nest and flying around soon, and their parents will have another brood before they fly off in the autumn.'

A swallow came flying in the door and, spotting them, did a lightning-quick about-turn and darted out again, chattering loudly.

'They want to feed their chicks, so we'd better go. We'll go and see if the hens have laid next.'

Bessie led Marigold across the yard and through a small gate in a hedge, which led into an orchard. There, rust-coloured chickens were pecking at insects in the dapple-shaded grass, watched over by a cockerel.

'That's Hector,' Bessie said as they paused to watch the large, brown cockerel strutting around, his chest puffed-out and curved glossy green tail feathers dancing in the breeze. 'He likes to think he's in charge of the hens, but they don't take much notice of him.'

Leaving Hector, they headed towards the chicken coop. 'Harry's beehives are over there.' Bessie pointed to where five hives stood at the far end of the orchard. 'Best not to go near them, or you might get stung.'

Reaching the coop, Bessie lifted the lid of the nest box and motioned for her to look inside.

'Eggs!' Marigold smiled at Bessie, a look of wonder on her face.

'Will you collect them for me?'

Marigold carefully picked up an egg, cradling it in her palm, gently stroking the brown shell with one finger. 'It's warm.'

'It's still warm from the hen. You can have it for your dinner if you like.'

'Can I?' Marigold's eyes were wide.

'Yes. We have a lot more eggs here than you get from rations.'

'Do they lay every day?' Marigold carefully put the egg in the basket and reached back into the nest box to collect more.

'Usually, though not as many in the winter.'

Once they'd collected all the eggs, they headed to where Harry was working in the large vegetable garden.

'Morning, Marigold.' He smiled at her, leaning on his hoe. 'Do you want to come and meet Daisy, our new calf?'

The little girl nodded. 'Where is she?'

'In the barn, the other cows are grazing down in the bottom meadow, I'll take you to see them later.'

Marigold looked uncertain. 'I've never been near a cow before.'

'They're lovely and gentle, there's nothing to be frightened of. Daisy's only small, yet. We'll go to her first and you can see what you think.' Bessie held out her hand to Marigold and the child took it and held on tightly as they walked with Harry towards the barn.

'You've got plenty of eggs this morning,' Harry said. 'We ought to send some to your mother in London.'

Marigold frowned. 'Can you send eggs in the post?'

'Yes, if we wrap them well enough,' Bessie said. 'Do you think she'd like some?'

Marigold's face lit up. 'Yes, she loves eggs and we hardly have any because of rationing.'

'Then we must send her some.'

'I dip my hand in the milk, like this, then put my fingers up to her mouth. See.'

Marigold watched in fascination as the calf sniffed Harry's fingers and then started to suck on them.

'I'm going to lower my hand into the milk, and she'll follow.' Daisy, the beautiful little calf, followed Harry's hand down into the pail and once her mouth was in the milk, he eased his fingers away. Daisy kept her head down for a few seconds, then jerked it up out of the pail which sent streams of creamy milk dribbling off her chin.

Harry laughed. 'They take a while to learn how to do it properly. She's used to feeding from her mother, so drinking from a pail's strange. Do you want to try?'

Marigold stared at Harry. Did he think she could do it? She wanted to try but was scared.

'Go on, have a go if you want to,' Bessie encouraged her. 'She won't hurt you.'

She'd try once, Marigold decided, and if she didn't like it, she wouldn't do it again. She knelt in the clean straw next to Harry.

'Ready?' he asked.

She nodded.

'Dip your hand in the milk first.' Marigold did as Harry said and put her hand into the warm milk. 'Now bring it up to her mouth and put your fingers on her lips.'

Harry took hold of her hand and guided it into the right place. As soon as Marigold's fingers touched Daisy's lips, the calf sucked strongly on them, drawing them into her mouth.

'Oh, her tongue's all rough!' Marigold giggled. 'And

she's sucking hard.'

'Good. Now we'll draw her down to the milk.' Slowly, Harry moved Marigold's hand downwards, with Daisy still sucking on her fingers, and into the pail of warm milk. Marigold felt Daisy's sucks drawing the milk into her mouth.

'Now, gently ease your hand away,' Harry said. 'Nice and slow.'

Marigold did as he said, and to her delight, Daisy kept her head down, drinking steadily from the pail.

'You did it!' Bessie squeezed Marigold's shoulder.

'Well done,' Harry said. 'You did a good job.'

Marigold smiled happily. She'd never done anything like it before. Until yesterday she'd never even seen a cow, and now she'd helped a calf learn to drink from a pail.

'Daisy will need some more help again tonight, until she's got the hang of it,' Harry said.

'I could help her,' Marigold said. 'Can I?'

Harry nodded. 'If you want to.'

'Yes please.' Marigold turned her attention back to Daisy, gently stroking the calf's soft ears as she drank. Peter was right. She was beautiful, with big brown eyes, and her fur really was the colour of toffee. Marigold didn't feel as worried about meeting the other cows, Beauty and Buttercup, now, not if they were as lovely as Daisy.

5

Bessie's knitting needles made a gentle clicking noise, her fingers seeming to move of their own accord in a steady rhythm, weaving the wool around the needles, in and out, every stitch making the sock grow.

She loved this part of the day. The day's work was done, the tea finished and cleared away, and she could sit down for a while. They'd listened to the news on the wireless earlier, and now Harry and Peter were pouring over the map spread out on the table, talking about the reports from France and moving the flags around to mark the Allies' latest position.

At the other end of the table, Marigold was drawing a picture to put in with the letter she'd written to her mother, her tongue sticking out in concentration.

'Peter, how do you spell Daisy?' Marigold asked.

'It's D.A.I.S.Y. Why do you want to know?'

'I need to write it on the picture I'm doing for my mother. See?' She held up the paper covered with drawings of the people and animals living at Orchard Farm.

Peter took it from her and studied it closely. 'You've done a good job.'

'It's so she'll know everyone who lives here,' Marigold explained.

Bessie was glad to hear Marigold sounding happy and at home. Over the past couple of days, she'd spent a lot of time taking her around the farm, introducing her to the rest of the animals, showing her their wood and the stream running through the bottom meadow.

25

The little girl had settled in well, and that's what Bessie had written in her letter to Grace. She would put it in with the parcel of eggs along with Marigold's letter and drawing, and they'd post it in the village tomorrow. Bessie hoped that knowing her daughter was happy would reassure Grace that she'd been right to put her trust in Bessie and Harry.

The front door opened and Dottie and Prune came in from cleaning their boots outside.

'Oh, look!' Dottie leaned over Marigold, examining her picture. 'Aren't you good at drawing?'

Marigold beamed at Dottie. 'It's for my mum.'

'I'm sure she'll be pleased with it,' Prune said. 'I expect she's missing you.'

'I miss her too,' Marigold said, softly.

'She'll be able to come and visit you here,' Dottie said. 'Would that be all right with you, Bessie?'

'Of course,' Bessie said. 'Anytime she wants. I've already asked her to visit in my letter.'

'It would be a lovely holiday for her, out in the countryside.' Dottie put her arm around Marigold and gave her a hug. 'Make a nice change from London.'

'She might not come,' Marigold said. 'She can't get leave from work easily, not with the doodlebugs.'

'Don't worry, she'll come when she can.' Bessie leaned across and put her hand on Marigold's arm.

Although how Grace would feel about coming to Orchard Farm and seeing her and Harry, Bessie didn't know. She'd told Grace in her letter that she could visit anytime she wanted, but it was up to Grace whether she would accept their invitation. She must, at some point, as she wouldn't be able to keep away from her daughter forever, and when that day came, they'd welcome her with open arms. Living now was what was important, not dwelling on what had gone before. What was done, was in the past and would have been forgiven and forgotten long ago, if only Grace had given them the chance.

★ ★ ★

Marigold couldn't sleep. She lay on her side with Blue safe in her arms thinking about the drawing she'd done for her mother. It would show her all the people and animals here on the farm, but she'd rather have told her mother about them face to face. Marigold sighed . . . but that was impossible because she was miles and miles away in London . . . She didn't even know when she'd see her again.

Since Marigold had arrived here, she'd been busy with so many new things to learn about and places to see. There'd been little time to think about home, but now in the quiet of her room, a gnawing ache for her mother was growing inside her. She missed her so much. Marigold started to cry again, muffling her sobs with Blue so no one would hear.

Worried thoughts flickered through her mind like a film at the pictures. Was her mother safe? Where was she now? At home, or working at the hospital?

It was nice here in this little house on Orchard Farm. Bessie, Harry, Peter, Dottie and Prune were all kind to her, but they weren't the same as her mother, and that's who Marigold desperately wanted to be with. The need to go home tugged at her heart. She had to return there and as soon as possible, but she didn't know how.

When she'd come here, her mother's friend, Mrs

27

MacDonald, had brought her, but she wouldn't be able to take her back again. If Marigold asked Bessie to take her home, she'd probably say no because it was safer here, and it was where her mother wanted her to be. If she was going home, then she'd have to do it all by herself. When, or how, she needed to work out, but she would get back there again. Somehow.

Later, when Bessie popped her head around the curtain to check on her before she went to bed, Marigold pretended to be asleep. Her eyes were heavy, and all her body wanted to do was sleep, but her mind kept going over and over how she was going to get home. By the time she eventually drifted off, she still didn't know the answer.

6

It was late afternoon by the time Bessie and Marigold left the farm to walk into the village, carrying the parcel of eggs for Grace in a shopping basket. Each egg had been carefully bound in a strip of cloth and packed securely in an old OXO tin. Their letters were placed on the closed lid and the whole thing then wrapped in brown paper and tied up with string.

'How long do you think it will take to get there?' Marigold asked.

'It should be there tomorrow.'

Bessie glanced at the little girl, who'd been subdued all day. Her face was pale and there were dark smudges under her eyes as if she hadn't had enough sleep. Maybe tiredness from the excitement and newness of everything over the past few days had finally caught up with her. It was nothing a good night's rest wouldn't put right, Bessie thought.

'Perhaps your mother will read your letter to Mrs Fox. I expect she'd like to know how you're getting on.'

'Mummy can tell her about me feeding Daisy. I've never done anything like feeding a calf before.'

'Life must be so different for you here, compared with in London.'

'Have you ever been to London, Bessie?'

'No, I've never needed to go there, but maybe I will one day.'

'You could come and visit me when I go home.'

Whenever that is, Bessie thought. Grace had said

nothing about how long Marigold would live with them. While London was still being targeted with doodlebugs, it was safer for the child to be here. She might even stay until the war ended, but when that would be, nobody knew. If Bessie had her say, it would be over today. Now. It had been going on for too long, every day more people being injured and killed. The Allies might be battling their way across France, but the Nazis were putting up a fight, they would not give in easily.

Bessie closed her eyes for a moment and sent up a silent prayer that it would be over soon, and all those far from home would come back safely. She touched the envelope lying in the bottom of her basket along-side Grace's parcel. It was for her son, George. She didn't know exactly where he was. Somewhere in France was all he could tell her, but Bessie hoped it would reach him. Writing to him every week helped her by making him feel a bit closer.

'Will you, Bessie?' Marigold's voice interrupted her thoughts, 'come and see me in London?'

'Yes.' She smiled. 'If you'd like me to.'

Marigold reached out to hold Bessie's hand. 'Yes, I would.'

★ ★ ★

'So, this is your little evacuee?' Nora Chambers peered at Marigold from behind the post office counter. 'Settling in all right, are you?'

'Yes, thank you,' Marigold said.

'I'd like to send this to London, please.' Bessie handed Nora the parcel of eggs. 'And can I have a stamp for a letter to George as well?'

30

Nora busied herself dealing with the parcel and finding the correct stamps, but kept taking quick, furtive glances at Marigold.

'Here, you can stick this on the letter for me.' Nora passed a stamp to Marigold, who stuck it on George's letter.

'Looks like you've got a good one there.' Nora took the money Bessie had put on the counter. 'But not all evacuees are like yours.' She leaned forwards, her thin lips pressed so tightly together they almost disappeared. 'I expect you'll have heard about the new ones staying at Mrs Potter's, causing a lot of trouble they are. They . . .'

Bessie turned to Marigold. 'Why don't you put the letter in the post box outside, I won't be a minute.' She watched her go out of the door, then turned back to face Nora who stood poised, open-mouthed, ready to carry on with her gossip. 'We must remember it's difficult for children coming to live with strangers so far from home.'

Nora closed her mouth and sniffed derisively.

'It must be bad in London with all those doodlebugs falling all over the place,' Bessie said. 'Terrifying when nobody knows where or when they'll fall next.'

'Your girl didn't come with the new lot of evacuees who arrived here last week, did she?'

'No, it was a private evacuation. Her mother asked us to look after her.'

'She's lucky she had you and Harry to come to.' Nora narrowed her eyes, studying Bessie's face. 'How did her mother know you?'

'Oh, from way back.' Bessie looked Nora straight in the eyes. 'I knew her in the last war.'

'Ah!' Nora raised her eyebrows above her horn-rimmed glasses. 'Not family then, I wondered . . .'

Bessie forced herself to smile. 'I'd better find Marigold; she's settling in well, but she doesn't know her way around the village yet. I don't want her getting lost. Cheerio then.'

Not waiting for a reply, Bessie strode towards the door, her stomach knotting. Nora didn't need any encouraging to sniff out gossip and spread it around. Her probing about how Marigold had come to them had made Bessie uneasy. What she had told her hadn't been a lie, she'd just been selective with the truth and said enough to answer the question, but no more. She didn't want the likes of Nora spreading it around the village who Marigold might be, not when the child didn't know it herself.

Bessie was relieved to see Marigold waiting for her by the post box. 'Did you post it?'

The little girl nodded.

'Good. Your mother's parcel won't take long to get there and then she'll be able to have eggs for tea.' She held out her hand to Marigold, who took hold of it. 'I need to do a bit of shopping, then we'll head home. If you want, you can wait for me on the seat under the tree, it'll be cooler there.'

Bessie pointed to the wooden seat circling the old chestnut tree standing on the village green. Its wide canopy cast a cool, inviting shade.

'What do you think, come in the grocer's with me or sit over there?'

Marigold considered for a moment. 'It's hot, so I'll wait in the shade.'

'I'll join you when I've finished the shopping and cool off for a bit before we walk home.'

Bessie watched Marigold cross the road and settle herself down on the wooden seat.

It took longer than Bessie expected to be served, as there were several people in the shop already, and all the ration books had to be checked.

While she waited her turn, she looked out through the front window to check on Marigold. She was doing what many children had before her, swinging her legs back and forth because they weren't yet long enough to reach the ground.

'That's a lovely name,' Edith, the grocer's assistant said, as she checked Marigold's ration book a few minutes later. 'How's she settling in?'

'Very well. It's so different from London, but I think she's enjoying it. I left her sitting outside on the old seat in the shade.'

'Best place to be in this heat.' Edith fanned her red face with her hand. 'So, what would you like today?'

Bessie handed over her list.

'Any news from George?' Edith asked, checking the list and reaching for a packet of tea and placing it on the counter, before moving on to fetch the next item.

'Not for a couple of weeks, but I'll probably get a bundle of letters in one go, that's how it is sometimes.'

'We get the same with our Stan. I write to him every week to keep him in touch with home. He said he likes to hear what we're doing and what's happening in the village.' She carefully tipped a little more sugar into the blue packet on the weighing scale pan, to reach the exact weight. 'It's a bit of normal life for them while they're living through war.'

'It makes me shudder when I think of it going on in France and our boys out there mixed up in it . . .' Bessie sighed. 'I suppose it's got to be done.'

Edith pulled a face. 'Yes, if we don't want that man over here telling us how to live. Hitler's time is running out.'

'The sooner the better,' Bessie added.

When she stepped out of the grocers a short while later, her basket full of packages, the seat under the tree was empty. She hurried across the road, circling the tree to check Marigold hadn't moved to the other side, but she wasn't there. Where was she? With her heart racing, she looked up and down the street, but there was no sign of the child.

Bessie had been longer in the shop than she'd intended. Perhaps Marigold had gone to look for her, and somehow, they'd missed each other. She dashed back across the road and into the grocer's but there was no one in there except for Edith, who was weighing out more sugar into blue paper bags.

'Edith, has a girl with blonde plaits been in?'

'No, love. No one's been in since you left a minute or two ago. Is that your Marigold you're looking for?'

'Yes.'

'I expect she's not far away. Something probably caught her eye, and she went to have a look.'

Bessie hoped so. Grace had trusted her to look after her daughter, not lose her. Keep calm, she told herself. Marigold couldn't have gone far. She went back outside and hurried along the street, searching in the shops and around the village green. But there was no sign of her anywhere.

Could she have gone home on her own? Marigold wouldn't have left without telling Bessie first, would she? But where else would she go?

7

Peter was in a hurry. As much as he'd loved his first year at grammar school, he couldn't wait to begin the summer holidays. He was looking forward to helping Harry on the farm and having time to watch the Liberators. He had plenty to do, and he wanted to get started as soon as possible.

He was ready, hand on the door handle, as the train steamed into Rackbridge station. He knew that if he pedalled hard enough on his bicycle, he could be home in ten minutes and then the holidays would begin.

The moment the train jolted to a halt, Peter opened the door and jumped down. Slinging his satchel over his shoulder, he rushed along the platform towards the booking hall and out through the exit. But then he stopped. He'd noticed someone who he didn't expect to see there. Turning on his heels, he went back through to the platform and looked at the lone figure sitting on a bench. It was Marigold.

'What are you doing here?' He called out, walking over to her. 'Have you come to meet me?'

She shook her head. 'I'm going home.'

'So am I, come on.' Peter gestured for her to follow him.

But Marigold didn't move. 'No. I'm going to my home in London. I want to be with my mother.' Her bottom lip trembled as she folded her arms across her chest.

He sat down on the bench beside her. 'But what

about Bessie and Harry, do they know you're going home?'

'No. They wouldn't want me to.' Marigold's blue eyes filled with tears.

'Here, have my hanky.' Peter pulled a folded white handkerchief out of his blazer pocket. 'It's clean. I haven't used it. Look, you can still see where Bessie ironed it.'

Marigold took it and gave him a watery smile. 'Thank you.' She wiped her eyes. 'I don't know which train to get, or even if I've got enough money.' She delved her hand into her dress pocket and held out a couple of pennies in her palm.

'That's not enough to get you all the way to London. You'll need more than that.'

Marigold sighed. 'But I have to go back.'

'Why? Don't you like it at Orchard Farm?'

'Yes . . .' She scrunched the handkerchief tightly in her hands. 'But my mother's not there. I worry about her and miss her . . . I just want to go home.'

Peter nudged her arm. 'I'm sure she misses you too, but it's safer here than in London.'

She turned to face Peter, her eyes flashing with anger. '*You* don't know what it's like to miss your mother and be in a strange place with people you've never met before!'

Peter's stomach clenched. 'Yes, *I do.*' He sighed. 'I know exactly how it feels.'

'How can you when you're still living at home with Bessie and Harry?'

'They're not my parents.' He frowned. 'Did you think they were? I don't call them Mother or Father, do I?'

'No . . . I didn't realise . . .' She hesitated, looking

36

confused. 'But how...?'

'I'm not even from this country, Marigold. I'm Austrian. I haven't seen my parents since they put me on a train in August thirty-nine.' He sighed. 'Or heard anything from them for nearly three years, and I don't know where they are now.'

'I'm sorry, I didn't know.' Marigold took hold of Peter's hand. 'I shouldn't have said what I did.'

He smiled at her. 'It's all right, I understand how you're feeling. You're upset and you miss your mother. I miss my parents too.'

'You don't talk like an Austrian, although I'm not sure how they sound.' Marigold gave a little shrug. 'But you don't sound foreign.'

'I was only seven when I came here. I hardly knew any English, so I had to learn it from scratch. But now I can't remember much German.'

'Why did your parents send you away?'

'So I'd be safe.'

'Why wasn't it safe there?'

'Because my family is Jewish, and the Nazis don't like us. After they invaded Austria, they started making rules for Jewish people and it made life difficult. I wasn't allowed to go to school anymore.' Peter frowned. 'They took our apartment away from us. My parents decided it would be safer for me to leave them and come to England.'

'On your own?'

He nodded.

'How did you get here?'

'By train to Holland first, then we got a boat to England. I travelled with lots of other Jewish children, and we all left our families behind.'

'Did you know Bessie and Harry before you came

here?'

'No. They'd heard what was going on and wanted to help a child. Bessie told me she couldn't stop a war coming, but she could get a child away from it. So, she arranged to have me and came to meet me from the boat, then brought me back to Orchard Farm.'

'Will you go home to Austria after the war?'

'It depends on what my parents want to do.' He paused for a moment, watching the chattering swallows wheeling in the blue sky above the station. 'Before I left, my papa told me to look at the moon every night and remember it would be shining down on them as well. He said that they'd be looking up at it thinking of me. When I look at the moon it helps them feel a little closer. You could try it too.'

They fell into silence for a few moments.

'What do you think I should do?' Marigold spoke so softly he could hardly hear her.

He looked her straight in the eyes. 'I think you should stay here and not give up. Remember, your mother sent you here for a good reason. She'd rather you were at home with her, but it's too dangerous there now.'

Tears welled up in Marigold's eyes again. 'She said she couldn't risk losing me as well as Daddy. He died on D-Day . . . landing in France.'

'I'm sorry.' Peter squeezed her hand. 'I think you should stay here because it's what your mother wants you to do. Orchard Farm's a good place to be if you have to be away from home.' He smiled at her. 'You can write to her and she can come and visit you.'

Marigold nodded.

'And there's plenty to do here. I've finished school for the summer now, so I can take you places. Show

38

you the American airbase where you can see the aeroplanes. If you stay till Christmas, then you'll be able to go to the party there. They are wonderful. There's ice cream and candy to eat. Come on.' Peter stood up and pulled Marigold to her feet. 'Let's go home, they'll be wondering where you are.'

'I ran off while Bessie was in the grocer's,' Marigold admitted. 'Do you think she'll be angry with me?'

'I think she'll be worried.'

Peter led her out through the booking hall and collected his bicycle from where he always left it in the stationmaster's shed. As they walked out of the station yard, they ran straight into a frantic-looking Bessie.

'Marigold!' Bessie threw her arms around her and hugged her tightly. 'Where have you been?'

'I found her on the platform,' Peter said.

Bessie stepped back from Marigold, her hands resting on the girl's shoulders. 'What were you doing there? I came out of the grocer's and you'd gone. I've been looking for you . . . I was so worried.'

Marigold started to cry, and Bessie hugged her again.

'Your mother trusted me to look after you . . . so when I couldn't find you . . .' Her voice caught and she stopped, biting her lip.

'She was trying to go back home,' Peter explained.

'To London?' Bessie looked horrified.

He nodded. 'But she didn't have enough money or know which train to get.'

Bessie took hold of both of Marigold's hands in hers. 'Why do you want to go home? Don't you like it here?' She frowned. 'You've been getting on so well, and I thought you were settling in.'

'I . . . miss . . . my . . . mother . . . so . . . much . . .'

Marigold stammered; her words punctuated with sobs. 'I . . . worry . . . about . . . her . . .'

'Of course, you miss her, but she wants you to be here so you're safe. Lots of children are living away from home now because of the war.'

'Like me,' he said.

Bessie smiled gratefully at him. 'Peter knows how you feel. We all understand how hard it is for you, but you can write to your mother as often as you want, and she can come and visit whenever she can.'

'But writing a letter's not the same as telling her face to face,' Marigold said.

'I know, but it's the best way to keep in touch when you're apart. The good thing about letters is that you can read them as many times as you like, and that helps you feel closer to the person who wrote them. I do that with George's letters.'

'Do you?' Marigold asked.

Bessie nodded. 'I probably know them all off by heart.'

'I'm not very good at writing letters, I don't know what to put in them. Last night's was easy because there were so many new things to tell her, but I can't write that every time, can I?'

'No, but all you need to do is tell your mother what you've been doing,' Peter said.

'I'll forget what I've done.'

'You could keep a diary,' he suggested. 'Write in it what you do each day, then use it to help you write your letters.'

'I kept a diary a long time ago,' Bessie said. 'I enjoyed writing in it. How about if I gave you a little book to use as a diary, would you like that?'

'Could I draw pictures in it, as well?'

40

'Of course. Whatever you want. Shall we go home?' Bessie asked.

Marigold nodded.

Bessie looked relieved. 'Peter, will you ride ahead and tell Harry we're on our way? He'll be wondering where we've got to.'

'Of course, I'll see you back at the farm.' Peter swung his leg over his bicycle, pushed off and rode out of the station yard, glad that Bessie had met them and had sorted Marigold out. Now he could get home and properly start his summer holidays.

8

Bessie rummaged through the drawer, feeling between folded clothes, reaching into the farthest corners with her fingers. She knew it was in there somewhere.

Harry climbed into his side of their double bed. 'What are you looking for?'

'My old diary.'

'I thought you'd already given Marigold a notebook to use as a diary?'

'I have. She took it to bed with her to write in, but it got me thinking about my diary, and I thought I'd like to have a look at it again. Ah, here it is!' She pulled out a blue cloth-bound book and waved it in the air.

'You haven't written in that for years.'

'I know.' Bessie pushed the drawer shut and climbed into bed beside him. 'It was an important part of my life for a while. It helped me get through some hard times.'

Harry put his arm around her, and she snuggled into him.

'I felt like reading it again.' She stroked the faded cloth cover, then opened it and looked at the inscription inside.

'Who gave it to you?' he asked.

'Sergeant Harmer. Look.' She pointed to his signature.

'To Dear Nurse Carter,' Harry read aloud. 'With warmest wishes and thanks for all your care. Sergeant Frederick Harmer, 4th March 1918, Marston Hall, Auxiliary War Hospital.'

'I can vouch for you being an excellent nurse.' Harry kissed her cheek. 'I remember how much the men used to enjoy drawing and writing verses in the nurses' autograph books. What verse did he use?'

Bessie cleared her throat and read aloud the neat copperplate handwriting.

'Whatever you are — be that.
Whatever you say — be true.
Straightforwardly act.
Be honest in fact.
Be nobody else but you.
Be nobody else but you.
All that is best for thee.
That best I wish for thee.'

Harry nodded. 'He certainly picked the right verse for you.'

'What do you mean?'

'You're as honest as the day is long, Bess. True to yourself more than anyone I know.'

Bessie's stomach knotted; the verse was anything but true about her. Her thoughts drifted off to a place she seldom dared let them go, a place Harry knew nothing about and never would.

'Are you going to read it, then?'

His words dragged her back to the present. 'Beg your pardon?'

'The diary, are you going to read it?'

'Do you want me to read you some?'

'No, it's your private diary, with your thoughts and for your eyes only. No, I mean, are you going to read some tonight, or shall I blow out the candle and we'll get some sleep?'

'I'd like to have a look at a page or two. You settle down, I won't be long.'

Turning the page, Bessie read what she'd written over twenty-five years ago. Back then, another war had been raging, the one they'd called the Great War, the war to end all wars. But it hadn't.

4th March, 1918
My name's Bessie Carter, and this is my diary. I think that's how I should start, but I don't know if it's the right way or not, because I've never had a diary before. This was given to me by Sergeant Harmer, one of my patients, and I promised him I would write in it. He told me writing a diary had helped him, and it would be a good place to put my thoughts and feelings. Perhaps I should say something about myself. I'm twenty-one years old, and I'm working as a VAD (that's short for Voluntary Aid Detachment) nurse at Marston Hall Auxiliary War Hospital. I do some seamstress work for Lady Heaton too, when I've got the time. That's what I used to do here before the war, working as a seamstress for her ladyship. When she turned the Hall into a hospital at the beginning of the war, most of her staff started working in it.

As Bessie read on, it felt as if the years in between dissolved away and she was back at Marston Hall.

* * *

'It's for you, Nurse Carter. Please, I want you to have it.' Sergeant Harmer folded Bessie's gloved hands around the cloth-bound notebook which he'd handed to her.

44

'I'm sorry, but I can't take it.' Bessie's breath plumed in the crisp, cold air. 'You know the rules, nurses mustn't accept gifts from patients.'

'But who's to know? It's my spare one and I don't need it. If you won't take it, then I'll just leave it there on that seat.' He nodded towards a bench on the platform, then looked at her with a mischievous glint in his eye. 'Would be such a waste.'

Bessie sighed and returned his smile. 'It's kind of you, but I can't.' She handed it back to him.

'But I think you can. It's for you to use as a diary, write in it what you've done, your thoughts and feelings. I kept one all the time I was in France, and it helped me.'

'But I'm not in France. This is England and it's safe here.'

'I know, but you young women witness things you never ought to see. You have to deal with the horrors of what war can do to a soldier. That's hard.'

Bessie bit her bottom lip and nodded.

'You have as much need to write a diary as any soldier fighting in the trenches. I'm not taking no for an answer.'

'Hurry along, Nurse Carter, we need to get all the men on board. No time for long goodbyes,' an orderly said, smiling cheekily, as he wheeled a patient in a bath chair past them towards the waiting train.

'Let's get you on the train and then you'll be on your way home, and out of the war for good.' Bessie took hold of the sergeant's arm and walked him slowly towards an open carriage door. She shortened her stride to match his slow, dragging limp which he counterbalanced with a stick in his other hand.

Sergeant Harmer stopped by the door and turned

to Bessie. 'Please take it, with my warmest wishes and thanks.' Before she could say anything, he slipped the diary into a pocket in her greatcoat and slowly climbed into the train. 'It's yours now.' He smiled at her as he settled back into a seat.

Bessie tapped her pocket. 'All right, I can see you're not going to give in. I appreciate your kind gift, thank you.'

'Will you use it?'

'Yes, but only if you promise to look after that leg of yours; no overdoing it, then it will keep you upright.'

'Nurse Carter?' An orderly called to her from the doorway of another carriage. 'Can you help here, please?'

'I'm coming. Goodbye then, and . . .' Bessie smiled at him, 'remember to take care.'

★ ★ ★

Walking back to the hospital, a short while later, with the rest of the nurses and orderlies as they returned to Marston Hall, Bessie mulled over her morning's work. She always enjoyed taking the men to meet the train. It was satisfying seeing them on their way again, their job done, and their patients healed.

The lucky ones, like Sergeant Harmer, were going home for good. The war was over for them, but other men would return to France. Some would get a short leave, but if they were badly needed out there, then they'd be straight back to the war.

Knowing that the men she'd nursed would be sent back into battle was hard. Realistically, she knew that some wouldn't survive the next time they came into contact with a German bullet or piece of flying shrapnel. Bessie desperately wished the war was over and everyone back home again where they belonged.

An icy wind was picking up, Bessie turned up the collar of her coat and quickened her pace. It was good to be out of the ward for a while, but there would be plenty to do when she got back, as everything must be cleaned and prepared for the next lot of incoming patients.

Pushing her gloved hand into her pocket, she touched the diary that Sergeant Harmer had given her. He'd told her to write down her thoughts and feelings, but it wasn't the sort of thing she was used to doing. A fanciful thought is what her mother would call it, and the best way she'd say to cure that, was hard work. But then her mother had never witnessed what Bessie had, or had to deal with the things she did every day. Perhaps the sergeant was right, and she should write these things down, let her thoughts free on paper. Although it would have to wait until later, from the look on the face of the orderly who came running down the Hall drive to meet them.

'A telegram's arrived . . . more patients on their way,' he gasped between breaths. 'They're expected on the afternoon train, so Matron wants everyone back at the double.'

Bessie picked up the long blue skirt of her uniform and hurried back to the hospital with the others.

* * *

'Did they reach the train in one piece?' Ethel, Bessie's friend and fellow VAD asked, as they worked together stripping empty beds.

'Yes, and they were in fine form.'

'They sounded like it, going by all the cheering and whistling they did when they left here.' Ethel tipped another armful of sheets and pillow slips into the laundry basket. 'They don't make noise like that when they arrive.'

Bessie smiled. 'We did a good job with them.'

'Yes.' Ethel sighed. 'But there are always more to fill their place.'

'We'd better hurry, otherwise Matron will want to know why the ward's not ready.' Bessie added the last of the sheets to the basket. 'If we're lucky, there'll be time for something to eat and a cup of tea before the ambulances arrive. Do you know where they're coming from?'

'Matron didn't say. Let's hope it's not straight from the front this time.'

As Bessie started on the next job of disinfecting the beds, her thoughts drifted to her brother, Robert. He was out there at that place they called the Front, somewhere in France, and she hoped and prayed he was safe. She'd seen enough injured men to know how badly soldiers could be maimed. If . . . God forbid, Robert was hurt, Bessie hoped an excellent nurse would look after him, give him the finest care they could. That's what she always tried to do. Every man who came to their hospital was someone's son, brother or husband, who'd done their bit and deserved nothing but the best.

Swallowing hard to fight back the sudden tears stinging her eyes, Bessie wiped faster, worked harder. It was the only way to deal with worrying about Robert; keep herself so busy she only had time and energy to think about the job in hand, not the 'what ifs' and the worst that might, please God, never happen. She'd had to cope with it once before and hoped she would never have to face it again. The best thing to do was concentrate on what she needed to do, lockers to wipe out, floors to disinfect . . .

By the time Bessie, Ethel and the other VADs and orderlies had made the ward ready, with beds made up and hot water bottles tucked inside warming them for the next occupants, it was past one o'clock. They'd only been sitting down for a short while, eating bread and jam and drinking tea, when an orderly put his head around the kitchen door.

'The ambulances are on their way up from the station. Be here in about ten minutes.'

'Thanks,' Bessie said. 'We'd better eat up quickly. We don't know when we'll next get a chance to have something.'

It all depended on where the men were coming from. If they'd come straight from France, then they'd be in a sorry state, still wearing their muddy, lice-ridden uniforms, and their Blighty wounds would only have been quickly dressed in a field hospital. After travelling so far, they'd be exhausted, shocked and in pain. Bessie found it upsetting to see the soldiers arrive in that state, but she'd learned not to show it, outwardly she'd be calm and professional for the men's sake, but it wasn't easy.

Bessie and Ethel joined Sister Williams, Matron, and the others waiting at the front door, watching as the ambulances came slowly up the drive. Jolts and bumps would send pain searing through wounded men, so the drivers did their best to give them a smooth trip and always drove with the utmost care.

As soon as the first ambulance came to a halt, everyone stepped into action. They all knew what needed to be done to get the men inside and comfortable as quickly as possible after their journey. Bessie loved the way they all worked together, VADs, Sister, Matron and the men from the army's Medical Corps, each knew exactly what to do after plenty of practice; together they were like a smoothly oiled machine.

Bessie gave an inner sigh of relief when the back doors of the first ambulance were opened and a soldier wearing hospital blues was helped out. These men had already been treated in a bigger war hospital. They hadn't come straight from France.

'Where have you come from?' Bessie asked, as she guided a patient who walked with the aid of crutches in through the front door, and the short distance to the ward in the old ballroom.

'Norfolk and Norwich hospital, nurse,' he said. 'It's good to be sent out here to convalesce. Fresh air, peace and quiet.' He grinned at her. 'Just what the doctor ordered.'

'I hope you'll like it here.' Bessie steered him towards one of the empty beds. 'Now then . . .' She looked down at the notes the soldier had brought with him from the hospital. 'Private Dennis, this will be your bed and locker, we'll soon have you settled in and comfortable.'

'Nurse Carter? When you've finished there, hurry along and tell cook to organise some tea, and bread and butter; the men need some refreshment after their journey. Then straight back and start on the observations,' Sister Williams said, as she bustled past, guiding some orderlies carrying stretcher cases to their beds.

'Yes, Sister,' Bessie said. 'Right, Private Dennis . . .'

'I'll be all right now,' he whispered. 'You go and get that tea organised; I could do with a cuppa and I'm

50

sure the rest of the lads are the same.'

'Well, if you're sure? We don't want you keeling over from lack of tea. I'll be right back to check on you.'

Passing other new patients being helped into the ward on her way out, Bessie hurried down to the kitchen, going as quickly as she could without running. Matron was strict about that. They must walk, never run.

Down in the kitchen, the VAD cook and kitchen hands were already busy preparing the evening meal, and looked up when Bessie walked in.

'Tea, bread and butter?' Mrs Taylor, the cook, asked.

Bessie nodded. 'Yes, please. Sister's orders.'

'We've got the kettles on ready.' Mrs Taylor nodded towards the black kettles coming up to the boil on the big range. 'We put them on as soon as the ambulances drew up. Agnes . . .' she said to one of the kitchen maids, 'you start on the bread and butter.'

'Thank you, Mrs Taylor, the men are gasping for a cuppa, and it'll warm them up after their journey.' Bessie smiled at the woman who always reminded her of a friendly little bird in her pale brown cook's uniform.

'Where are they from?'

'Norfolk and Norwich War Hospital.' Bessie said. 'I must go, or Sister will wonder where I've got to.'

'You can tell us about them later,' Mrs Taylor said. 'When you have time to sit down and have a cup of tea yourself.'

'I will, but it won't be for a while, we've got lots to do.'

That was always true, Bessie thought as she hurried back to the ward. Not only on days when a convoy arrived, every day was busy, they were never short of things to do. Now, with the arrival of new patients, everyone would work hard to get them settled and comfortable. Her next job was to take the temperatures and pulses because the men couldn't have their cups of tea until it was done.

★ ★ ★

Another busy day and I'm tired. New patients arrived from the Norfolk and Norwich hospital, so no lice-ridden uniforms or mud to deal with today. So strange to see unfamiliar faces in the beds. I still expect the old ones to be there, but they've gone on their way again, our job with them finished. I wonder what this new group of men will be like. It's always interesting to get to know the characters who come our way, they're all different and keep us VADs on our toes. Must sleep. Goodnight.

Bessie closed the diary and leaned back against her pillows. She could still remember the bone-aching tiredness at the end of a long shift, when her only desire had been to fall into a deep, dreamless slumber.

9

'I needed that.' Dottie put the stopper back in her bottle of cold tea and tucked it under the shade of a bush, then lay down on the grass, her hands behind her head, and let out a deep sigh. 'This is lovely.'

'Sure is.' Prune sat nearby, her arms wrapped around her knees, looking across the wildflower-dotted meadow from their picnic spot at the edge of the wood.

Dottie laughed. 'Hark at you! You sound like an American.'

Prune's cheeks flushed. 'I don't.'

'Sounded like one to me. Sure is . . . that's the sort of thing a GI would say. You're picking up the language from Howard.'

'Not intentionally.' Prune plucked a daisy out of the grass and twirled it between her fingers.

'No, but I suppose it's only natural. The more time you spend with someone, the more you pick up from them. The Americans get things from us, too. Look at Clem, he loves learning our different British words. Did you know he writes them down? Remember when he called Harry's waistcoat a vest?'

'He didn't know that a vest's a completely different thing for the British!'

'They speak English, but it's certainly not the same as ours.'

They fell into silence for a few minutes in the warm

53

sunshine, listening to bees droning from flower to flower, and a skylark overhead which was filling the air with its crystal-clear song.

'The fact is, you are spending a lot of time with Howard. Every chance you get.'

'I enjoy being with him. What's wrong with that?'

Dottie rolled onto her side, propping her head up on one hand. 'Nothing, nothing at all, but I think you might be falling for him.'

Prune looked at her and shrugged. 'Perhaps.'

'Come on, can't you be more exact?'

'Well . . .' Prune strung out her reply. 'Yes, I like him. I enjoy his company and he makes me laugh.'

Dottie let out a long whistle. 'You're not giving much away, are you? Have you fallen in love with him?'

'I think I might have.'

'He'd better watch out or you'll be taking him home to meet your mother next.'

'No!' Prune snapped, her face flushing. 'Definitely not.'

Dottie held up her hand. 'I was only joking. There's no need to get upset.'

'I'm sorry. I shouldn't have spoken so rudely.' Her friend leaned back on her hands and looked up at the clear blue sky. 'My mother wouldn't approve.' She sighed. 'If she knew I was spending *any* time with a GI, she'd be furious; she doesn't agree with them being here.'

'Well, they're not here on holiday, are they? Who knows where we'd be now if the Americans hadn't joined the war?'

'Unfortunately, she does not think that way.'

'She doesn't know what she's missing.' Dottie

checked her watch. 'Five more minutes rest, then we must get back to work.' She rolled onto her back again and closed her eyes against the sunlight.

'What about you?' Prune asked. 'Wouldn't you like to find a nice GI to fall in love with?'

'Me?' Dottie opened her eyes, shielding them from the sun as she looked at Prune. 'No. I'm staying carefree and not getting romantically involved with anyone. I've got plans for a career after the war's over, I have no intention of being side-tracked by any man.'

'Doesn't Clem count?'

'Not in that way. He's a good friend, a brilliant dancer, and we enjoy each other's company, but because he is an honourably married man, that's it — no romance involved.'

'But don't you wish, deep down, you could find someone to love?'

Dottie's stomach twisted, and she forced a bright smile. 'That's for you, not me. Trust me when I say I know what I'm doing; now be quiet and let me have a rest before we start work again.'

★ ★ ★

London

Grace slipped quietly out of the door at the end of the ward and stepped onto the balcony. The night air was cool and its slightly salty, tarry tang from the river, was a refreshing contrast from the clinical smell of the hospital. As her eyes adjusted to the London black-out, she could pick out familiar landmarks bathed in pale moonlight.

Sited on the banks of the Thames, St Thomas' hospital had a fine riverside vista. Grace loved to come out here on night shifts to take in the view. Leaning forward on the cold stone of the balcony balustrade, she watched some coal barges floating past along water streaked with faint, silvery ripples of moonlight. Casting her gaze further to the opposite bank, she could see the Houses of Parliament, which had miraculously survived the Blitz.

Leaning a little further over, Grace picked out the dome of St Paul's curving against the sky; it stood proudly amongst the jagged ruins littering the skyline. She loved that the grand old cathedral was still standing, like a symbol of Londoners' resilience against the enemy's attacks. They hadn't destroyed St Paul's, or the spirit of the people who'd lived through the Blitz and had come out the other side still strong, still there.

But there was one thing missing from London, Grace thought: her daughter. She felt in her pocket and touched Marigold's letter, which had arrived that morning. She didn't need to read it now because she almost knew it by heart after reading it so many times. The words had eased Grace's worries about sending her child away. Marigold was safe and enjoying her new life, which was all Grace wanted for her. Although she missed her with every ounce of her body. Not knowing when she would see her again made Grace's heart ache, but her feelings must come second to Marigold's safety; she'd lost her husband and couldn't face losing her daughter too.

She smiled as she recalled the things Marigold had told her about in her letter; collecting eggs, teaching a calf to drink from a pail, and the description of the house. Grace could picture all of it, the smells and tastes, the feeling of a calf's rough tongue. She knew exactly what her daughter was experiencing . . . because she'd done those same things . . . but that was all a long time ago, in another lifetime.

The parcel of eggs which Bessie had sent was a lovely surprise, and so typical of her and Harry's kindness. Grace had rushed to show Ada, and together they'd carefully unwrapped the precious brown eggs, which had arrived still as perfect as when they were laid. Eating them would be a treat, so much nicer than the awful, powdered egg.

Bessie's letter had told Grace all she needed to know, even down to the little details of how Marigold was eating and sleeping. It helped knowing that her daughter was happy. Bessie had invited her to come and visit whenever she wanted, but when she'd be able to accept her invitation, Grace didn't know. She was desperate to see Marigold, but to do so would mean facing up to her past, and that wasn't so easy.

She sighed and checked her watch. A couple more minutes and she must get back to work, returning to the enclosed world of the ward with its bricked-in windows, and a steady stream of patients injured by doodlebugs. Soon after a flying bomb exploded, the first casualties would come in; it didn't matter if she was about to go off duty, she'd stay and do her bit like all the other nurses and doctors, but it made for long, hard shifts.

Filling her lungs with fresh air, and with a last glance at the moon shining down on the city, Grace opened the balcony door and went back to work.

10

Norfolk

'They're huge!' Marigold shouted.

She stood beside Peter watching the queue of silver B24 Liberators waiting to take off. The ground and the air around them, was throbbing and shaking from so many thrumming engines. Marigold had never seen planes close up before, and was surprised how big and heavy they looked, and thought it was a miracle they could ever fly.

'They're late leaving this morning,' Peter shouted back. 'See that one.' He pointed to the plane closest to where they stood, on the road outside the boundary fence, which was waiting to leave its hardstand. 'That's the Peggy Sue. Prune's Howard is the navigator in her.'

'Are they full of bombs?'

'Yes, if they're going on a bombing mission.'

Marigold shivered. She'd been on the receiving end of many such missions when the bombs had landed with a sickening crump, killing and injuring people. Her bones seemed to turn to jelly inside her as she recalled the wailing of the air-raid siren . . . the urgent dash to reach shelter before the droning enemy bombers arrived overhead to drop their load. Afterwards, when the all-clear sounded, they'd emerge into the morning, picking their way through damaged streets, anxiously making their way home, not knowing whether their house would still be there. They'd been lucky, their house had escaped the bombs, when others only a street or two away had been flattened.

Peter touched her arm. 'Are you all right?'

She nodded. 'I was thinking about what it's like to be on the side getting bombed.'

'Did that happen to you?'

'Yes.' She took a deep breath. 'The Blitz was terrible. They bombed us night after night.'

'Were you scared?'

She nodded. 'Wouldn't you be?'

'Of course.' He frowned. 'What do you think about these planes going to bomb the Germans?'

Marigold poked at a stone with the toe of her shoe, not knowing what to say. Part of her thought that because they did it to us, then we should bomb them back. An eye for an eye. But then she knew what it was like to feel the fear of them coming . . . the way it made your heart race because you didn't know if it was going to be you who got it this time. If a bomb had your name on it. Or not.

It should stop, Marigold thought. They should all stop fighting each other. The British and the Germans, the Americans, the Russians and the Japanese. Everyone. Children aren't supposed to fight. Teachers always stopped any fights at school, pulled them apart and sent them to the headmaster. So why was it right for adults to do it when they tell children not to? Only their fighting was worse, it killed and injured people.

'I wish the war would end. No more bombs dropped anywhere.'

'We all do,' Peter agreed. 'Especially those men in there.' He gestured towards the planes.

'Then why are they fighting?'

59

'To stop Hitler. Trust me, you wouldn't want the Nazis to invade England. So, we must fight back, until it's safe again.'

'Was it bad in Austria before you came here?'

'Yes, and it was getting worse all the time. My parents did their best to hide it from me, but I listened to them talking. They were scared. They tried hard to get us out of the country, writing and applying for jobs here in England, but couldn't find any, and were getting desperate . . . so when the chance came for me to leave on the train with other children, they grabbed it.'

'Did you want to come here?'

Peter shrugged. 'Yes, and no. It was exciting to travel to England. An adventure, my parents called it, but I had to come alone and leave them behind.'

Marigold nodded sympathetically. 'I know how that feels.' She turned her head as a green flare suddenly shot up in the air. 'Hey! What's that?'

'It means they can go.'

The noise increased as the lead plane revved its engines hard and then hurtled down the runway. Just when Marigold thought it was going to run into the field at the far end, it took off and slowly climbed upwards, like a heavy bird taking off.

'Here goes another one!' Peter shouted.

'But the first one's only just gone.'

'They go about forty-five seconds apart.'

'But won't they hit each other?' Marigold asked.

'They try not to, but it sometimes happens in poor weather, though not today I hope.' He waved his hand up at the blue summer sky, which had cleared after the misty start.

They watched as one by one; the planes took off

and the Peggy Sue left her hardstand and joined the queue of waiting planes. Peter counted each one as they lifted off the ground, and began climbing higher and higher, circling round and round as they went.

'That's the last one,' Peter said as it sped down the runway and took off. 'That makes twenty-nine up today.'

'What happens now?' Marigold asked, her voice back to a normal level.

'They'll join up into a huge formation with planes from other American bases, then head off over the North Sea to wherever they're heading for today's target. They've nearly flown a hundred missions from here, and there's going to be a big party soon to celebrate.'

'Where are they flying to?'

'It's a secret!' He turned and looked behind him, first to the right and then the left, then pressed his finger to his lips. 'Shh! Careless talk costs lives; there could be a spy around.'

Marigold giggled. 'Do you know?'

'No. They tell the crews at a meeting before they fly, where there's a large map on the wall which shows where they're going.'

'When will they be back?'

'This afternoon sometime, I'll come back here and watch them land. Do you want to join me?'

Marigold nodded.

'You can help me count them in again. All twenty-nine, I hope.'

11

Bessie's arm was aching. She let go of the churn handle and opened the lid. Peering inside she saw that small granules of yellow butter were bobbing in the pale milk. It was nearly there. Shutting the lid firmly, she'd just started to churn again when Marigold walked in the door.

'Hello, Bessie, we're back. Peter's gone to find Harry.'

'Did you see the planes?'

The little girl nodded. 'They were huge . . . and full of bombs.' She pulled a face. 'I didn't like it that they were going to bomb people, the same as happened to us in London.'

'I know, but it's what Churchill thinks we must do to win the war.'

'I wish it was over.'

'So, do I, as do millions of people.' Bessie turned the churn handle faster. 'You should write about seeing the planes in your diary.'

Marigold pulled out a chair and sat down at the table near where Bessie was working. 'What did you write about in your diary?'

'About things I did every day, like you do. I was a nurse during the Great War, so I wrote about my work in the hospital and sometimes about what I thought and felt.'

'My mummy's a nurse, at St Thomas'. What hospital were you at?'

'Marston Hall Auxiliary War Hospital. It wasn't

as big as St Thomas'. It was in Marston Hall, a big house where I worked as a seamstress before the war. After the war started there were so many wounded men that they needed more hospitals. Lady Heaton, who I worked for, volunteered her house to be used as a hospital. I became a nurse there. A VAD.'

'What's that?' Marigold asked.

'It stands for Voluntary Aid Detachment. I wasn't a proper nurse like your mummy is. I had some nursing training, but my job was mainly to help look after the men and run the ward.'

'Did you enjoy it?'

Bessie stopped churning and smiled at her. 'Yes, I did. It was hard work, and I was on my feet all day rushing around. It was sad to see the men with such terrible wounds, but I enjoyed caring for them and helping them to get better.'

'Mummy says her feet ache at the end of a shift, did yours?'

'Oh yes, and I'd be so tired that all I wanted to do was sleep, but I always wrote in my diary first. I'd let all my thoughts out and then I'd be able to rest better. I think writing them down was like letting them go, and then I didn't lay awake worrying about things so much. It helped me.'

That's what Sergeant Harmer had told her when he'd insisted that she take the diary, and he'd been right.

★ ★ ★

6th March,
1918 A letter from Robert today. He says he's well, in good spirits and having a few days' rest from the

*Front, with a chance of a bath and some clean clothes.
I can imagine what he's like from the state of the soldiers who come here straight from the Front. He got
the socks I knitted him, and the scarf from Mother too.
He's worrying about them at home, Mother, our little
sister, and especially Father, now he has to work at the
forge on his own. Robert's concerned about me seeing
wounded men too. That's so typical of him to be fretting about us when he's the one in real danger! I can
manage perfectly fine. I'm used to it now and enjoy
doing my bit to help.*

★   ★   ★

'Here we are, nurse.' Private Dennis placed his empty
mug on the tray. 'Lovely cup of tea, thank you.'

'You're welcome.' Bessie smiled at the young man.
He'd quickly made himself at home, she thought, making her way around the ward collecting more mugs.

Each time a convoy of new patients arrived, it shook
the ward up and took a while for things to settle down
again, and for everyone to get to know one another
and feel comfortable together. The latest group of
men, who'd arrived a week ago were a happy, talkative
bunch, except for one: Sergeant Rushbrook. He was
an amputee, one leg gone below the knee, and was
still bedbound. His bed was at the end of the ward,
facing the window which he spent most of his time
staring out of, rather than joining in with the cheerful
banter of the other men. Despite being quiet and
withdrawn, he was always polite and as helpful as he
could be when they changed the dressing on his leg.
Bessie had the feeling he was far away, and he intrigued
her.

She watched him as she approached his bed, where he lay staring out the window again with an expression of sadness on his face.

'Sergeant Rushbrook?'

He started at Bessie's voice and turned to face her. 'Nurse?'

'I've come for your mug. Have you finished your tea?'

He reached over and picked it up from the top of his locker. It was still half full, and he gulped it down and handed the mug to her.

'Was it cold?'

'It was fine, thank you.'

'Would you like a book to read . . . or a newspaper?'

'No, thank you.'

Bessie regarded him for a moment. 'I've noticed you often look out of the window, what are you looking at?'

'Trees, grass, birds. The sky.'

'Spring will soon be here. The daffodils are coming up in the garden and there are some snowdrops out. You'll be able to go outside and see them for yourself once you're up.'

Sergeant Rushbrook didn't say anything. Bessie had the distinct feeling he didn't want to talk, and she wasn't going to push him. She'd learned that patients would talk when they wanted to, and not before. In the meantime, she would keep talking to him and, hopefully, he'd become less withdrawn and begin to enjoy being on the ward with the other men.

'If you change your mind and would like me to fetch you a book or something, call me.'

He gave a nod and resumed staring out of the window.

She left him to his thoughts and carried on collecting up the rest of the empty mugs.

'Nurse Carter?' called one of the other bedbound men, with both his arms bandaged from fingertip to shoulder, as she walked past.

Bessie stopped by the end of his bed. 'What can I do for you, Private Wade?'

'I'd like to write a letter to my girl, only . . .' he held up his bandaged right arm and shrugged. 'I can't hold a pencil. I know what I want to say, but I need someone to write it down for me.'

'I'd be happy to help you. I'll take these along to the kitchen, then be straight back.'

Five minutes later, Bessie drew up a chair alongside Private Wade's bed, ready with a pencil and paper. The first time she'd written a letter to a Tommy's sweetheart she'd felt awkward, as if she were intruding in their special world, but she'd now done it so many times it no longer bothered her. She was merely acting as a secretary, and besides, all the men were used to their letters passing through the censor while they were in France. Every word they'd written to loved ones back home had been scrutinised for anything which might prove useful if the letter fell into enemy hands. The censor's stamp was on each one she'd received from her brother.

'I'm ready. You dictate to me and I'll write in my best handwriting.'

'Dear Lizzie.' He stopped, looking awkward.

Bessie smiled at him encouragingly.

Private Wade cleared his throat and continued. 'Nurse Carter is writing this for me . . .'

★ ★ ★

The ward was settling down for the night. The men were changed into their pyjamas and in bed, with some reading and others already dozing off. Bessie glanced at the clock on the wall. Fifteen more minutes and she'd be off duty. She was more than ready for her bed. Since she'd come on duty at midday, she'd been almost non-stop on her feet the whole time, except for the time sitting beside Private Wade writing his letter for him. Bessie was happy though, she loved doing this work, helping the soldiers who had been through so much.

'No!' a loud shout came from the end of the ward. 'No! No!'

'It's Rushbrook, nurse,' Private Dennis called from his bed. 'He's asleep. He does that sometimes.'

Bessie nodded at Private Dennis and strode down the ward to the end bed where Sergeant Rushbrook was still asleep. His face was contorted in anguish, beads of sweat stood out on his brow, while his eyes danced rapidly under their lids.

She pulled up a chair and sat down beside him and gently took one of his hands in hers.

'Sergeant Rushbrook?' she whispered. 'It's Nurse Carter.'

Her voice must have broken into his dream as he woke with a jolt, his eyes darting around, checking where he was.

'Everything's all right, you're safe. You were dreaming.' Bessie squeezed his hand.

She'd seen plenty of men having nightmares; some would thrash about in their beds, screaming and crying out as they relived the terrors of the trenches. The best thing to do was hold their hands and be there for them. Talk to them if they wanted to when they woke up. But with Sergeant Rushbrook, Bessie doubted he would want that.

'A dream?' His clear blue eyes met Bessie's.

She nodded. 'You were crying out.'

'What did I say?'

'No, several times over.'

He sighed heavily, glancing down at the space in the bed where his right leg should be. Was that what he was dreaming of? Bessie wondered; the time when his leg was injured. She wanted to ask him, but knew she shouldn't push him, so waited quietly for him to speak, still holding onto his hand, which to her surprise he hadn't snatched back when he woke up and realised what she was doing.

'My leg,' Sergeant Rushbrook said several minutes later when Bessie was thinking perhaps it would be best to leave him alone. 'It was about my leg.' His eyes caught hers for a few seconds, then he looked away again. His glance had been brief, but enough for her to see his pain.

'Was it about when you were injured?' Bessie gently probed.

He shook his head. 'It was when they told me they'd amputated it.' He swallowed hard. 'I needed it. One leg's no good to me.'

Bessie's heart ached for him. 'Better to lose your leg than your life.' She tightened her hold on his hand. 'I know it's easy for me to say, but the doctors wouldn't have removed it unless they had to. Trust me, you would never want to have gangrene.'

'But one leg's no good for . . .'

'There you are, Nurse Carter.' Sister William's voice interrupted them. 'It's time you were off duty.'

What bad timing, Bessie was sure he'd been about

to say something significant, but she would not give in now, she'd stay on in her own time. It wouldn't be the first time she'd be late going off duty. Nursing wasn't a regular office job, in at eight, out at five. If something like this happened, it was her duty to follow it through, and this, she had the strongest feeling, was important.

'Yes, Sister, I'll be along soon.'

Bessie waited until her footsteps retreated to the other end of the ward and then quietly said, 'What's one leg no good for?'

'You should be off duty; you've been on the go since midday.'

'I have, but . . .' Bessie began. How did he know how long she'd been working for? 'Are you keeping a check on when we come on duty?'

'I watch what's going on.'A hint of a smile played on his lips. 'You started at midday, brought me my dinner.'

'Yes, I did, but you're trying to distract me. You haven't answered my question, tell me . . . what is one leg no good for?' Bessie smiled at him. 'Please?'

'For my old life.' He stared up at the ceiling as he spoke. 'I can't go back to it now.'

'What did you do?'

'Worked on a hill farm in Cumberland where I come from. Up on the fells with the sheep. You need two working legs to walk about up there. A wooden leg's no use.'

'The artificial legs are good for walking on, but I don't think they'd stand up to jumping around the fells.' She frowned. 'Isn't there something else you can do?'

'I love farming,' Sergeant Rushbrook said. 'It's all

I ever wanted to do, right from when I was a lad. I enjoy looking after animals and working outside.'

'Perhaps you could think of another way to do it.'

'My old boss would never employ a one-legged man.' His voice was tinged with bitterness.

What could Bessie say? She knew the farmers around her home village wouldn't take on a worker who couldn't do the job as well as a man with two legs. Not even if he lost a leg fighting for his country.

'I know it's hard for you, but you're alive, and you still have your entire life ahead of you,' she said gently. 'It might not be the one you hoped for, but you mustn't give up. Something will come up for you to do, but you need to get fully better first, up on crutches and then learn to walk again with an artificial leg.' Bessie fixed her eyes on his face. 'Nurse's orders,' she added with a smile.

She waited for him to respond, his expression unreadable as he stared at the hump his remaining foot made under the covers. He sighed and turned to face her, his eyes meeting hers.

'It's time you were off duty, Nurse Carter. Thank you for talking to me.' He paused, looking down at their joined hands. 'And for holding my hand.' To her surprise, he squeezed her hand before releasing it. 'Goodnight.'

His message was obvious. He didn't want to talk about it. For now, Bessie thought. She had at least cracked his hard shell and he'd revealed his worries to her. It was an important first step. She was satisfied for the moment, but she hadn't finished with him by a long way. She was determined to get him up and out of bed, onto crutches, then well enough to go on to St Mary's in Roehampton where he would be fitted with a new leg. There would be a life worth living for him. Perhaps not the one he'd planned, but she had the strongest feeling he would find a role which made him happy.

'Goodnight then, Sergeant Rushbrook.' Bessie stood up. 'I'll be back on duty at midday tomorrow and will see you then. Sleep well.'

12

Peter paced up and down the road, stopping now and then to listen, straining his ears for the sound of approaching engines. But there was nothing. Only the distant caw of crows and the chattering of swallows flying overhead. He glanced at Marigold, who was sitting on the bank making a daisy chain.

Waiting for the planes to come back was always bittersweet. Peter loved being there to welcome them home, but at the same time, he dreaded it too, worrying what sort of condition they would be in? Would they all return? He sighed. They'd already been here nearly an hour because he could only guess when they might arrive. It depended on where they were going, the further away, the later they'd be back.

Over on the base, Peter could see the control tower where tiny figures stood on the high balcony around the top. If they were out watching and waiting, the planes must be expected anytime now.

Then it came . . . the first sound of droning engines. He searched the sky in the distance and could just make out some tiny dark specks heading towards them.

'Look! They're coming!' Peter pointed to the planes, which were growing bigger by the second.

Marigold jumped to her feet, scattering daisies off her skirt. 'Where?'

'See, there! Remember, we need to count them in.'

'Twenty-nine planes went out,' she reminded him.

'And I hope twenty-nine come home.' Peter hated it when they didn't all come back. He'd got to know some of the crews and losing them made him cry. He wanted everyone to get through their thirty missions safely, and then they could go home to America. But not all of them made it. It was a bitter fact of war, though it was hard to bear.

'Here comes the first one in.' Marigold grabbed hold of his arm as a B24 descended towards the runway. It landed with a bounce, rushing along the airstrip so fast it looked like it would plough into the cornfield at the far end. But it slowed, turned in time and headed in their direction around the perimeter track on its way back to its hardstand.

'First one in,' Peter said. 'It's the Laughing Jenny, see the picture and name painted on the nose. It looks fine. No holes.'

That wasn't always the case, though. Sometimes the B24s came back damaged, with ragged tailplanes, holes in the wings, engines not working, or worse. If the damage was bad enough, then landing could be a problem. Peter had once seen a plane land with no wheels, it had skidded along on its belly and ploughed off the runway at the far end. The men had been lucky that time, they'd all got out.

'Here comes another,' Marigold said. 'Number two.'

They watched as each plane landed and made its way back to where it had started from that morning. Some of them were damaged, with chunks missing out of tails and holes peppered in their fuselage, but at least they'd returned safely.

'Twenty-eight,' Peter said. 'One more to go.' He

looked around for any sign of the final one, but the sky in the distance was empty. His stomach knotted.

'Where's the last one?'

'I don't know!' He snapped. Marigold stared at him, her eyes wide. 'Sorry, I didn't mean to snap at you, I'm worried what's happened.'

'Is Howard's plane back?'

Peter shook his head, gesturing his hand at the empty hardstand in front of them.

'What . . . ?' Marigold began. He hushed her and listened.

'There!' He pointed to the distance where a speck had appeared and was slowly coming towards them. 'Is that them?'

His heart was thudding as they watched the plane come in, flying lower than the others had. It skimmed a few feet over the trees at the far end of the base before touching down.

Peter let out a sigh of relief. 'Twenty-nine, Marigold! Twenty-nine out, and twenty-nine back.'

As the Peggy Sue rolled down the runway and turned to head back to her hardstand, Peter could see what the problem was. One of her propellers was still, she'd had an engine knocked out, which had made her slower than the others.

'Don't forget Bessie's message for Howard,' Marigold reminded him.

'I'll tell him as soon as he gets out, before they go off for debriefing.'

'What's that?'

'It's when they talk about what happened on the mission. If they saw enemy planes, whether they hit the target, that sort of thing.'

Like all the other boys he knew at school, Peter

was fascinated with the planes which filled the skies above Norfolk, and the airmen who flew them. He often talked to Howard about how things worked when he came to Orchard Farm to visit Prune. Peter had wanted to know what they did before and after a mission. What it was like flying thousands of feet up over enemy territory, and Howard had told him what he could.

Howard was the fourth to climb down out of the plane, and he waved to them.

'Hey! Peter.' He strode across to them dressed in his thick sheepskin jacket, trousers and boots, and spoke to them through the perimeter fence. 'Has the school vacation started?'

'Yes, last Friday,' Peter said. 'What happened to the engine?'

'We had a disagreement with a Focke-Wulf 190 over the Dutch coast. Nothing to worry about though; Peggy Sue brought us safely home. You must be Marigold. Prune's told me about you, I'm glad to meet you.'

'Hello,' Marigold said shyly.

'Come on, Howard, time to go,' one of the Peggy Sue's crew shouted, as they piled into a jeep which had come out to fetch them.

'Okay, be right there.' Howard waved to him.

'Bessie said to remind you and Clem about tea on Saturday,' Peter said.

'Thank you, I'm looking forward to it. I'll see you guys soon.'

Howard jogged over to the waiting jeep and climbed on board with the rest of his crew, waving as he was driven off.

13

Marigold laid the last of the knives and forks in place and stood back to look at the table in case she'd forgotten anything. She'd had to lay eight places instead of the usual six because they were having visitors.

'You've done a good job.' Bessie put her arm around Marigold's shoulder. 'There's the bread to slice and then I think we're ready. Howard and Clem should be here any minute. Are you sure you don't want to go with the others to meet them?'

'Yes. I'd rather stay here.'

'Can you go and tell Harry to come in for tea?' Bessie asked.

'Where is he?'

'In the garden.'

Marigold slipped out of the back door, running past the washhouse where Bessie heated water in the big copper for baths or washing clothes, then along the path to the large vegetable garden.

'Harry!' she called.

'Over here.' He was standing in the row of cabbages, examining the leaves.

'What are you doing?'

'I'm checking for caterpillar eggs. If they hatch out, they'll eat the lot.'

'Are there any?'

'Not yet, but I've seen the cabbage white butterflies flying around, so I'm keeping an eye out for them.'

'Bessie said you're to come in for tea. The American visitors will be here soon.'

'You'll like them, they're full of fun.'

'I saw Howard when his plane landed,' Marigold said.

'Peter told me. They were lucky to get back.'

'Howard said it was nothing to worry about.'

'He would say that.' Harry patted Marigold's shoulder. 'Come on then, it's time for tea.'

She could hear strange voices coming from indoors as she and Harry climbed up the steps to the house — the Americans had arrived. Marigold held back behind Harry, lingering in his shadow, as she followed him into the house.

'Hello, sir,' Howard and the other American both said, coming over and taking it in turns to shake Harry's hand.

'Hello, Howard, Clem. Good to see you both.'

'Here's Marigold, Clem,' Howard smiled at her.

'I'm glad to meet you.' Clem held out his hand to her. 'I guess my daughter's about the same age as you.'

'Hello,' she whispered, shaking his hand.

Clem was different from Howard, he was older and wore glasses, but they were both dressed in the smart American uniform.

'Look what Howard and Clem brought us,' Bessie said, her arms full of tins of peaches and luncheon meat, and bags of sugar.

'And they gave us these.' Peter waved some comics and two Hershey chocolate bars in the air. 'There's Superman and Captain Marvel.'

'It's kind of you,' Harry said. 'But we don't expect you to bring us something if you come to tea.'

'We're glad to.' Clem smiled. 'We appreciate you inviting us to your home, it means a lot.'

'Come on then, sit yourselves down everyone,'

77

Dottie said. 'Howard, you go next to Prune there. Clem, you go beside Peter.'

'Can I get your chair for you?' Clem asked Marigold, as she pulled her chair out from under the table.

She nodded. 'Thank you.'

Marigold watched as he and Howard did the same for Bessie, Dottie and Prune, before sitting down themselves. The Americans had pleasant manners and were friendly. She decided she was going to enjoy getting to know them.

★ ★ ★

'What do you think of her?' Peter leaned over the side of the pen and scratched Daisy's ears.

'She sure is a fine calf.' Howard ran his hand appreciatively along Daisy's back.

'A heifer too,' Harry said. 'We were pleased.'

'Tell us about your cows in America,' Peter said. 'Are they like ours?'

Howard stroked under Daisy's throat, and the calf stretched out her neck, enjoying his touch. 'No, our cattle are a bigger, hardier breed, used to being outside most of the time. Your girls are much prettier, but they wouldn't do well on our ranch.'

'Do you lasso them?' he asked.

Howard grinned at him. 'Sure do. I guess you don't with yours, do you?'

'They wouldn't like it!' Harry shook his head. 'They're so friendly they'll come when we call them. We don't need to catch them.'

'Would you show me how to lasso?' Peter asked. 'Not on our cows though, it would scare them.'

'Sure, we'll find something else to lasso instead.

78

Have you got some rope?'

Peter thought it looked as if the Wild West of the pictures had come to Orchard Farm, when five minutes later, Howard stood in the middle of the farmyard circling the lasso around his head.

Round and round the rope went, then effortlessly, Howard flung the lasso away from him and it slipped cleanly over the end of Harry's sawing stool. Then, with one swift movement, he pulled the noose tight.

'There you go,' Howard said. 'That sawhorse's not far off a cow shape. It's got the four legs and horns. You wanna have a turn, Peter?'

'I'll try.' He would love to swing the rope as effortlessly as Howard had, and if he could get it to go over what he aimed for, well, that would be swell, real swell, as the Americans would say.

'No problem. I can teach you how, and Harry, if you like, sir?'

'Turn us into cowboys?' Harry laughed. 'Why not?'

'Okay, first up, you need to hold your rope like so.' Howard held the loop in one hand and the end coiled up in his other. 'You need to stand in front of your target and let your wrist relax . . . then slowly swing it, right to left, like this.' Howard brought the rope up and swung it above his head. 'Then . . . cast the loop forward.'

Peter watched as he swung the lasso, and once again, sent it straight over the sawhorse's horns.

'Pull the loop tight.' Howard shrugged his shoulders. 'Nothing to it, once you know how. Who's turn first?'

'Let's see you have a go, Peter,' Harry said.

Howard guided Peter, helping him to start off holding the rope the right way.

'You've got it,' Howard said. 'Now remember, relax your wrist and swing it above your head.'

Concentrating hard, he brought the rope up and started the swinging motion, but he didn't have to look at it to know it was nowhere near as perfect as Howard's.

'Okay, Peter, you're doing great. When you're ready, cast it forward and over the sawhorse's horns.'

Peter launched the loop in the sawhorse's direction, but it landed short on the ground with a thud. He sighed. Howard made it look so easy, but it wasn't.

'Good try, have another go,' Howard encouraged him. 'It took me weeks of practice to do it right. You'll get there if you keep at it.'

★ ★ ★

Howard and Harry leaned against the gate leading into the orchard, watching Peter practising.

'He's getting the hang of it much better than I did,' Harry said. 'And won't give up until he gets there.'

'Practise is the only way, that's what I did after my pa taught me. Kept on practising until I could do it every time.' Howard turned to face Harry. 'I'd like to ask you something, sir. You know the Peggy Sue lost an engine on our last mission?'

Harry nodded.

'She's being fixed up, and we'll have a trial flight in a day or two to check her out before we go on the next mission. I wondered if Peter would like to come with us. We'll only be flying up as far as the coast, and I know he'd enjoy it, but I didn't want to ask him without checking with you first.'

'I'm sure he'd love to, only . . .' Harry hesitated.

'I'd take real good care of him.'

'I know you would, but it's Bessie . . . she'd say no.' He rubbed the back of his neck. 'But it's a chance to fly and I think the lad should have it, if he wants to.'

'But what about Bessie? I don't want to upset her.'

Harry patted the young man's shoulder. 'You leave her to me. If Peter's happy to do it, then we'll keep it between ourselves, Bessie can know afterwards when it's over and done with.' He would deal with the aftermath when it came. This was too good an opportunity for Peter to miss out on.

'You're sure about that?' Howard asked.

'Yes. Come on, let's tell Peter.'

'Really? You'll take me flying in a Liberator?' Peter stared at Howard. 'In the Peggy Sue?

'You bet.'

The boy's face broke into a wide smile. 'Yes, please, I would love to go! Thank you very much.'

'But you mustn't tell Bessie what's going on, because if she knows, then she won't let you go,' Harry warned him.

'But . . .' Peter began.

'She'd be too worried about it to say yes. But I think you should grab the chance to do it if you want to.' Harry smiled at him reassuringly. 'We'll tell Bessie when it's over and you're back, then she won't have to worry about a thing.'

14

London

'Grace!' A voice called.

Opening her eyes and shielding them against the bright sunlight, Grace spotted her friend, Helen, hurrying towards her.

She got up from the bench overlooking the lake in St James's Park, and went to meet her. This was the first time Grace had seen Helen since she'd taken Marigold to Norfolk. Although her friend had been back for a few days, their conflicting shift patterns at the hospital hadn't allowed them a chance to get together until now.

'Hello.' Grace smiled warmly at Helen and put her arms around her.

'It's lovely to see you.' Helen returned her hug. 'How are you?'

'I'm fine. Glad to have the day off though, it's been busy as usual.'

Helen stepped back and looked at Grace. 'You should take a holiday too. I feel like a new woman.'

'It was good then?'

Helen nodded. 'It was marvellous. I didn't want it to end . . .' She looked wistful. 'But we both had to return to our work.'

'Shall we walk around the lake?'

'Yes, why not?'

Grace linked her arm through Helen's, and they wandered along in the warm August sunshine, passing other people out enjoying time in the park.

'Have you heard from Marigold?'

'Yes, she's settled in well and seems to be happy, and has been helping on the farm. Even helping to teach a calf how to drink milk from a pail.'

Helen laughed. 'It's a wee bit different from around here then.' She stopped walking and her eyes met Grace's. 'You did the right thing, sending her to live in Norfolk. I know it wasn't easy for you, but Marigold's safe there.'

She nodded and swallowed hard, forcing back the emotion threatening to overwhelm her, waiting until she was sure she could talk without crying. 'But I miss her so much . . .'

'Of course, you do.' Helen squeezed her arm. 'Bessie seemed like a lovely woman. I only met her for a few minutes, but she had a genuine warmth about her. Her face when she saw Marigold . . . I thought she was going to scoop her up in her arms.'

Grace wasn't surprised at Bessie's reaction. 'Did she?'

Helen shook her head. 'But I could see it in her face that she wanted to.'

A thorn of guilt pricked at Grace's conscience. Perhaps she was wrong, insisting that Marigold not be told who warm-hearted Bessie was. But it would have exposed Grace's past and revealed to her daughter that she'd not been completely honest with her.

'You've no worries about your daughter not being cared for properly with Bessie,' Helen added.

'What about Marigold, how was she when you left her?'

'Quiet. I think she was resigned to it by then. After we left you at Liverpool Street station, there was no

83

going back, and she seemed to accept it.'

'I hated seeing her so upset.'

'I know, but she soon settled down once we were on the way. It's difficult for wee children being evacuated, but thousands of them are, and it is the safest thing for them right now.'

Grace sighed. 'I keep telling myself that. I'll go and see her there in a while.'

'I . . .' Helen began, but then paused. 'Listen!'

They both halted, hardly daring to breathe, listening to the ominous droning sound which was heading towards them. Around them, other people had stopped having heard it, too.

'Doodlebug!' someone shouted.

Grace scanned the sky, looking for it, her heart racing.

'There!' Helen pointed as it came into view, travelling fast over them and heading northwards. 'It's still going.'

Seconds later, the doodlebug's drone altered to a *phut, phut* sound, and then the engine cut out, and it started its deadly glide downwards, heading for a spot behind some trees and tall buildings in the distance.

Grace sighed with relief. They were safe from that one, but some poor souls were about to have their world blown apart. She clung onto Helen's arm as they waited for the explosion. Then it came. *Whoomph!* They couldn't see the flash as it exploded, only the pall of smoke rising high into the still summer air, marking the spot where innocent people had probably been injured or killed.

'Are you all right?'

'Yes . . . they're hideous things!' Helen's voice was shaky, her face turned chalk white.

Grace put her arms around her friend and held her close. Any doubts about sending Marigold away had vanished . . . the doodlebug was a harsh reminder of why she'd had no choice. With deadly weapons like that falling out of the sky, London wasn't a safe place for her daughter. Or safe for anyone now.

15

Peter stared at the Peggy Sue; she was beautiful and so much bigger close up. He could hardly believe he was going to fly in her.

'Are you ready?' Howard asked.

He nodded.

'Great, I just need to double-check your harness before we climb on board.' Howard tested the buckles on the parachute harness Peter was wearing. 'Remember, I promised Harry I'd take good care of you. I guess Bessie still doesn't know about this?'

'No, we've kept if from her. I didn't like not telling her, but Harry said she wouldn't let me come if she knew.'

'It's because she cares about you. My mom's the same, she worries about me.'

'Bessie's not my mother though.'

'No, but she's looking after you for your parents. I suppose that's even harder in a way . . . she feels responsible for you.'

'All aboard, you guys,' Walt Stewart, the pilot, called over to them.

Peter's heart was galloping and his legs trembling, as he followed Howard to the belly of the Peggy Sue, where the bomb bay doors hung open.

'This is where we get in, and you need to remember, it's where we'd jump from if we had to parachute down. Understand?'

He nodded, hoping that wouldn't be necessary.

86

Howard climbed in first and held out a hand to help him in. Standing upright once he was inside, Peter was surprised at the difference between the smooth outside skin of the Peggy Sue, compared with the inside. In here it was a network of rib-like joins, where sections of the plane were riveted together.

'You okay?' Howard asked.

'It looks so different in here.'

'Yup, I guess so, you kinda get used to it. Walt wondered if you'd like to go to the cockpit for take-off?'

'Oh, yes, please. I'd love to.'

'I'll fix you up with some headphones and a throat-mike first, then you'll be able to hear us and talk back once we're airborne.'

Peter couldn't stop smiling as he followed Howard along the length of the Peggy Sue to the cockpit, a few minutes later. Wearing his harness and chute, headphones and a throat-mike, he looked the part of an airman. He'd have so much to tell Harry when he got home.

'Welcome aboard,' Walt said, when Peter arrived at the cockpit. 'John's flying copilot with us.'

John looked up from his last-minute checks and smiled a welcome at him.

'Thank you for letting me come flying.'

'It's a pleasure,' Walt said. 'If you want to stay in here for take-off, you can kneel here between our seats.'

Howard laid a hand on Peter's shoulder. 'I'll go back to my base for take-off. I'll see you once we're flying.'

He knelt where Walt had told him, watching every move the pilots made as they prepared to fly.

As the four engines roared into life, the whole plane seemed to come alive, shuddering and throbbing. Peter listened in as Walt talked to the control tower, and once they'd been given clearance to go, they started to move. They were the only plane going out on a check-out flight that afternoon. The others had gone out on a mission earlier that morning.

At the end of the runway, they turned to face the long ribbon of tarmac, where Walt applied the brakes and revved the engines hard. The entire plane thrummed and juddered with the engine noise, it was as if she was straining to go, like a dog desperate to be off its lead. Then, on word from the control tower, Walt released the brakes, and they were off.

The Peggy Sue hurtled down the runway, faster and faster, and Peter had the strongest urge to go even quicker. He loved the sensation of speed. When it seemed as if they could go no faster, Walt eased back the control column and the plane's nose tilted skyward.

Peter had the strangest sensation as they swung upwards, a sudden lightness, but his stomach felt like he had left it behind on the ground. It quickly caught up with him and then Peter knew he was flying . . . actually flying! He wanted to jump around with excitement, but he kept still, holding on to the back of Walt's seat as the plane climbed higher.

There were clunks and whirrs as the undercarriage came up and the wing flaps moved. The inside of Peter's ears tightened, then popped. Howard had warned him he'd need to keep swallowing as they went up and down, but he'd forgotten with the excitement and wonder of it all.

'Peter, how're you doing?' Walt's voice came through the headset.

'It's wonderful.' He smiled at Walt, who grinned back and gave him a thumbs-up.

'We'll be out for about an hour, doing some circuits around the base first, then go up to the coast and you can see the ocean. Howard said you'd like to buzz your folks?'

'Yes, please. They'll be looking out for us.'

'You live on the farm to the east of the base?'

'Yes, Orchard Farm.'

'I know it. Howard's going to take you down to the nose turret, you'll get a magnificent view in there, and your folks will be able to see you.'

Sitting in the nose turret, a short while later, with only the Plexiglas between him and the air, made Peter feel he was as close to flying like a bird as he could be. He had a bird's-eye view, and everything looked so small and neat. The treetops were spongy looking, and the fields, hedges and woods spread out like a patchwork quilt of different tones of gold, brown and green.

'We're on approach,' Howard warned him. 'Orchard Farm's up ahead. I can see the elms on the lane. Where did Harry say they'll be?'

'In the yard, with Bessie and Marigold.' Peter fished in his trouser pocket and pulled out a scarlet scarf. 'Dottie gave me this to wave, so they'll be able to see me. She and Prune will be watching out for us in the field near where they're working.'

Howard grinned. 'I told Walt we should give them a buzz too. Right, you'd better start waving, we're going in!'

★ ★ ★

'Bessie! Marigold! Come out here. Quick!'

Bessie stopped turning the mangle's handle and

turned to look at Harry, who'd stuck his head around the wash-house door. 'What's the matter?'

'Come on quick, or we'll miss it.' He beckoned to them. 'Hurry.'

'What on earth's going on?'

'You'll see.'

They followed Harry out into the cooler air, and it was a relief to be out of the steamy heat of the wash-house.

'What are we supposed to see?' She asked, peering around and seeing nothing unusual.

Marigold turned in a circle, looking in all directions. 'I can't see anything different.'

'Just wait . . . any minute now,' he said. 'All we have to do is stand here and wait.'

'Harry Rushbrook, I have a lot of washing to get through. If you think I have time to play silly games you've got another think . . .' Bessie's words failed at the sound of engines approaching. Loud, fast engines.

She whipped around to face the direction from which they came, gasping at the sight of what was heading towards them. A Liberator. It was coming in so low, barely clearing the church tower in the village. Was it going to crash?

'Harry!' Bessie clutched his arm.

'It's all right, love. Look!' He pointed to the front of the plane, where something red was being waved around inside the nose turret.

Harry waved back, laughing.

'Wave, you two. Come on, wave at the lad.'

Bessie glanced at her husband's beaming face, as he looked up at the plane. Had he taken leave of his senses?

Marigold jumped up and down, waving madly.

90

'Who's in there?'

Harry's reply was drowned out by the noise of the Liberator bearing down on them, and as it flew straight over head, they all instinctively ducked down.

Harry laughed. 'Did you see him?'

Her heart was hammering. 'What's going on? Who was that?'

'Peter.'

Bessie's knees trembled, and she thought for a moment her legs were going to buckle, but they held fast. '*Peter's up there?* Flying in that thing?' She jabbed her finger towards the plane, which was banking around looking like it was about to make another pass over the farm.

Harry nodded. 'He had the chance to go for a flight in the Peggy Sue.'

'When was this arranged?' Bessie's voice sounded surprisingly calm; it didn't betray the way she was churning up inside. 'Why wasn't I told?'

'Here they come again.' Marigold jumped up and down, waving as the huge plane came rushing towards them, barely higher than the elms lining the lane. 'Look at Peter.'

Bessie stood still, her arms hanging limply at her side, while Harry waved his arms above his head. She could just make out Peter's face looking down at them as the plane passed over, and this time it kept flying straight on and was soon lost from view.

'That was amazing!' Marigold said. 'Do you think I could go for a ride in one?'

Bessie didn't reply, but stalked back to the wash-house, slamming the door shut behind her and leaning against it. The sticky heat immediately enveloped her, and tears stung her eyes as the image of Peter's face looking down from the nose of the plane filled her mind. Harry had a lot to answer for when she could trust herself to speak to him, but in the meanwhile she had work to do. Grabbing the mangle's handle, she turned it with far more force than it needed.

* * *

'Here he comes!' Dottie squealed, grabbing hold of Prune's arm.

Prune stared at the plane bearing down on them.

'Come on, wave.' Dottie pulled the pink scarf off her hair and waved it in the air enthusiastically. 'Look at the red in the nose turret, it's Peter.'

Prune swallowed down the bubble of unease welling up in her throat and joined in, waving both her arms over her head. Howard was in that plane somewhere too, and although she couldn't see him, no doubt he could see her.

As the plane thundered towards them, Prune had to fight the urge to throw herself on the ground for fear it was going to hit them. But it didn't, roaring overhead, its engines making the air and earth around them throb.

'Did you see his face?'

'Yes.' They stood watching the plane head northwards, growing smaller and smaller until it disappeared.

'I bet Peter's loving it. We'll hear all about it when he gets home. It was good of Howard to arrange it for him.'

'He's a kind man,' Prune agreed as they walked back up the track to the woods where they were working. 'I wish that was the only flying he did, with no more dangerous missions over enemy territory with guns shooting at them, and fighter planes waiting to pounce.'

Dottie put her arm around Prune's shoulders. 'We all wish they didn't have to do it.'

'You know what some men call the planes . . . flying coffins.'

'There's only one way to deal with it.' Dottie stopped, looking back in the direction the plane had gone. 'You have to take it one day at a time. Worrying yourself sick won't make any difference, it will only make you miserable. Cheer up, remember, we've got the hundredth mission party to look forward to.'

'I know, you're right, but it's the way I am. I care about Howard so much.' Prune sighed. 'Sometimes I wish I could be like you, carefree and easy, but I'm not.'

'We're all different.'

'But don't you wish you had . . .' she paused. 'A proper beau? Someone to marry, even?'

'No!' Dottie's voice brooked no argument. 'Come on, back to work.'

Was her friend's attitude the right way to be? Prune wondered. It would certainly save herself the anguish and heartache that she went through every time Howard flew on a mission. But knowing him brought her much happiness too, and she couldn't have one without the other, at least while the war was on . . . And if it hadn't been for the war, they'd never have met. Howard was worth every minute of worry, even if it was hard.

★ ★ ★

Bessie was folding a sheet into four, ready to put it through the mangle, when the wash-house door opened, and Harry stepped inside.

'Are you all right?'

She ignored his question. 'Where's Marigold?'

'I sent her to collect the eggs after she helped me move the cows out of the barn and down to the meadow.'

'Why were the cows indoors at this time of day?'

'I thought the plane might frighten them if they were outside. They're fine.'

Bessie fed the sheet into the mangle and turned the handle, squeezing it between the rollers and out the other side. 'So, what have you got to say for yourself?'

Harry looked at her, his clear blue eyes full of concern. 'First, I'm sorry I upset you. I knew how you'd feel about Peter going flying . . . what you'd say . . .'

'No!' Bessie snapped. 'I would have said, no.'

'I was right then.' A smile flickered across his mouth. 'But I said yes. The lad was desperate to go, and it was a good chance for him. When Howard asked, I had to say yes. You know I'd go too if I had the chance.'

Bessie shook her head. 'I thought Howard was a nice, sensible young man. Wait till I see him.'

Harry held up his hand. 'Wait a minute, you've got the wrong idea. Howard wanted to ask your permission too, but I told him not to. He wasn't happy about you not knowing.' He took a step towards her. 'He'll take great care of Peter; we can trust him.'

Bessie stopped turning the handle and glared at him. 'But that's not the point. I'm sure Howard is trustworthy and will keep his word . . . but things can go wrong. Planes don't have to be shot at to crash; they can do it all on their own when engines fail or....

You've seen the palls of smoke when that happens.'

'I hope nothing will happen.'

'It could, though.'

'And I could get run over next time I go into the village. Sometimes you have to take a risk.' Harry rubbed the back of his neck. 'It was an opportunity for Peter to do something he desperately wanted to. Who knows what's going to happen to him in the future, or if he'll ever see his parents again, so if he can have some joy out of this, then he should?'

'Don't you understand?' Bessie gripped the handle so tightly her knuckles turned white. 'I gave my word to his parents that I'd take care of him. Who knows what's happened to them or where they are?' She sighed. 'Or even if they're still alive. But I promised them that I'd look after Peter, and then you go and give permission for him to go flying. If anything happens to him . . .'

'It won't.' Harry reached out and took hold of her hand. 'I know you promised to care for Peter, and you do, extremely well, but he needs to have the chance to live life to the full, too. Sometimes you have to let things go.'

Bessie shrugged. There was no point in being angry now. Peter was up there flying in the Peggy Sue, and all she could do was wait and hope he came back in one piece.

'If there is a next time, I want to know about it, Harry. No more hiding, understand?'

'Yes, ma'am.' He gave a mock salute, then held his arms out wide to her. 'I'll go to the base and meet Peter if you like.'

'No, I'll go.' Bessie wanted to see him safely back for herself.

'Am I forgiven?' Harry asked, opening his arms wide.

'Partly . . .' Bessie smiled at him and went into his arms, leaning her head against his chest. 'The rest will come when Peter's safely back on solid earth.'

16

Peter couldn't take his eyes off the sea. It was a deep sapphire blue and had the hint of waves rolling across its surface in lines towards the shore. It was perfect and so beautiful. He'd spent most of the flight looking down on the world from inside the Plexiglas nose of the Peggy Sue, loving the way it looked from up here.

'Peter? We're going to head back to base now.' Walt's voice came through the headphones as the plane banked round towards the shore. 'Would you like to come up to the cockpit and fly the Peggy Sue?'

'Can I, really?'

'Sure, if you'd like to.'

Walt didn't have to ask twice. With a last look at the sea, he made his way up to the cockpit where John, the co-pilot, got out of his seat and beckoned for him to take his place.

Peter's heart was pounding as he climbed into the co-pilot's seat. Did Walt really think he could fly the plane?

'So, take hold of your control column, like me.' Walt nodded towards the co-pilot's controls.

Peter tentatively took the column in his hands and held it like Walt.

'Great, now hold it steady and keep your eye on this.' Walt tapped the front of the artificial horizon indicator. 'It will hold us straight and level.'

He nodded.

'Okay then, you have control.' Walt removed his hands from his column and smiled encouragingly at

97

him. 'There you go . . . you're flying the Peggy Sue, but no looping the loop though. This old ship couldn't take it.'

Peter could hardly believe it . . . he was flying a plane. He was both terrified and ecstatically happy. He held onto the column as if his life depended on it, sitting completely still in case he jogged the controls.

'You're doing great.' Howard patted Peter's shoulder. 'You can relax a bit, nothing will happen.'

He nodded and tried to loosen the tension in his shoulders, taking care to fly straight and level, concentrating on the artificial horizon indicator and keeping the column still. If he hadn't been so focused on what he was doing, he'd have been smiling so hard his face would've ached.

Part of Peter was relieved when Walt took back control, and he slipped out of the co-pilot's seat. His arms and legs were aching from holding them so rigid while he was in control.

'How was that?' Howard asked.

'I loved it, but it scared me, too.'

Howard clapped him on the back. 'You did a magnificent job.'

Peter stood between the two pilots as they headed towards their base, thinking they made flying the Peggy Sue look so easy. One day, he'd like to fly like them.

As they neared the base, Walt heard over the radio that they'd been instructed to join the incoming formation of Liberators returning from the day's mission. Peter watched out of the cockpit window as they seamlessly joined the formation and circuited around the base, waiting for their turn to land.

He'd seen the formations many times from the

ground, but now flying as part of one was something else. It gave him another perspective and rounded off his first flight perfectly.

* * *

The first Liberator landed as Bessie arrived at the base's perimeter fence, close by Peggy Sue's hardstand. She heaved her bicycle onto its stand and stood watching them come in one by one. Bessie had spotted the planes coming in from the distance as she'd cycled along. They looked like a flock of enormous birds returning home to roost, only they hadn't been out pecking in the fields all day, but on a raid somewhere.

Some Liberators were battle-scarred with bullet holes and ragged tails, or with knocked out engines, but at least they'd made it home. Had they all come back? Bessie wondered. She shuddered; the thought of men going out and not returning was heartbreaking, but it happened. There were ten in each one, meaning many lives lost every time a plane went down.

Where Peter was, Bessie had no idea. Howard had told Harry the flight would be about an hour, and that was almost up now. She'd arrived early, desperate to see Peter and know he was safe. The sight of him in the nose of the Peggy Sue had been such a shock.

Harry admitted it was only her and Marigold who hadn't known. Marigold wasn't told because they thought she might let the secret out, and Bessie knew very well why he hadn't said anything to her. She wouldn't have let Peter go, but would that have been the right thing to do? Perhaps it was better that she hadn't known and had the chance to stop him.

Her protectiveness of Peter had begun the moment she saw him coming down the gangplank off the ship, which had brought him to safety. She could still picture him, a seven-year-old with big anxious eyes and crumpled clothes, carrying a single brown suitcase. Bessie's heart had melted at the sight of him. She'd wrapped her arms around him and held him tight.

The first few months had been hard for Peter. He'd only been able to speak a few words of English, while they knew little German, only a few phrases which Harry had picked up in the trenches. But Peter was determined to learn English, and now no one would suspect that he hadn't spoken it all his life.

At first, his parents had kept in touch by letter, telling him they were safe and well, and they'd always include a note to her and Harry, thanking them for looking after their son. But then the letters suddenly stopped coming, and Peter had been devastated. Now they had no idea where his parents were or what was happening to them. Bessie thought about them often, and she desperately hoped he would be reunited with them one day when all this was over. Until then, it was her job to look after him for them.

The sound of engines turning into the nearby hardstand brought Bessie's thoughts back to the present. It was the Peggy Sue. They'd returned.

Howard and Peter were the first ones out of the plane, appearing from its huge underbelly. They headed straight over to where she stood waiting on the other side of the fence. As they drew closer, she saw they both looked guilty and worried. Folding her arms, she waited for them to speak.

'Good afternoon, Bessie.' Howard rubbed the back

of his neck. 'I owe you an apology.'

'I'm sorry, I didn't tell you.' Peter quickly added. 'Harry told me not to because he said you wouldn't have let me go.'

'He was right, I wouldn't have.' She looked hard at them, the expression on their faces told her they were bracing themselves for what she had to say. 'But Harry told me why he thought you should. First, because you wanted to.' She paused for a few seconds, then went on. 'Second, because it was a wonderful chance for you to fly, and lastly, because Howard would be with you and he'd take excellent care of you. They're all good reasons . . .' She put her hands on her hips. 'But I would still have said no . . . because I promised your parents that I'd keep you safe, and flying can be dangerous. Planes crash!'

'But it was all right, Bessie. Nothing has happened to me, I'm here, safe and in one piece.' Peter held out his arms wide and smiled at her. 'It was wonderful up there. Everything looks so small and neat. We went out over the sea, and I flew the Peggy Sue for a bit on the way back.'

'It's true, ma'am,' Howard said. 'He took control of her and did a fine job.'

'I want to be a pilot when I'm older,' Peter said. 'And fly a Liberator to help win the war.'

'I hope this war will be over long before you're old enough.' Bessie caught Howard's eye, and he nodded, no doubt thinking the same thing. 'But you could still learn in peacetime though and fly people around for pleasure.'

'I could take you flying. You'd love it.'

'Oh . . . I don't know. It frightened me seeing you waving down at us.'

'I guess you might like it if you tried,' Howard said.
'It's beautiful up there.'

She shrugged. 'Perhaps one day I will.'

17

Bessie couldn't get back to sleep. She'd had a nightmare in which Peter had been trapped inside the nose of a Liberator, desperately waving a red scarf, as the plane spiralled downwards with smoke trailing from its engines. Thankfully, she had woken up in a cold, clammy sweat, moments before it hit the ground.

It was only a dream, she reminded herself, one which played on her fears from yesterday when thankfully nothing had gone wrong. But the fear of what could have happened haunted her, rattling around her mind and stopping her from going back to sleep.

Beside her, Harry lay fast asleep, oblivious to her wakefulness. She should get up, Bessie thought, read for a bit until she was tired; she hadn't had a chance to look through her old diary again for a while. Now the house was quiet, it was a good opportunity and would take her mind off the dream, transport her back to another time when there were no huge bombers falling from the sky.

Swinging her legs out of bed, Bessie pushed her feet into her soft slippers and wrapped her dressing gown around herself. She took the diary from the top of the chest of drawers and padded softly out of the room, carefully closing the door behind her.

She lit the lamp and settled down in an armchair by the stove. Opening her diary at the place she'd marked with a piece of ribbon, her eyes fell on the first words and her stomach instantly clenched into a tight knot.

★ ★ ★

23rd March, 1918
Terrible, terrible news . . .

Bessie snapped it shut. She didn't need to read on because that day was etched in her memory . . .

★ ★ ★

'Nurse Carter?' Sister Williams hurried along the ward to where Bessie and Ethel were putting clean sheets on a bed. 'Matron wants to see you in her office.'

She caught her friend's eye across the bed, the surprised look on Ethel's face reflected her own thoughts. What did Matron want to see her for? She hadn't done anything she shouldn't have, at least not to her knowledge.

'I'll take over here.' Sister spoke kindly, stepping into place and tucking in the sheet. 'Hurry along now.'

'Yes, Sister.'

Ethel gave Bessie an encouraging smile as she left the ward.

Stopping outside the small sitting room, which was Matron's office, she checked her cap was straight and smoothed down her apron, then tapped on the door.

'Come in,' Matron called.

Taking a steadying breath, Bessie went in and her gaze immediately fell on the person sitting in the armchair opposite Matron. Her father. Bessie's heart quickened. What was he doing here? Something must have happened.

Bessie's eyes darted between him and Matron, but neither of them gave any indication of what was going

104

on. Her father didn't even look her directly in the eye as he normally would.

'Nurse Carter, your father,' Matron tilted her head towards him, 'has come with some bad news, I'm afraid.' She paused again and looked at Bessie's father, who nodded at Matron, giving her his permission. Matron cleared her throat and continued. 'I'm so sorry to tell you this. Your brother has been killed in France.'

Bessie heard the words come out of Matron's mouth, saw her lips move, but didn't want to take in what they meant. They were words that she never wanted to hear about Robert. Ever.

'I'm so sorry, my dear.' Matron stood up, laying her hand on Bessie's arm. 'Your mother needs you at home.'

Bessie looked at her father. His bleak eyes now met hers and held them briefly before he looked down at his hands again, which, she noticed, clasped his hat so tightly that his knuckles had turned white. He still hadn't spoken, but Bessie knew him, understood how he'd be feeling. It was written on his face for all to see, he'd lost his only son. Robert had gone to France and wouldn't be coming back, just like . . . Bessie's legs trembled.

'Come and sit down for a moment.' Matron took Bessie's arm and led her over to the armchair she'd just vacated. 'Stay there until you're ready. I think some tea's in order here.'

Matron didn't wait for an answer, but bustled out of the room, closing the door quietly behind her.

Bessie's throat was tight with emotion. 'How? When?' Her voice sounded hoarse.

'The twentieth. We don't know how. Not yet. I

expect there'll be a letter telling us more . . .'

Bessie reached out and touched her father's hands. 'How's Mother?'

'She wants you home . . . I know this job's important and you're doing good work, but we need you to come home for a while. Matron's given her permission.'

Bessie nodded. If her mother needed her at home, then she must go. Although she feared there was little she'd be able to do to make her mother feel better. Nothing she could do, or say, would bring Robert back. His death left a massive hole in their family which would stay with them for the rest of their lives.

★ ★ ★

The first thing Bessie noticed when she arrived home, was that the curtains were drawn. It was only one o'clock in the afternoon, not even dusk, and yet they were closed, as was traditional when someone died. She'd seen it done too many times since the war had begun. Parents who'd received the dreaded telegrams telling them their sons were no more, shut the curtains and blocked out the world to mourn.

Bessie glanced at her father, who walked silently along beside her. He'd hardly spoken to her all the way home from the hospital. Not on the walk to the station, or on the train, and not even now on the last leg through the village, and back to their home next to his blacksmith's forge. Her father was a quiet man, but he seemed to have retreated even further inside himself, like a snail tucked away in its shell.

The door flew open as Bessie raised her hand to turn the doorknob, and the sight of her mother standing in the shadowy inside shocked her. She'd aged. Her usual upright stance was bowed, she looked haggard and weary.

'Bessie!' Her mother's voice was raw, and her blue eyes stood out starkly against their red, puffy lids.

'Mother.' Bessie stepped inside and reached out to take her mother's hands.

With surprising strength, her mother grabbed hold of Bessie, wrapping her arms tightly around her, and then began to cry with heaving sobs which shook her entire body.

'I'd best go through to the forge.' Her father closed the front door behind them, plunging the room into a gloomy dusk befitting the atmosphere of grief which filled the room.

Bessie looked over her mother's shoulder and nodded at him. He looked relieved to go. The sight of his normally strong wife reduced to a sobbing wreck was probably too much for him. He would feel safer and more at ease amongst the familiar heat and smell of the forge. In there, he could deal with his feelings in his own way while he worked. Even after what had happened, he still needed to work if the family were to eat. Keeping busy was the best way to deal with it, Bessie understood that well enough.

'Bessie?'

A little hand tugging at her skirt drew her attention to her sister, Grace, who stood staring up at her, her eyes wide and glistening with tears. Poor little mite, Bessie thought. It wasn't good for her to see their mother like this. She was only three years old and wouldn't properly understand what was going on.

'Hello, Grace.' Bessie reached out and ruffled the little girl's blonde hair. 'Come on, Mother, let's get you a cup of tea. Sit down and I'll see to it.'

Prising her mother's arms from her, she led her to the armchair by the stove and helped her sit down. Then Bessie checked the fire was banked up and pushed the kettle onto the hotplate to boil. The best thing she could do now was to be practical. As much as she wanted to cry herself, she mustn't. Not now, not here. She'd save her tears for when she was alone. She needed to be strong for the sake of the family, Robert would have wanted her to do that.

Swallowing hard to relieve the tightness in her throat, Bessie forced herself to smile. 'I'll hang my coat up then make the tea.' Her voice sounded artificially high, but no one seemed to notice. Her mother sat bowed in the chair, self-absorbed as silent tears ran down her cheeks, while little Grace had settled down on the rag rug in front of the stove and was playing with her doll.

★ ★ ★

Bessie watched her mother reading the letter the postman had just delivered. It was from Robert's commanding officer and brought news of how her brother had died. Her mother's pale face crumpled, and she let the letter drop onto the table.

'My boy!' she wailed, slumping forward in her chair, and sinking down onto the table, resting her head on her arms.

Her father picked up the letter and read it in silence, his mouth a grim, straight line. When he'd finished, he drew in a sharp breath and Bessie saw a glint of tears in his eyes.

'Stay with your mother.' He handed Bessie the letter and laid his hand briefly on his wife's shoulder, then went out of the door back to the forge. Moments later, they could hear a hammer beating iron, over, and over again.

Bessie steeled herself and looked at the letter.

Dear Mr and Mrs Carter, she read.
It is with my deepest sympathy that I write you this letter. Your son, Robert Carter, was a fine young man, with a cheery disposition, who was well liked by all the company. He was a conscientious worker who shall be greatly missed by all of us.
Robert was killed by a sniper while digging out a fellow soldier who had been buried in a shell explosion. Rest assured, he did not suffer in any way.
Yours sincerely,
2nd Lieutenant Charles Pearson.

A sniper. Killed by a sniper, while helping someone else. She bit down hard on her bottom lip. It was typical of Robert to help others, only this time he'd paid the ultimate price for it. Bessie tasted blood. She wouldn't cry, she mustn't. At least it would've been over quickly for him.

'He didn't suffer, Mother. We've got to be grateful for that.'

Her mother's shoulders stiffened, and she lifted her head. 'He's dead! And you expect me to be grateful for a sniper's bullet?' She spat out her words, glaring at Bessie as if she were responsible for pulling the trigger which had ended her son's life. 'Get out of here, I want to be alone.'

Bessie patted her mother's arm; she was in no state to reason with. She couldn't tell her now, that there were far worse ways for a soldier to die. Slow, painful deaths, from wounds that maimed a man, took him through painful operations, brought him back to Blighty and still killed him in the end. Her mother didn't want to know that. If Robert had to die, then a clean sniper's bullet was the kindest way.

'Come on, Grace, let's go for a walk.' She held her hand out to the little girl, who looked from Bessie to her mother and back in confusion. 'It's all right, Mother just needs some time on her own.'

Grace nodded and slid off the armchair where she'd been sitting, watching the whole proceedings, her doll clasped tightly in her arms.

★ ★ ★

A shower of tiny sparks flew off the metal as her father's hammer hit it. Again, and again, he hammered, working on the glowing hot iron, moulding and forming it. He was so focused on his work, that he wasn't aware of Bessie and Grace standing in the doorway.

'Father.' Bessie called when he'd stopped hammering and plunged the hot metal into a bucket of cold water, making it sizzle and hiss.

He looked up, and she felt a surge of love towards him at the sight of the pain in his eyes. 'Mother wants to be alone, so I'm going to take Grace out for a walk. She could do with some fresh air.'

Her father nodded and wiped his brow with his sleeve. 'I'll look in on her in a while. She's taken it hard.'

'I know.'

'Don't fret yourself, she'll come around in a day or two. It's the shock of it . . .' his voice wavered. 'You run along now, and I'll see to your mother, don't you worry.'

Grace tugged at Bessie's hand, desperate to get going. She'd been a patient little girl since Bessie had arrived home two days ago, quietly playing on her own, making no demands on anyone, clearly aware of the grief-stricken atmosphere in the house.

'Are you ready, Grace?'

The little girl nodded.

'We'll see you later, Father.'

They walked out onto the road, turned left and headed out of the village, and for the first time since she'd come home, Bessie was aware of the birds singing. There was the smell of spring in the air, and a sense of the world reawakening after winter. She breathed in deeply, filling her lungs with fresh air. It was a relief to be outside again.

It looked like Grace felt the same. The farther they'd walked from the house, the more talkative she became. She chatted about the things they saw, clumps of frogspawn in the pond, the shapes of white clouds dotting the blue sky. Grace stopped often, looking carefully at anything which caught her interest. Walking at this slow pace gave Bessie a different view of the world, where life was still going on outside the gloomy room where their mother sat, wracked with grief for Robert.

What did Grace make of it all? Bessie wondered. Did she fully understand what had happened? Since she'd come home, Bessie had noticed that their mother had hardly spoken to the little girl. Or to any of them. She had no idea what her sister had been told.

'Grace,' Bessie said, as they started walking again after looking at the smashed snail shells scattered around a thrush's anvil stone. 'Do you understand what's happened to Robert?'

Grace looked up at Bessie. 'He's dead.'

'Yes, he is. Do you know that means he can't come home again, that we won't see him anymore?'

'Never?'

'Yes, never. He's buried in France now and he'll stay there forever.'

Grace stared at Bessie, her deep blue eyes wide, while she absorbed what she'd been told. Bessie expected her to say something, but she didn't. Instead, she put her hand in Bessie's and walked alongside her for a few minutes until something in the hedge caught her attention, and she skipped over to investigate. From the look of her, no one would guess they'd just had a conversation about their dead brother.

Bessie sighed. Thank goodness she seemed to accept it, but whether Grace fully understood the meaning of what had happened, she couldn't be sure, but at least she'd explained it to the little girl, and hoped it made sense.

Grace had seen little of Robert for the past year since he'd been called up, just a few fleeting visits before they had sent him to France. Would she remember him in the future? She wouldn't have the memories of him to look back on that Bessie had. Robert would become a faint shadowy memory for Grace, only a brother in a photo on the mantelpiece, but he'd been so much more, and her sister would never know. Bessie's throat tightened. A sniper's bullet had stolen Robert from them all, taken away their parents' son and their brother . . . this time she couldn't stop her tears from falling.

* * *

Martha Carter's back was ramrod straight as she walked out of the church, arm in arm with Bessie's father, after the service on Sunday morning. Walking behind with Grace, Bessie was relieved that her mother was now out and engaging in life again. The days since they'd found out about how Robert had died had been long and painful. Her mother's grief was raw, and she'd sunk into a deep, dark pit, but suddenly this morning, she was first up, and the table had been set and breakfast made, by the time Bessie had come downstairs. Her mother had come back, almost to her former self, except for a veil of sadness about her eyes.

Bessie held Grace back, watching her parents accept the kind words from their friends. People who'd briefly come to the house, bringing with them cooked food, caring that the family shouldn't starve while they grieved for Robert. Simple kindnesses, which Bessie knew her mother had done for other families when they'd been in similar situations.

They would carry on. Robert was gone, but he'd never be forgotten. Bessie's chest tightened. One day, she promised herself, she would go to France, visit his grave and put some flowers on it.

Tomorrow she'd be going back to Marston Hall, returning to help the soldiers who were injured. It was what Robert would want her to do. Keeping busy, banishing her thoughts and worries, was what she needed now more than ever. Working hard had stopped her worrying about Robert before . . . now it would help stop her from thinking about the vast gap he'd left in her life.

18

31st March, 1918

Bessie closed the front door behind her and stood still, soaking in the familiar atmosphere of Marston Hall Auxiliary War Hospital. The pervading smell of carbolic was comforting, and she could hear a cheery song being played on the gramophone in the ward. It was good to be back.

'Nurse Carter?' Bessie saw Matron bustling towards her. 'You're back so soon?'

'Hello, Matron. Yes, I needed to get back to work.'

The older woman raised her eyebrows. 'If you're sure? How are your parents?'

'They're fine, thank you. Carrying on as best they can.'

'It's the only thing they can do.' Matron sighed. 'Too many families are losing their sons.' She drew in a sharp breath, and then smiled at her. 'I'm glad to see you back, we've missed you. I'm sure the men will be delighted to see you return to the ward in the morning.'

'Oh, but I'd like to start work straight away.' Bessie looked down at her clothes. 'At least when I've changed into my uniform.' The thought of sitting around doing nothing for the rest of the day didn't appeal to her, she needed to be busy.

'Well, if you're sure, there's always plenty to do, but you're not to start until you've had something to eat. Come along, this way.' Matron motioned for Bessie to accompany her.

She knew better than to argue, so fell into step beside her. The train had been delayed, and it was a long time since breakfast.

'I'm sure cook can find you something warm and filling. Then, and . . .' she looked Bessie directly in the eye, '*only* then, can you start work.'

Reaching the door of the kitchen, Matron opened it and stood aside to let Bessie go in.

'I've found a stray who needs feeding, Mrs Taylor,' Matron announced. 'Something warm and filling please.' She laid a hand on Bessie's arm. 'There's no need to hurry. Take your time and we'll see you on the ward when you're ready.'

She nodded. 'Thank you.'

Matron smiled, then turned on her small feet and went out, closing the door quietly behind her.

Bessie looked around the kitchen at the faces staring at her. It was as if everyone were frozen on the spot. Mrs Taylor, her hands floury from the pastry she was rolling out, and the two kitchen maids, who were peeling vegetables at the sink.

'Bessie!' Mrs Taylor broke the silence and hurried towards her, wiping her hands on her apron. 'How are you, dear? We were all so sorry to hear about your brother.' Her eyes were full of sympathy.

Bessie's throat tightened. 'Thank you.'

'How about some nice hot broth? It will warm you and fill you up in one go, and a nice slice of bread and butter to go with it. How does that sound?'

'Lovely, thank you.'

'Take off your coat and sit down. I'll fetch some for you.'

'I can do it,' Bessie protested. 'You're busy cooking.'

'I want to do it.' Mrs Taylor smiled. 'Agnes, you'll cut the bread and butter it for Bessie, won't you?'

Agnes, the tallest kitchen maid, nodded and smiled shyly at Bessie.

'Thank you.' She pulled out a chair and sat down at the table. 'It's good to be back here with you all again.'

The cook had just placed a bowl of steaming broth in front of Bessie, when the kitchen door burst open and Ethel came rushing in.

'You're back!' She hurried over, pulled Bessie to her feet, and hugged her tightly. 'It's so good to see you again.' She stepped back and held her at arm's length. 'I'm so sorry about Robert.'

'Thank you. I'm sorry I didn't have a chance to see you before I left. There wasn't time if we were going to catch the train home.'

'Matron told us, and . . . and about Robert.' Ethel frowned. 'I was worried you might not come back.'

'I wanted to . . . I needed to. There are always patients here who need looking after . . . my brother would have wanted me to carry on.' Bessie blinked back sudden tears. 'I'll be starting work this afternoon.'

'But not until you've got some food inside you,' Mrs Taylor said. 'Matron's orders. Have you time for a cup of tea, Ethel?'

Ethel shook her head. 'I'd love to, but I can't. I should be sorting out some bandages, but when Matron said Bessie was back . . .' she shrugged. 'Well, I had to come and see her for myself.'

'I'm glad you did.' Bessie smiled at her friend. 'I'll be back on the ward as soon as I've eaten my broth and changed into my uniform.'

'Good. Everyone's looking forward to seeing you,'

Ethel said, making her way to the door still in full flow. 'The men all missed you. You'll see how well they're doing, especially Sergeant Rushbrook. You're in for a surprise when you see him!'

* * *

Dressed in her familiar uniform again, Bessie glanced in the mirror on top of her chest of drawers, checking her cap was straight. Her reflection seemed just the same as before she'd gone home. Same uniform, same face, same cap, but underneath it all, she wasn't the same and never would be again. It was as if there was a big hole somewhere inside her chest which Robert had filled, but now he was dead, it was empty. Although for something empty, it was strange it should hurt so much. She sighed, heavily. The best way to forget about it for a while was to be busy . . . so busy that she wouldn't have time to think or feel. It was how she'd coped once before . . .

With a last tug of her cap to make sure it was secure, Bessie left her small attic bedroom and made her way down to the ballroom where twenty men needed looking after. Pausing outside the door, she took a deep breath, plastered a smile on her face and went in.

The gramophone at the far end of the ward was trilling out one of the men's favourite songs, *If you were the only girl in the world, and I were the only boy . . .* Some men were playing cards, others drawing or reading. Bessie's eyes were drawn to the figure slowly making his way down the ward towards her, with a smiling Ethel walking along beside him.

Sergeant Rushbrook was up. Bessie could hardly believe it. He was out of bed and walking towards her

117

on crutches, a look of determination on his face. He was tall, much taller than her. She watched his every move, silently willing him on, not daring to speak in case she broke his concentration. Every swing of his crutches brought him closer, his one good leg stepping through and his arms working in coordination to propel him along.

When at last he was within a couple of feet of Bessie, Ethel gently laid a hand on his arm. 'Stop there, well done.'

He came to a rest and stood in front of Bessie, looking her in the eye and smiling warmly. 'Welcome back, Nurse Carter, we missed you.'

'It looks like you've been busy while I've been gone,' Bessie said. 'I'm happy to see you upright, Sergeant Rushbrook. You were still flat on your back and going nowhere when I left.'

He raised his eyebrows. 'I decided it was time I got up.'

'He's been working hard at this,' Ethel informed her. 'Started the day after you left. He practised getting his balance and since then, there's been no stopping him. Could you walk alongside him for a while, I need to do the observations?'

Bessie nodded. 'I'd be delighted to. Where shall we go?'

'The main hall is good for practising,' Ethel said over her shoulder as she headed towards another patient. 'It's quieter out there.'

'Shall we then, Sergeant Rushbrook?' Bessie gestured for him to move off, and walked slowly beside him, her pace fitting in with his, keeping ready to catch him if he faltered.

Outside in the hall, he stopped and looked down at

Bessie, his blue eyes meeting hers. 'I'm sorry to hear about your brother. Truly, I am.'

'Thank you.' Bessie's voice came out in a whisper.

'If there's anything I can do to help . . .'

'You already have.' She blinked against threatening tears. 'Seeing you up is a real tonic. I didn't expect that when I got back.'

'I'm not surprised, I was a right miserable so and so, feeling sorry for myself.' He frowned. 'Got a kick up the backside . . . beg your pardon . . . and it made me stop and think about things . . .' he paused. 'I decided it was time to get going again.'

'What made you change your mind?'

'You.'

'Me? How?'

'What you said to me about finding another way. When I heard your brother had been killed, it made me realise how lucky I am . . . I'm still here.' He looked down at his foot and then up at Bessie again. 'After you suddenly disappeared, we all wanted to know where you were. Matron said you'd had to go home for family reasons. She wouldn't tell us why, but Ethel told me.'

'She shouldn't . . .'

'Don't be angry with her, she only told me because I kept on badgering her until she did, and I promised I wouldn't tell the others — and I haven't.'

'Why did you want to know?' Bessie asked.

'Because I was scared that you'd gone for good and I wouldn't see you again.' His eyes held hers. 'I didn't know if I could cope here without you . . . you made it bearable.'

Bessie's cheeks grew warm. 'All I did was care for you like all the other nurses. It's my job.'

'You made a tremendous difference to me.' He swallowed hard. 'When Ethel told me about your brother, I felt ashamed of lying there feeling sorry for myself. I'm alive and I've got a chance . . . a lot of men aren't so lucky. I've got to get on with my life and live it well in memory of those that lost theirs.'

'I think you're doing the right thing.' Bessie smiled at him. 'Life's never going to be the same without my brother . . . and all the others that won't ever come home.' She bit her bottom lip. 'But we've all got to carry on and live our lives. Live them well. It's what they would have wanted.'

Sergeant Rushbrook smiled, his eyes crinkling up at the corners. 'Welcome back to life at Marston Hall, Nurse Carter. I'm so happy you're here.'

'So am I. Now are we going to stand here talking all day, or are you going to practise walking?' Bessie tried to sound firm but couldn't stop the smile from playing on her lips.

'Yes, nurse,' he said. 'Your wish is my command.'

19

'Ta-da! How do I look?'

Bessie glanced up from where she was mending Prune's hem, and watched Dottie twirl round, sending the skirt of her blue dress swirling outwards. It was good to see her in something other than the brown dungarees she usually wore for work. She was such an attractive girl and looked beautiful tonight, her curly blonde hair loose around her shoulders.

'Lovely.' Bessie spoke carefully, her lips full of pins.

'You look pretty,' Marigold said, looking up from where she was sitting at the table doing some drawing.

'Thank you, my angel.' Dottie plopped a kiss on the little girl's cheek. 'Whoops! I've given you a lipstick print.'

'Where? Let me see.' Marigold jumped up from the table and rushed across the room to check in the mirror, touching her skin where Dottie's lips had left a red mark.

'I'll clean you up.' Dottie whipped a fresh hanky out of her bag and gently wiped away the lipstick. 'There you are, as good as new!'

'Thank you. I wish I could come with you.'

'I know.' Dottie put her arm around Marigold's shoulders. 'But it's not for children. I promise I'll tell you and Bessie all about it in the morning.'

'I want to hear about everything, the music and the

dances.'

'And the band,' Prune added.

Dottie laid her hand on her heart. 'I give you my word.'

'Will you be dancing with Clem?' Marigold asked.

'Definitely. He's a great dancer, so we'll probably be on the floor most of the evening. Once the music starts, it gets my toes a-tapping and I just can't stop myself dancing.' Dottie looked at her watch. 'Are you nearly finished, Bessie?'

'Just a few more stitches.' Bessie quickly passed her needle back and forth through the fabric, while Prune stood patiently on the chair towering above her.

'I don't know how I didn't see it before.' Prune said. 'I'm glad you spotted it, Bessie.'

'We want you looking your best for Howard.' Dottie looked up at Prune with a broad grin on her red lipsticked lips.

'He probably wouldn't have noticed,' Prune said.

'Probably not.' Dottie agreed. 'He's only got eyes for you and not what you're wearing.'

Prune blushed.

'There you are, all done.' Bessie put her needle and pins back in her workbox, then smoothed Prune's skirt down, checking how it looked. 'It's as good as new.'

'Thank you.' Prune steadied herself with a hand on Bessie's shoulder as she carefully climbed down from the chair and slipped on her shoes. 'Right, I'm ready to go.'

'Have a lovely time.' Bessie followed them outside a few moments later after they'd gathered their jackets and bags. 'We'll want to hear all about it tomorrow.'

'Don't worry, you will! We'll be talking of nothing

else for days.' Dottie laughed, running down the steps into the yard. 'Goodbye.'

Bessie and Marigold stood in the doorway and watched the two young women walk out of the farm gate and turn in the direction of the base. It was wonderful to see them looking so happy and off to have some fun. They were bound to have a great time as it was the one hundredth mission celebration dance. The pair of them had been talking about it for days, planning what they were going to wear and how they'd do their hair. Celebrations had been happening all day at Rackbridge base, and this evening's dance was the grand finale and promised to be wonderful.

'I wish I could go with them.' Marigold sighed.

'I know, but like Dottie said, it's not for children.' Bessie put her arm around the little girl who leaned against her. 'Why don't we go for a walk? It's a lovely evening and I fancy being outside for a bit. We can see how Harry and Peter are getting on with that fence in the orchard.'

Marigold nodded and slipped her hand into Bessie's as they headed for the orchard, where the chickens were still scratching around in the light evening.

'Did you ever go to dances, like Dottie and Prune?' Marigold asked.

'You mean during the Great War?'

'Yes.'

'Not often, I was working most of the time, but we still had fun where we could.'

'What did you do?'

'We used to put on concerts for the men. Hold fetes . . .'

★ ★ ★

123

4th May, 1918

Bessie stood on the side-lines, hardly daring to watch. On the blast from Matron's whistle, the three men started their race and set off down the course marked out on the lawn. Each man had a look of concentration on his face, and that, combined with the egg and spoon tightly clamped sideways on, between his teeth, made them all appear fierce and determined. They'd jokingly named this the 'three-legged egg and spoon race', because each contender had just one leg of his own and two from the crutches.

All around Bessie, other patients in their hospital blue suits, nurses, orderlies and visitors alike, were cheering the men on, shouting words of encouragement. She wanted to add, 'and be careful', but couldn't speak without betraying her anxiety and the way her heart was thumping. This must be how a mother feels, watching over her child when it first learns to walk, Bessie thought. Worrying that it might lose balance and tumble onto something and hurt itself. Only if one of these men fell, any injuries could undo weeks of healing.

'Look at them go!' Ethel came to stand beside her. 'Who do you think will win?'

'I just want them all to stay upright,' she whispered.

Ethel glanced at Bessie, her eyebrows raised. 'Don't worry, they will. Taking part in sports is good for the men's spirits. Look at that!'

The cheering around them grew louder as the three men drew abreast and crossed the finishing line together, side by side. Taking the spoons out of their mouths, they heartily congratulated each other on making it all the way. All of them were winners.

She sighed with relief, and her heart slowed to its usual steady rhythm. They had done it. All of them had finished in one piece and still standing on their three legs. It would do each man the world of good, boosting their confidence and raising their spirits . . . and that's what today's fete was all about, Bessie reminded herself. Raising both men's spirits and money for the hospital's fund.

Satisfied that all the men were fine, she headed back to the stall where she'd been helping. It was full of handmade goods, embroidered handkerchiefs, tablecloths, knitted socks, and decorated hats — some of which Bessie had made in the little spare time she had. There'd been a steady trade all afternoon, with visitors keen to buy something to support the hospital.

Bessie had just sold a straw hat, trimmed with silk daisies to a woman, when Sergeant Rushbrook appeared at the stall.

'Congratulations!' She smiled at him. 'You did a fine race. Finishing all together was perfect.'

'Thank you. We thought it was the best way to do it, we didn't want anyone being daft trying to win and taking a tumble.' His eyes met hers. 'I looked for you afterwards. I wasn't sure if you'd watched us.'

'I was there watching; I wouldn't have missed it for the world. But I had to get straight back to the stall afterwards.'

He nodded and turned slightly as if to go, and then changed his mind. 'I was worried about the race, you know . . . in case I fell . . .'

'So was I,' she admitted. 'But I was proud of you . . . of all of you for doing it, especially after what you said . . .'

'That I was good for nothing?' He raised his eye-brows.

'No . . . about how you felt when you first came here,' Bessie said. 'You have come far since you arrived here, Sergeant Rushbrook.'

He smiled, bowing his head slightly. 'Thanks to you, Nurse Carter. You're an excellent nurse, with a lovely way about you.'

Bessie's cheeks grew warm. Before she could say anything, a shout went up for the tug of war to begin.

'You're not planning on taking part, are you?' she asked, hoping he wasn't.

'I would have before . . .' He looked down at his remaining leg and shrugged. 'But I have to make allowances now, so I'll just watch this one and give some moral support instead. Put my energy into cheering them on.'

'I'm glad to hear it. You'd best get over there and start encouraging them.'

He nodded, his eyes holding hers for a few moments before he turned and made his way over to where the crowd had gathered, ready to watch the two mixed teams of able-bodied patients and visitors pull against each other.

As Bessie watched him go, she thought how well he had done since he first arrived at Marston Hall, when he'd lain so quiet and withdrawn in his bed. She was happy that he'd made such a good recovery, there was something about Sergeant Rushbrook . . . Right from the start, he'd intrigued her, and his determination to get himself going once more when she'd returned after Robert's death, had impressed her.

Soon, he would be ready to leave here and go to have an artificial leg fitted and start the next phase of

126

his life. To her surprise, Bessie's heart clenched at the thought of not seeing him again.

★ ★ ★

This was the perfect way to end the day, Bessie thought, looking around at the men joyfully singing along to the music Ethel was coaxing out of the piano, which they'd pushed into the ward. They always loved an impromptu concert, and their spirits were still soaring after the afternoon's fete. The sports had been a great success, starting with the races and ending with the cricket match, where the local boy scouts had been runners for men who could only bat and not run themselves.

'What shall I play next?' Ethel asked after bringing the last song to a close.

'Long Way to Tipperary, please, nurse,' Private Dennis shouted out.

Ethel nodded her agreement and started to play, the men singing along with her. Bessie added her own soft voice to the mix, but it was drowned out by the men's deeper tones. The sound of their voices singing in harmony, happy after the day's events, brought a lump to her throat, and she had to stop for a moment. If only things could stay like this, and none of the soldiers would have to go back to France when they were well again. If only the war would end.

The last notes of Tipperary had softened and faded away when Matron walked into the ward and came to stand by the piano.

'Beautiful singing.' She smiled warmly at the men. 'But it's time for a cup of cocoa and then bed, so just one more song.' She nodded and slipped away as quietly as she'd arrived.

'What's it to be, then?' Ethel asked, looking around.

'If You Were The Only Girl,' a voice called out.

'Good choice, Sergeant Rushbrook.' Ethel turned back in her seat and began to play.

As the men sang, their voices swelled gently over the words making each one sound special. Bessie joined in with the popular song, which they often played on the ward's gramophone player. As she sang, her sixth sense told her she was being watched. Taking her eyes off Ethel at the piano, she glanced around and saw that she was right, someone was looking at her. It was Sergeant Rushbrook. He was singing full-heartedly, clearly enjoying it from the way his eyes twinkled as they caught and held hers. He bowed his head slightly to acknowledge her, smiling as they moved on to the second verse.

'If you were the only girl in the world and I were the only boy,' everyone sang.

She knew she should break his gaze but couldn't.

'Nothing else would matter in the world today. We could go on loving in the same old way.'

'Last verse,' Ethel called.

Bessie looked back at Ethel, who was playing with great enthusiasm. The men responded with extra vigour in their singing, bringing with it a warm cheeriness to the ward, with thoughts of love and hope for the future. She inwardly thanked her friend for drawing her attention away from Sergeant Rushbrook's gaze. As she sang the last verse, Bessie knew he was still watching her, but dared not look at him again.

20

August, 1944

'Do you like it?' Howard asked.

Prune looked around the inside of the enormous hangar, which had been cleared of planes and turned into a dance hall just for tonight. Straw bales were set up along the sides to sit on, and the whole place was decorated with bracken and lit up with blue lights. On a raised platform at the far end, a band was in full swing, belting out *In the Mood*, making Prune itch to get on the dance floor and join the throng of dancing couples.

'It's wonderful.' She smiled at Howard and tugged at his hand. 'Come on, let's dance.'

'Wait a moment, take a good look at the band.'

It was hard to see them clearly, but they didn't look like the usual base band, The Galloping Gators, who played at all the dances. 'They look new to me.'

'It's Glenn Miller and his band. You can't get better than that.'

'Glenn Miller!' Prune loved listening to him and his band on the wireless, so to see and hear them in real life, made tonight even more special.

He nodded. 'So come on, what are we waiting for?'

As they danced, Prune caught glimpses of Dottie and Clem, who were also enjoying themselves on the dance floor. The whole atmosphere was electric, everyone in a jovial mood as they enjoyed the climax of the one hundredth mission celebration. The Americans knew how to relax and enjoy themselves and were making the most of some time off to have fun.

'Wanna have a beer?' Howard asked after Glenn Miller announced the band would take a quick break.

'I'd love one.' Prune's throat was parched after jiving and lindy hopping her way through several songs.

'I'll grab us a couple. I won't be long.'

Waiting while Howard went to the bar, she looked around for Dottie and Clem and spotted them sitting at a table on the far side of the dance floor, sipping some drinks.

'Shall we join Dottie and Clem?' Prune asked when Howard came back with two beers a few minutes later.

'In a while, I'd like to sit outside for a bit to cool off.' He handed her a beer, then took hold of her elbow and guided her out towards the doors.

They weren't the only ones spilling out of the hangar for some fresh air. The grass nearby was dotted with people sitting down, resting after their vigorous dancing.

Howard led her to a spot a little way off from the others, who were chatting and laughing loudly between them.

Settling down on the grass, side by side, Howard put his arm around her shoulders.

'Cheers.' He knocked his glass against hers.

'Bottoms up,' Prune said. They both took a long draught of the golden liquid. 'That tastes marvellous.'

'Sure does.' He put his glass down and took hold of her free hand. 'I'm glad you're here, it wouldn't be half as fun without you.'

'Thank you so much for inviting me.'

Howard laughed. 'I love the way you talk, Prune. It sounds so formal sometimes.'

She shrugged. 'That's the way we English do things.'

'I like it.' He stroked her palm with his thumb. 'I think about you a lot when we're flying. It keeps me happy, makes me feel good, and takes my mind off where we're going.'

Prune's chest tightened. She hated him flying on missions, worrying that he might be shot down, but she'd never tell Howard that. It wouldn't be fair. 'Tell me then, what do you think about me?'

His eyes met hers. 'The way you look. Your beautiful, big brown eyes. How you make me feel. Your laugh.'

'You're having me on.'

'No, I'm not. I am being totally honest with you.' He stroked her cheek gently. 'I love you, Prune. You've bewitched me with your funny, Limey ways, and I'm under your spell.'

'I love you, too.' There, she'd said what she had been feeling for weeks now. Prune's heart was thudding so hard in her chest, she was sure Howard must be able to feel it when he pulled her into his arms and kissed her.

21

London - September, 1944

Grace folded the letter and put it back in its envelope. She'd thought it would get easier with time, but it hadn't — she still felt as if part of her was missing. Contact with Marigold through their letters helped, although sometimes they left her feeling that her daughter was so far away, both in miles and the lifestyle she was now living. It scared her that her daughter might be slowly drifting away from her.

Shrugging off her coat, Grace slumped down in an armchair, and eased her shoes from her throbbing feet. She was exhausted and in dire need of some sleep, but it would have to wait as she was due down at Ada's shortly. They'd taken to eating together as it made sense to pool their rations, and Ada enjoyed cooking for someone. And they were company for each other too. The older woman was sure to ask about Marigold's letter though, having left it out on the hall table for Grace to collect when she got home from work. Usually, she enjoyed sharing Marigold's news, but tonight she would rather not talk about it. Her emotions were too near the surface, and she feared that she might not be strong enough to gloss over how she felt. Sighing heavily, Grace settled back in the chair and closed her eyes — she would have five minutes rest and then get ready.

A tapping on the door woke her with a start.

'Grace! Tea's ready.' It was Ada.

Glancing at the clock, she saw it was nearly six; she must have fallen asleep. She sprang to her feet, shaking her head to try to relieve the after-sleep mussiness.

'Come in, Ada.' She smiled as the old woman appeared around the door. 'I'm sorry, I only sat down for five minutes and must have dropped off.'

Ada chuckled. 'I thought you might have, it's no wonder you're tired after being on your feet all day. The tea's ready, so come down as soon as you can.'

'I'll wash my hands; I won't be long.'

Grace was about to go out of the door when she spotted the letter on the table, she picked it up to take with her, thinking it was only fair to share the latest news with Ada. She'd been such a support to her, and missed Marigold very much, too.

★ ★ ★

'That was lovely.' Grace placed her knife and fork together on her empty plate. 'Thank you, Ada.'

'You're welcome, dear. If you cook it for long enough, even a tough bit of meat will soften up . . . eventually.'

'Shall I start on the washing up?' She pushed back her chair and stood up.

'No, you make the tea and then you can tell me what Marigold's been up to.'

Grace didn't want to talk about it. 'Why don't you read it, while I put the kettle on? She's written such a lot and I might miss something out.'

'You sure?' Ada asked.

'Yes.' She usually just told Ada snippets of Marigold's news, rather than giving her the letters to read herself. Her daughter wrote to Ada separately, so she received her own letters from her.

133

Standing with her back to Ada, waiting for the kettle to boil on the gas ring, Grace mulled over how she'd felt earlier after reading the letter. It was a reaction from being so tired; she reasoned. All mothers whose children were away in the country missed them; it wouldn't be forever, and that's what she had to hold on to, to keep telling herself. Marigold would come home one day. She must focus on that and be glad that her daughter was safe.

But most mothers went to visit their children if they could, a treacherous thought whispered in her head as the kettle whistled. Grace suddenly wanted to scream in unison with the shrieking steam. It wasn't as simple as that for her, though; she couldn't just go and see Marigold when she wanted to. She wished she could, but . . .

'Grace! The kettle.' Ada's voice made her jump.

'Oh.' She turned off the gas and poured the boiling water into the teapot.

'You are so tired tonight,' Ada said as Grace put the teapot down on the table and sat back in her place. 'Been busy today?'

Grace sighed. 'Every day's busy with those rockets falling on us.'

Ada shivered and tapped a finger on Marigold's letter. 'It makes me thankful she's safe in Norfolk.'

'That's what I tell myself.'

'It sounds like she's settled in well at school and made some nice friends.'

Grace nodded. Marigold was turning into a wonderful letter writer, filling pages with descriptions of what she'd been up to. Today's was all about her starting school, her new friends, her teacher, what games they played. It painted a picture of a world far away from London and the life she'd had here.

Going to a new school wouldn't have been easy for her. Grace knew her daughter would have been nervous. Her mind drifted back to when Marigold first started school and how she'd looked to her for reassurance, only this time it would have been Bessie that she'd turned to . . . a pang of longing sliced through Grace.

She felt Ada touch her arm and stared down at the old woman's veiny hand.

'I don't think you've listened to a word I've said.'

'I'm sorry.' She looked at her friend's concerned face. 'The only thing I'm good for tonight is sleeping.' She stood up. 'I'll wash up quickly and then go to bed.'

Ada grabbed hold of her arm and pulled her down into the chair again. 'Leave the pots, I'll do them. I want to know what you're going to do about Marigold's last line.'

'What do you mean?'

'Here.' Ada traced her fingers under the last row of handwriting.

Grace closed her eyes as her friend read it aloud. She knew it by heart because Marigold always ended her letters the same way.

'I miss you, Mummy. When are you coming to see me?' Ada read aloud, and then fixed her shrewd brown eyes on her. 'Have you sorted out a date to visit her?

'Not yet. It's been so busy on the ward with all the doodlebug casualties.' She shrugged. 'You know how it is. Look at me! I'm a wreck from exhaustion.'

'I appreciate that, love.' Ada patted Grace's arm. 'But everyone's entitled to some time off, even a couple of days. It's weeks since Marigold left here, and

135

she wants to see you. Norfolk's not that far away.'

'I will visit her. I want to, believe me, but it's not as easy as you think.'

Ada studied Grace's face for a few moments. 'Are you making it harder for yourself than it need be?' She raised her eyebrows. 'I've got the feeling there's more to this than simply getting the time off.'

'We're often short-staffed, so how can I go off and leave them when we've got so many patients to look after?'

'I understand that, but if by some magic means I could wave a wand and you had no more patients to care for, plenty of staff, and time off allowed, would you go straight away?'

Grace hesitated, then quickly said, 'Of course I would.'

'Call me an old fool, but there's something here that doesn't quite add up. No doubt you've got your reasons, and maybe you'll tell me when you're ready, but I think you're putting excuses in the way of going to visit your daughter.'

'But . . .'

Ada put her hand up. 'Let me have my say, then I'll shut up about the matter. I know it's not because you don't want to see her. It's clear from your face how much you want to be with Marigold, so is it something to do with where she is?' she probed, looking her straight in the eye.

Grace sighed and looked down at the teaspoon she was fiddling with. 'It's complicated, and best left alone. Marigold's safe where she is, and I'm truly grateful for that. I just have to put up with missing her.'

'But she wants to see you.'

'I know and I will go, but not yet. I need more time.'

Ada clasped Grace's hand. 'Don't leave it too long, eh?'

22

Norfolk - Christmas Day, 1944

'One, two, three, four, five, six . . .' Bessie hopped her counter across the board and landed on a snake's head. 'Oh no, not again!' She slid the counter down the snake's curving body and onto a square close to the start of the board. 'Look! I'm right back near the beginning.'

Harry, Peter and Marigold all laughed. They'd been playing for a while, with no one reaching the finish.

'That's snakes and ladders for you.' Harry picked up the dice and shook it in his cupped hands. 'You think you're getting somewhere and then you land on a snake.'

'You might get a ladder next time,' Marigold said.

Bessie smiled at her. This was all part of Christmas, having a chance to play games and relax for a bit. She looked over to the kitchen area where Dottie was washing up, Clem and Howard were drying, and Prune was putting away. They'd insisted on doing it, saying she should put her feet up after cooking such a lovely dinner. It had been good. With goose, crispy roast potatoes, batter puddings and vegetables, nearly all of it reared or grown on the farm. Even the Christmas pudding had turned out well, made with the dried fruit she'd saved up.

The house was looking beautiful too, Bessie thought. They'd trimmed the living room up with holly and ivy, draping sprigs over the mantelpiece and around picture frames. The pine-scented Christmas tree, which Harry had cut down, was laden with decorations. Old ones which had been in their family for years, and some new ones made by Peter and Marigold. They'd collected dropped silver foil window, from bomber planes, which gathered in hedges, and turned it into decorations that glittered and twinkled prettily against the green tree.

'I've got a five!'

Peter's voice brought Bessie's attention back to the game, and she watched as he moved his counter along to the finish.

'I've won!' Peter beamed.

'Well done,' Harry said. 'At last, someone's made it to the finish.

'Shall we play another game?' Marigold asked. 'Do you want to join in?' She directed her question to the group who'd just finished in the kitchen.

'I was kinda hoping Prune and I could go for a short stroll before Clem and I head back to base,' Howard said. 'Do you mind if we do?'

'Not at all.' Bessie understood the young couple needed some time on their own. A crowded house wasn't the place to be if you wanted to be alone together for a while.

'I'll play,' Clem said.

'And me,' Dottie added.

They sat down at the table and each took a counter and placed it with the others on the first square on the board.

'Who's going first?' Marigold asked.

'Clem. He's our guest,' Bessie said.

'Thank you,' Clem said. 'You know, Bessie . . . Harry . . . Howard and I really appreciate you inviting us to spend Christmas with you all. You always make us so welcome when we visit; Orchard Farm's become a proper home from home for us.'

'We're glad you could join us.' Bessie patted his arm. 'We've enjoyed your company, and it can't be easy for you being away from your own families at this time of year.'

'No, ma'am, it isn't.' Clem shrugged. 'But maybe we'll be home for next Christmas.'

'I hope so,' Harry said. 'Now, shake that dice and let's get this game started.'

★ ★ ★

'Look at all those stars,' Howard said.

Prune stared up at the thousands of pinpricks of light in the inky blackness above them. 'They're beautiful.' She leaned back against Howard's chest and he wrapped his arms around her, keeping them both warm.

'They sure are. Some of them are the same ones we see back home. Look at those, there,' he pointed to one group of stars. 'I used to see them out of my bedroom window in Montana. I love it that they look down on us here as well. Makes it feel connected and not so far away.'

'Do you miss your home?' she asked.

'You bet. I miss lots of things about it, but I like it here too.' He rested his head against Prune's. 'There's something I'd miss about here if I went home.'

'What?'

'You.' He laughed, loosened his arms and turned her around to face him, then gently kissed her. 'There's something I want to ask you.' He hesitated, before going on. 'Would you do me the honour of becoming

140

my wife? Will you marry me, Prune?'

Her heart did a bunny hop jump. Howard had just asked her to marry him! She'd never expected that. They hadn't known each other that long, just six months, and their meetings had to be snatched when they could fit them between his missions and her work. Nothing was ever guaranteed because the USAAF ruled his life, meaning they could cancel leave passes at a moment's notice. However, a few months in wartime wasn't the same as in peacetime, it sped relationships up and they had to make the most of every precious second together.

'Prune . . .' Howard's voice sounded unsure. 'Are you okay?'

'Yes, yes, I'm fine. You just surprised me, that's all.'

'Well, what do you think? Will you marry me? I love you, and I want to spend the rest of my life with you. Grow old with you.'

What should she say? Should she be sensible and suggest they wait until the war was over, and they'd known each other for longer? Or should she follow her heart, say yes to this man whom she'd fallen in love with. The old Prune, the one she used to be before leaving home to become a Timber Jill, would have said wait. But she wasn't that person anymore.

'Yes!' Prune's voice came out in little more than a whisper. 'I'll marry you, Howard.' This time she spoke it loud and clear.

He picked her off her feet and swung her around.

'We'll get married as soon as possible. There are forms to sign, and your mother will have to give permission because you're not twenty-one yet. You must meet the chaplain to show him you are serious about wanting to be my wife, and once we've got approval, we have to wait sixty days till we can marry.' He planted a kiss on her lips. 'So, we need to get it organised.'

'How do you know all this?'

'I found out about it. Thought I should know what to do before I asked you . . . in case you said yes.'

'Did you think I might turn you down?'

'Well, I hoped you'd say yes, but I wasn't sure. I was worried you might think it was too soon.'

Prune gently stroked his cheek. 'You make me happy. The happiest I have ever been, and I love you. Simple as that. I want to be your wife.'

Howard pulled her to him and hugged her tightly. She closed her eyes and savoured the moment. This Christmas Day had been the best she'd ever had, so different from the stuffy, rigid traditions of past Christmases at home with her mother. Her mother. The thought of what she'd say about her marrying him, was like dousing her flame of happiness with a bucket of icy water. Prune's stomach twisted for a few seconds before she took control. No, she wouldn't let anything ruin this moment. Howard wanted to marry her, be with her for the rest of his life, and that made her heart sing with joy. Nothing was going to spoil that feeling. She'd deal with what was to come later. Right now, this moment was hers and Howard's to enjoy. They had their entire lives together stretched out before them, and she was deliriously, wonderfully, happy.

★ ★ ★

London - Christmas Day

'Merry Christmas, nurse.' A visiting relative greeted Grace as they walked onto the ward.

142

'Merry Christmas to you,' she responded with a smile.

There was an air of jollity about the ward today, everyone making the best of being in hospital. She was glad to be on duty, volunteering to do an extra shift so that nurses who had families at home could be with them.

It was better to be busy and useful at St Thomas' than to brood at home, desperately missing John and Marigold. They'd always made Christmas Day such a fun, happy family time. Grace smiled at the memory of her daughter coming into their bedroom on Christmas morning, her face alight with joy that Father Christmas had been. She would climb up into their bed, snuggle down between them, and delve into her stocking to pull out gifts. A doll, some chocolate, an orange, a handful of nuts and a sixpence in the toe.

When Grace had woken up this morning, she'd been alone, the flat silent, and John and Marigold's absence keenly felt. She sighed, reminding herself to be glad that Marigold was safe in Norfolk with Bessie and Harry. She'd sent a parcel for her and knew Bessie would make sure she got it today.

Marigold had sent her a present wrapped in brown paper with *To Mummy, Happy Christmas, Love from Marigold*, written on it.

Grace had opened it in bed this morning. Inside was a lavender bag, made from pale pink cotton and with the word *Mummy* carefully embroidered on the front. Her eyes had blurred with tears as she'd stared at it, gently stroking the letters. Marigold had made it all by herself, so the letter that came with it had told her, after Bessie had taught her how to embroider. The lavender inside it, was from Bessie's garden and smelt wonderful.

She slipped her hand into the pocket of her uniform and touched the lavender bag, her fingers skimming over the letters spelling out 'Mummy'. Carrying it around with her while she was on duty helped Marigold feel a little closer.

23

Norfolk

Something had woken Bessie; she lay still, listening for it again. Beside her, Harry was sleeping, curled up on his side as usual. The sound came again, a faint rattling, as if someone was poking at the fire. Carefully pulling back the covers to avoid waking Harry, she slipped out of bed and tiptoed to an in-wards looking window. Tweaking aside the muslin curtain, Bessie saw a silhouetted figure hunched over the fire's red glow — someone else was awake. After putting on her slippers and dressing gown, she crept to the door, quietly opened it and slipped into the main room.

The figure in front of the stove started and turned around. It was Prune.

'Oh, Bessie! I'm sorry, I didn't mean to wake you. I just couldn't sleep and was trying to sort out the fire.'

'It's all right, don't worry.' She sat down in the armchair opposite the young woman, and in the faint red firelight could see something was wrong. Prune who was usually so calm and collected, looked distraught and began to weep silent tears which splashed down onto her thick, tartan-patterned dressing gown.

Bessie touched Prune's hands, which were tightly clasped on her lap. 'I'll bank up the fire so we won't get cold, then we can talk if you want to.' She busied herself adding some wood to the stove, taking care to not make any noise. The last thing they needed was anyone else coming in and seeing Prune like this.

"What's happened?' Bessie asked, settling back in her armchair.

'It's . . . Howard asked me to marry him tonight. And I said yes.'

'But that's good. Isn't it what you want? Or did you say yes, when you meant no?'

'It's what I want, more than anything.' Prune gave a watery smile.

'I don't understand why you're so upset; shouldn't you be happy?'

'The thing is, I can't marry him . . . I'm supposed to be marrying someone else.'

Bessie gasped. 'You're already engaged?'

'No.' Prune shook her head vehemently. 'Definitely not! Though, if Mummy had had her way, I would have been before I left home.'

'You've lost me. You'd better tell me the whole story, I never had you down for one who'd be involved with two men at the same time.'

'No, I'm not like that at all.' Prune bit her bottom lip. 'Mummy expects me to marry her best friend's son, Jeremy. I've known him all my life, we used to play together as children and grew up knowing each other. We're good friends. Only Mummy and Jeremy's mother have this dream that we'll marry, and fool-ishly we've let them go on thinking that to keep the peace.' She sighed. 'But there's never been anything romantic between us.'

'Do you intend to marry him?'

'No. We are like brother and sister. When the war came along it gave us both an escape route from our mothers, though they still think we'll marry when the war's over. In the meantime, Jeremy's escaped to the navy and I'm a Timber Jill. He's now engaged to a

146

Wren, but his mother doesn't know yet.'

Bessie took one of Prune's hands in hers. 'You must marry who you choose, not who your mother wants. Write and tell her you've met Howard and Jeremy's engaged to someone else. Simple as that.'

Prune sighed. 'You don't know my mother. She won't take this well after planning our marriage for years. If I marry a GI, she'll never speak to me again . . .' Her voice wavered. 'I know mother's difficult, but she's all the family I have left after Daddy died.'

'It sounds like she's trying to run your life for you. You need to follow your heart and trust where it leads you, even if it's against her wishes.' Bessie squeezed Prune's hand. 'Remember, it's your decision, not hers, and if she cares for you, she should understand that.'

'But what if mother doesn't and never speaks to me again? I'd have to choose her or Howard. One or the other, but not both.' Prune started to sob, her shoulders shaking.

Bessie moved over and sat on the arm of Prune's chair, putting her arms around the young woman. 'It won't be easy, but you need to tell her straight. I suppose you haven't told Howard any of this?'

Prune shook her head. 'I never expected him to propose.'

'He's a lovely young man. Harry and I are very fond of him. Everyone is.'

'What's going on?' Dottie's voice made them jump. She came over and knelt in front of her friend. 'What's wrong?'

'You'd best tell her,' Bessie said.

Dottie sat in the opposite chair and listened as Prune explained everything. 'You're a dark horse, you 'never let slip about this other engagement.'

'It's. Not. An. Engagement.' Prune's eyes welled with tears again. 'Not a proper one, just our two mothers' understanding. Jeremy and I never agreed to anything, to them, or each other. It was something we laughed at behind their backs.'

Dottie shook her head. 'You should never have let them get away with thinking like that, especially now with all this going on.'

Prune shrugged. 'I know. But with Mother . . . well, it was the easiest way. You don't know her.'

Dottie pulled a face. 'I'm not sure I'd want to either.'

'It's no good going over and over it,' Bessie said. 'You've got to be honest and do the right thing by Howard and Jeremy, and your mother. Write to her and explain everything. Warn Jeremy, too. Then when it's settled you can get on with getting married.'

'Tell her you can't help who you fall in love with.' Dottie said. 'It hits you when you least expect it, isn't that right, Bessie?'

She nodded. 'It's true.'

24

May, 1918

A flash of vivid blue and orange caught Bessie's eye as a bird flew off downstream, vanishing round a bend.

'A kingfisher!' Sergeant Rushbrook levered himself around in the wicker bath chair and looked up at Bessie, his face lit with pleasure. 'Did you see it?'

She nodded, smiling. 'It was beautiful. Shall we stop here as usual?'

'Yes, please.'

'Right, be careful how you steer; I don't want to have to fish you out of the beck.'

She pushed the bath chair up the gentle slope onto the wooden bridge, while Sergeant Rushbrook steered with the T-barred handle which turned the small wheel underneath the front.

Satisfied the chair was safely parked so it couldn't roll off the bridge, Bessie leaned against the handrail while keeping one hand on the push bar at the back for security. She breathed in deeply, savouring the fresh green smell of spring and the gentle gurgling of the water passing over the ford and under the bridge. It was a delight to be out here on such a beautiful day, with its cloudless blue sky soaring overhead. She sighed with pleasure.

'Was that a good sigh, saying you're happy to be here like I am? Or a bad sigh, because you're tired of bringing me here?'

'Oh, definitely a good one; I love coming here.' She

looked around them and across the ford towards the water meadows stretching along its banks into the distance. 'It's . . .'

'Lovely?' he suggested. 'Beautiful, gorgeous, marvellous?'

'All of those and more. It's so wonderful to be outside, especially on a day like this.' Bessie threw her free arm out wide to encompass everything around them.

The walks she'd been taking Sergeant Rushbrook out on over recent weeks, had often brought them to the beck. They both liked it there, usually stopping on the bridge for a while, watching the water flow past while they talked and laughed. Their outings were always good-hearted and fun, each of them enjoying being away from the hospital together. Matron said getting out was part of the men's healing process, it prevented them becoming institutionalised in the hospital.

'I'm going to miss this place when I go.' He glanced upstream and then turned to face Bessie, his eyes meeting and holding hers. 'Did you know I'll be leaving for Roehampton next week? Matron told me this morning.'

Bessie's stomach lurched. 'No.' She managed to smile. 'But that's fantastic news, isn't it?'

He shrugged. 'It is . . . and it isn't.'

'Your injury has healed up well enough to have an artificial leg fitted. That's marvellous. Think what you'll be capable of once you're walking again; you can move forward and start the rest of your life.'

'The thought of being able to walk again is incredible'

'It will be wonderful for you.' Bessie was pleased he

150

had the chance to go to Roehampton. Being mobile would give him back his independence, he wouldn't have to rely on a VAD pushing him around in a bath chair or hobbling along on crutches. But for that to happen, he had to leave Marston Hall. Their work with him would be finished, and he'd be sent on his way, another successfully healed patient. The perfect outcome. So why did her insides feel like they were being wrung out at the thought of him leaving? Bessie wondered. She would miss him . . . that's why.

'Have you decided what you'll do when you're finally discharged?'

'I've been giving it plenty of thought. I know what I want to do, it's just how, that I need to think about.'

'Is your father a farmer?' Bessie asked.

'No, it was the last job he'd have done.' He laughed. 'He was a shopkeeper, a neat and tidy man who kept his grocery shop the same way. I grew up in the house behind the shop, it was just me and him after my mother died. Father was more interested in weighing out blue bags of sugar than farming. He expected me to follow suit and work there after I left school.'

'Did you?'

Sergeant Rushbrook pulled a face. 'No. I worked in there helping before I left school, but I was determined to have a job on a farm once I'd finished my education. And I did. It's all I ever wanted to do, right from when I was small. I've always loved animals and being outside. I used to help on my aunt's farm — she's my mother's sister — who married a farmer. I knew what farming was about, and that it suited me. My father didn't like it, but he accepted it . . . eventually.' He paused, a pained look crossing his face. 'Although I think he thought I'd tire of working outside in all weathers, doing backbreaking, dirty jobs, and go back and join him in the grocers.'

'Is that what you're planning to do?'

'I can't. My father died suddenly in 1916, so I sold the shop and put the money in the bank for after the war. I'd planned to buy a hill farm of my own if I made it through, only that can't happen now.'

'So, what are you going to do instead?' Bessie asked.

'I've got an idea.' Sergeant Rushbrook's eyes met hers. 'It would give me the life I want, slightly different from what I originally planned, but it would still be right for me.'

'What is it?'

'I'm sorry, I can't tell you yet.' He smiled mysteriously. 'But I will one day, I promise. I won't allow what's happened to stop me.'

'Good. The war's changed things for all of us, sending our lives off in different directions from the ones we'd planned.' Her life had been altered too. If the archduke hadn't been shot, she'd be living another life now. 'I would've been a married woman if the war had never happened.'

'What stopped you getting married?'

'My fiancé, William, was killed. We were engaged and were going to marry on his next leave, but . . . he never came back.'

'I'm sorry,' he said, sympathetically. 'When did it happen?'

'1915'

'Did you join the VAD then?'

Bessie shook her head. 'No. I've been a VAD since November, nineteen fourteen when Marston Hall was turned into an Auxiliary War Hospital. I was already there with a job as a seamstress, and like the rest of

152

the staff, I started working in the hospital. And I'm still here.'

Falling into silence for a few moments, Bessie recalled when she'd last seen William, and then the terrible news coming of his death. At least time had dulled the pain and she could look back and remember him with love, and hope he rested in peace.

'Enough about me.' She stood up straight. 'I'm intrigued about your plan for the future, Sergeant Rushbrook, but if you won't tell me, then I must get you back to the hospital or you'll miss tea and Matron will be on the warpath.'

Taking hold of the handle at the back of the bath chair, Bessie prepared to pull it off the bridge. 'Steer straight backwards, if you please.'

Back on the road, she expected him to turn right and head down the lane leading to Marston Hall, but he kept going straight on.

'We should have gone right.' Bessie reminded him. 'We'd better turn around.'

'No. I'd like to go this way, past the wood.' He turned in his seat to look at her. 'Please, Nurse Carter, I just want to check whether the bluebells are out. They were still in bud last time we went past. It's been a long time since I saw bluebells.'

Bessie loved the beautiful spring flowers and would like to see them too. She couldn't be sure if she'd have another chance to see them, they might be over by the time she went that way again. 'Very well then, but we mustn't be long, or you really will miss your tea.'

The smell of the bluebells reached them before they saw the flowers. A gentle breeze blew their subtle perfume towards them as they approached the wood, where the beech trees were unfurling their fresh green leaves, while underneath the canopy, a hazy carpet of blue stretched out into the wood as far as they could see.

'They're out! And so beautiful.'

He turned and looked up at her. 'I want to go in there.'

She glanced at the uneven, rutted ground leading into the woodland. 'I'm not sure if I can manage to push . . .'

'I mean on these.' He held up the crutches, which he'd insisted on bringing out with them today. 'Please, I need to stand among the bluebells again.'

Looking at his face, which was filled with hope and longing, Bessie nodded. She helped him haul himself out of the bath chair, onto his crutches so he stood upright. Then, with slow, painstakingly careful steps, he made his way into the wood, with her right beside him, her hand on his back.

'Easy here.' Bessie pointed at a deep rut in the ground. 'Check each crutch is level and firm before you put your weight on it.'

A few minutes later, they stood surrounded by the fragrant flowers. Bessie gazed around at the blueness; it was stunningly beautiful. Being there amongst such beauty made her heart sing.

'Glad we came this way?' Sergeant Rushbrook asked.

She smiled at him. 'Yes, I am. I love bluebells, they're my favourite flower.'

'Hold on to my arm, will you?'

Bessie quickly grabbed hold of his arm, frightened he might fall. Perhaps it was too much for him walking on the wood's uneven floor. 'Have you lost your balance?'

'No, I'm fine, I just want to do this.' He put both crutches under one arm and then slowly bent forward, his weight still supported on his leg, and with Bessie holding onto him, he reached out with his free hand.

'What are you doing? Be careful.'

'This.' He plucked a single bluebell stem and slowly stood upright again. 'For you.' He held out the flower for Bessie to take, his eyes studying her face.

'Thank you.' She sniffed the bluebell, enjoying its delicate perfume.

'My pleasure. It's a perfect match for your eyes; they're the same colour. I always thought so, but now I know for sure.' He glanced around at the bluebells carpeting the wood, and then returned his gaze to Bessie's face. 'Do you remember I said, 'it is, and it isn't' good that I'm going next week?'

'Yes.'

'The bit which isn't good, is that I'll be leaving you behind. I've grown very fond of you. Forgive me if I speak out of turn, but I had to say something before I went.'

Bessie's heart quickened its pace. He was fond of her . . . The feeling was mutual. 'I . . .'

'It's all right if you don't feel the same way . . .'

'But I do, Sergeant Rushbrook. I do!' The words rushed out of her mouth before she had time to think. 'I've grown fond of you, too. When you told me you were leaving, I couldn't help thinking how much I'll miss you.'

He took hold of one of her hands. 'My name is Harry. Please, no more Sergeant Rushbrook.'

'But I have to call you that, it's hospital rules.'

'But we are not at the hospital now, though.'

She laughed, gazing around at the bluebell wood,

then returning to look at Harry. 'No, we're not. My name's Bessie. Short for Elizabeth.'

'Bessie, I like it. Sweet Bess.' He reached out and gently stroked her cheek. 'Will you be my girl, Bess?'

'Nurses aren't allowed to be involved with patients. It's against the . . .'

'Rules. I know, but I shan't be here much longer and after that, it won't matter because I'm not one of your patients anymore. So, will you be my girl, Bess?' His blue eyes were filled with hope and tenderness.

'Yes, Harry, I will, but not properly until you leave. It's not that I don't want to, but I have to keep to the rules. I hope you understand.'

Harry smiled happily. 'I do. I'll come back to see you as soon as I can.'

Bessie gently touched his face. 'I'll be waiting for you.' She put her arms around him and hugged him tightly, happy at the thought that she would see him again after he left. When he went to St Mary's, it wouldn't be the end . . . but the beginning.

Stepping back, Bessie gazed into his beautiful blue eyes, which always looked as if they were filled with the light of a clear summer sky.

'Now I must get you back for your tea, or Matron will send out a search party for us.'

25

Going out collecting firewood was a good antidote to Christmas Day feasting, Bessie thought, as they marched across the meadow towards the wood. Peter and Marigold ran ahead, towing the small cart behind them, their breath coming out in steamy billows in the crisp air, while she, Dottie and Prune followed on, their arms linked.

'Have you decided what you're going to do about your mother?' Bessie asked.

'There's no way around it but to write to her,' Prune said. 'Until I'm twenty-one in February, I'll need her permission to marry.'

'Do you honestly think she'll say yes, not when she's expecting you to marry Jeremy?' Dottie asked.

Prune shook her head. 'No, I don't.' She sighed. 'But what choice do I have? If I want to marry Howard before I'm twenty-one, then I must have her permission.'

'You could wait,' Bessie suggested.

'In normal circumstances, I would, but with the war on . . . And Howard wants to get married as soon as possible. We won't be able to marry immediately anyway, because of all the paperwork there is to do. I'll have to have an interview with his commanding officer or chaplain. Once we have permission, we still must wait another sixty days until the wedding, so the sooner we get started with all that, the better. But it

157

means getting my mother's approval.'

'What's the interview for, to check you'd make a suitable GI bride?' Dottie giggled.

'I suppose they want to make sure you're not rushing into things,' Bessie said. 'For some girls, marrying a GI's a one-way ticket to America.'

'Not for me, I promise you. I've never been more serious about anything in my life. Howard is the man for me.'

'You make a lovely couple. But if your mother says no, what will you do?' Dottie asked.

'The only thing I can do.' Prune pulled a face. 'And that's wait until I don't need her permission. It's only a few weeks, but time's precious these days, so I'd rather not have to hang on till then. I'm going to marry him anyway whether or not she approves, she's got to realise that, so it would be better to help us out.'

'I hope she'll see sense and it won't come to that,' Bessie added as they reached the edge of the wood. 'Right, let's get this cart loaded up.'

The physical work of finding fallen branches and loading them into the cart soon warmed Bessie up. The others were feeling the same, their cheeks glowing as they scouted around for suitable branches, then dragged them back to a growing pile. Prune and Dottie broke up long bits over their knees and loaded them up. It was a team effort which would warm them again later when the wood was burnt in the stove.

Dottie tipped an armful of short sticks into the cart. 'Have you thought about a wedding dress?'

Prune laughed. 'It's only been a few hours since he asked me. I'd rather wait until I know when the wedding's going to be.'

'You don't want to leave it too long though, it's difficult to come by wedding dresses these days.' Dottie snapped a thin branch in two.

'Who needs a wedding dress?' Marigold asked coming up behind them, dragging a branch.

'You'd better ask Prune,' Dottie said.

'Are you getting married?'

Prune blushed and nodded. 'Yes. I think I am.'

'Who to?'

Dottie laughed. 'To Howard, who else?'

'Congratulations,' Peter said. 'Will you live in America after the war?'

'I suppose we will. I just want him to get through the war first.'

'We all do.' Dottie put an arm around Prune's shoulders.

'When are you getting married?' Marigold asked.

'In a few months, I hope.'

'Bessie could make you a dress,' Marigold suggested. 'Would you?' she called over to Bessie, who was heading back to the cart, dragging a fallen branch in each hand.

'What's this about?' she said.

'Prune's getting married and needs a wedding dress. You could make her one, couldn't you?'

'Well, I could, but it's up to Prune, and depends on whether we could get some nice material.'

'Can I be your bridesmaid?' Marigold asked. 'I've always wanted to be one.'

'I don't think Prune's even thought about it yet,' Bessie said, gently.

'No, I haven't. Howard only asked me last night. But if I have one, I must think carefully about who I might choose.' Prune looked hard at Marigold. 'Do you think you might be interested in the job?'

'Yes, yes.' Marigold jumped up and down. 'Yes, please. I can, can't I, Bessie?'

'If it's what Prune wants, then I don't see any reason why not.' Bessie put her arm around Marigold. 'I think you'd make a lovely bridesmaid.'

'But what about, you?' Marigold looked at Peter, who threw some branches onto the pile.

He grinned. 'I wouldn't make a good bridesmaid, but I'll be there to watch you being one, Marigold.'

'It's going to be lovely to have a wedding to think about,' Dottie said. 'Give us something to look forward to.'

26

Bessie had brought patients to the station many times before, but none of those trips had ever made her feel the way she did today. Before, she'd always had a sense of happiness and satisfaction that the men were well again, especially if they were going home for good and the war was over for them. But now, it was as if a tide of sadness was welling up inside her and creeping around her heart. She was chilly, despite the warmth of the beautiful summer's day, because Sergeant Rushbrook — Harry - was leaving.

'Are you sure you've got everything?' Bessie stowed Harry's crutches in the corner of the compartment beside him, trying hard to be practical, ignoring the leaden weight in her stomach.

Harry leaned forward from his seat by the window to be nearer where she stood on the platform. 'Nearly everything.'

Bessie frowned. 'But we checked before you left the hospital, and you said you had.'

'I did then. I had all I needed with me, but now I'm about to leave something behind. Something important.' He reached out and took hold of her hand. 'I'm leaving you, Bess.'

She quickly glanced up and down the platform to see if anyone had noticed Harry was holding her hand. Fortunately, everyone else was occupied helping men into the train.

Swallowing hard against the growing tightness in her throat, Bessie met his eyes and smiled. 'You'll just have to come back for me then, won't you?'

'I will, I promise you, Bess. And I'll write to you.'

The guard started slamming carriage doors shut, making his way towards them from the front end of the train. Time was running out.

'I'm going to miss you.' Harry raised Bessie's hand to his lips and kissed it. 'Thank you for everything you've done for me.'

Bessie nodded, not trusting herself to speak. She wanted to throw her arms around him and hold him tight, but she couldn't, not here, not now. But in the future, she'd be able to do so without breaking any hospital rules. 'I'll miss you, too,' she said, her voice sounding hoarse. 'Look after yourself.'

He gave her hand a last squeeze as the guard arrived at the door.

'All set then?' he said. 'Mind your fingers.' He shut the door and hurried onto the next compartment.

Harry slid the door-window down and reached out his hand. Bessie linked her fingers in his. 'Have a good journey, be careful on your crutches.'

'I will. Next time you see me, I'll be walking on two legs.'

'I look forward to it. Goodbye, Harry.'

The guard's whistle blew from the far end of the train, and the engine up the front sent great chuffs of smoke puffing out of the chimney.

'Goodbye, Bess.' His eyes held hers as the train moved.

Bessie walked alongside it, her fingers still on his for a few seconds more, but then as the train picked up speed, she let go and waved to him. Even after she

162

lost sight of Harry's face at the carriage window, she kept watching and waving, only stopping when the train rounded the bend and was gone.

27

London - Early January, 1945

Grace walked towards the two anxious-looking women waiting by the ward entrance. They were huddled together, their faces drawn and exhausted, but their eyes as they watched her approach, still had hope in them that their missing relative was alive and would be all right. She hated this part of her job. It never got easier, no matter how many times she'd done it.

'Nurse, please . . .' The older, white-haired woman stepped forward. 'Have you got my daughter, Stella, here . . . we can't find her nowhere . . . red curly hair, blue eyes, thirty years old. Is she here?'

'If you'd like to follow me, please.' Grace led them into the small room just outside the ward, which they used to talk to relatives in. It was somewhere quieter, more private, and where they kept the brandy bottle and medicine glasses.

Taking a coat from the bundles of patients' clothes left on the table in there, for relatives to identify, she held it up. 'Is this your daughter's?'

The white-haired woman stared at the coat, that would once have been a smart royal blue, but which was now stiff with dried blood and impregnated with dust and plaster.

'That's Stella's. That's my sister's.' The younger woman said. 'Thank Gawd! Can we see her nurse, please?'

Grace swallowed hard. 'I'm sorry, but I'm afraid she

164

died a short while ago. Her injuries were too severe.'

The old lady let out a soft moan and the younger woman grabbed hold of her.

'Sit her down there.' Grace nodded at a chair and unstoppered the brandy bottle they kept ready on a small table, pouring some into two glasses, which she handed to the women. 'Drink this, it will help.'

She stood back and gave them some time to gather themselves together as they sipped their brandies, wincing as the liquid burnt their throats. At least their search was over; they'd found Stella, and she wouldn't be a nameless victim of the latest V2 rocket any longer.

Stepping out of St Thomas' at the end of her over-long shift, Grace turned left instead of the usual right and walked to the middle of Westminster Bridge. She leaned against the parapet and looked down into the water rippling underneath, feeling exhausted, physically and emotionally. They'd been rushed off their feet dealing with a wave of incoming patients from a V2 blast. Many of them had been badly injured, and several, like Stella, hadn't made it.

Grace sighed. This morning, all those people had been going about their business, and suddenly without warning, boom, they'd been injured or killed. Young, old, children, it didn't matter; the V2s didn't discriminate; they hurt anyone. These latest rockets were proving to be even worse than the doodlebugs, dropping with no warning, no chance to take cover.

A surge of anger flooded through Grace. It wasn't right or fair. But who said war was fair? How many more lives had been ruined just today? How many families had lost someone in this war? Not just away fighting, but here on home soil.

Normally, Grace tried hard not to think about it too

much. Dealing with what she had to do every day on the ward . . . it was the only way to keep going and cope with the things she saw, but sometimes, like today, it was hard not to dwell on it. Not to become emotional. How could she not become angry about Stella dying? She'd been so badly injured there was nothing they could do and had just slipped away — the mother of two young boys, who'd been evacuated to Devon, so Stella's sister had told her. Stella's husband had died on the North Atlantic convoys and now she was dead, her children were orphans.

What if it happened to you? a thought whispered in Grace's head. What would happen to Marigold if she was killed by a V2? She'd be an orphan too. Grace shuddered. She must make plans, ensure if anything happened to her, that her daughter would be looked after.

28

Norfolk - January, 1945

Prune's fingers were numb and her cheeks stinging from the biting wind, by the time she and Dottie turned their bicycles into the lane leading down to Orchard Farm. The sun had set, and the temperature was dropping fast; there'd be another sharp frost tonight.

'Last one in makes the cocoa,' Dottie shouted, putting on a spurt of speed and whizzing past her.

'Hey! Aren't you supposed to be tired after all the felling we've done today?' she called out, pressing harder onto her pedals, trying to catch up.

'It's the lure of a warm fire.' Dottie laughed back over her shoulder.

Prune pedalled as fast as she could and had almost reached her friend before she turned into the farm gate.

'I won!' Dottie panted, jumping off her bicycle.

Prune brought her bike to a halt beside Dottie and leaned over the handlebars, breathing heavily and laughing at the same time. 'You had an unfair start, you caught me out. How about a fairer race tomorrow? One we both know about, then we'll see who has to make the cocoa.'

'You're on, but tonight the cocoa's on you, and it might be tomorrow, too.'

'Is that a challenge?'

'Why not?' Dottie laughed. 'As long as you're not

afraid of being beaten twice.'

They were still laughing when they went indoors. Peeling off their coats, they hung them up in the porch and walked into the living room to find a visitor waiting for them.

'Clem!' Dottie said.

He stood up. 'Hello.'

'This is a pleasant surprise.' Prune went over to the stove and warmed her hands above it. 'Are you staying for tea?'

'I won't, thank you, not tonight.'

'Sit down, Prune.' Bessie took hold of her arm, guiding her to an armchair.

'What's the matter?' She looked at Bessie and Clem, her stomach knotting — something was wrong.

'I've come with some bad news.' Clem twisted his cap in his hands. 'I'm sorry to tell you . . . Howard's plane didn't make it back today. He's officially missing in action.'

Prune gasped. Bessie sat down on the arm of the chair beside her and put her arm around her.

'All we know is the Peggy Sue went down. One of the other crews saw she was hit by flak and was losing height. There weren't any chutes.'

'Chutes?' Her voice sounded odd. 'What do you mean?'

'Parachutes. They didn't see anyone parachuting out before they lost sight of her in the cloud.'

'But you don't know for sure what happened?' Bessie said.

'No. Only that the Peggy Sue was hit and was going down when she was last seen. Until we find out more, the crew are all listed as missing in action.'

'But there's always hope, isn't there?' Prune's words

felt thick in her mouth. 'Howard might be all right.'

She looked down at the engagement ring he'd given her. He had to come back to her, she couldn't bear it if she lost him. Prune shut her eyes and concentrated hard. It didn't feel as if he had gone. Howard was still out there somewhere. He had to be.

Clem nodded. 'We'll keep hoping.'

A sudden, loud sob made them all look at Dottie, whose normally pretty face was contorted with pain and her shoulders shaking.

'Dottie?' Bessie said.

She didn't answer but turned and yanked the door open and rushed outside.

'I must go after her.' Prune struggled to her feet.

'No, you don't.' Bessie pushed her down again. 'You've had a shock and need to sit down. Clem, can you stay with her?'

He nodded. 'Yes, of course.'

'Make her some tea and put sugar in it.' Bessie grabbed her coat from a hook. 'I must find Dottie.'

'We were going to have some cocoa. It was my turn to make it because Dottie won the race,' Prune said after Bessie had gone out. 'It was before . . .' she stopped. It was before she knew Howard was missing. He might be back . . . and he might not.

If he didn't . . . She couldn't bear to think about it.

'Prune?' Clem said, gently.

She started to shake and dissolved into gut-wrenching sobs.

★ ★ ★

Outside, Bessie scanned her torch around the farmyard, but there was no sign of Dottie. It was too cold

169

a night to be out here for long without a coat, so she'd probably gone into the barn or a shed. Hurrying across the yard, she wondered what had got into the young woman. The news about Howard was bad, but there was still hope.

Why would Dottie run off? It wasn't as if he was her fiancé. She'd always been adamant that she wanted a career and didn't want to get seriously involved with any man.

Bessie slipped in through the door of the barn, closing it quietly behind her. Inside, the whitewashed walls were dimly lit by the light of Harry's tilly lamp, and the smell of warm cow and sweet hay was familiar and comforting.

Harry and the children were settling the cows in for the night, as Marigold and Peter enjoyed seeing to the animals with him after school. Thank goodness they'd been in here with him, and not indoors to hear Clem breaking the news to Prune. They'd have to be told and it would upset them, especially Peter as he'd flown in the Peggy Sue with Howard, but she would deal with that later. Her priority was to find Dottie.

'Are they all settled?' Bessie tried to sound normal.

'Nearly done,' Harry said.

'I'm looking for Dottie. Did she come in here?

'No,' Peter said. 'It's just us. Is it time for tea?'

She smiled at Peter. 'Soon.'

Harry caught Bessie's eye. 'Is everything all right?'

Biting her bottom lip, Bessie nodded. 'Yes.' She didn't want to say anything in front of the children. Not yet. 'I expect she's gone in the bike shed, probably left her flask in her bicycle basket.'

She could tell from Harry's face that he knew something was wrong, but he just said, 'We'll be in soon.'

170

Bessie tried the bike shed next, but there was no sign of Dottie there, nor in the woodshed. She eventually found her in the wash-house, crouched on the little stool by the copper, which still gave out some warmth as it had been lit earlier for the washing.

'There you are!' She closed the door behind her. 'Are you all right?'

Dottie shook her head, her tear-streaked face looking ghostly in the pale torchlight.

Bessie knelt beside her and put her arm around Dottie's shoulders. 'We've got to hope Howard comes back. There's a chance he might, and we need to cling on to that for Prune's sake.'

Dottie threw off Bessie's arm and stood up. 'Only a fool does that!' she snapped, her voice hoarse with emotion. 'Don't encourage Prune to hope. He won't come back and hoping will only make it worse for her.' Her anger quickly subsided, and she sank back onto the stool, burying her head in her hands and weeping.

'If Prune wants to hope, then she should.'

'But it's useless.' Dottie looked at her and drew in a deep breath. 'I hoped and kept on, day after day, but it was pointless. He died and won't be coming back. Ever.'

'Who didn't come back?'

'My husband!' Dottie's face crumpled and Bessie wrapped her arms around her while she sobbed.

Bessie waited until she was calmer again, then took hold of the young woman's hands in hers. 'I'm sorry. You're so young to have lost your husband.'

'I'm not the only one. There's plenty out there like me.'

'Far too many . . . I didn't know you were married.'

171

'I don't talk about it. Too painful.' Dottie sighed. 'After Jim died in forty-two . . . I joined the Timber Corps and kept quiet about my past. Pretended it never happened. I thought it would be easier if no one knew.'

'What happened to him?'

'He was a flight engineer in a Lancaster. They went down on a raid over Germany. I kept hoping somehow he had parachuted out and would come home, but one of his friends wrote and told me he'd seen Jim's plane blow up in mid-air . . .' She halted. 'There were no survivors. They didn't get out.'

'I'm sorry.' Bessie squeezed Dottie's hands. 'Hearing about Howard has brought it all back to you?'

Dottie nodded. 'Prune loves him so much, and I can't bear to think of her going through what I did. Howard was like a breath of fresh air to her.'

'Your plan for the future . . . to be a career girl . . . it's because of what you've been through?' Bessie asked gently.

'I thought it was the best way forward, there's too much risk of losing someone all over again if you become involved. I've learned the hard way.'

'That's a shame. You're young and might meet someone else one day who's right for you.'

'I'd rather walk a safe path. Just look after myself and not get embroiled with anyone again. Look what a state I'm in now and it's nearly three years since I lost Jim.'

'Probably because you've bottled it up for a long time.' Bessie smiled. 'No wonder you blew like a ginger beer.'

'I'm sorry.'

'Don't be, I understand.'

172

'I must talk to Prune, explain it to her. I do hope Howard comes back. Honestly, I do. But the fact is most of them don't when their plane goes down.'

'I know, but if hoping helps Prune cope for now, then we've got to support her. It'll give her something to cling on to until we know more.' Bessie stood up. 'Will you come in with me?'

Dottie shook her head. 'I need a few minutes.'

'All right, but don't be too long, you need to eat after a day's work.'

★ ★ ★

'Clem?' Bessie hurried across to the American who was walking towards the gate. 'How's Prune?'

'She's quiet but okay. Harry and the children are indoors now, so I thought it was time to go.'

'Do Peter and Marigold know?'

He shook his head. 'Harry knows, he came out on the steps when I left, so I told him.'

'Thank you. We must tell the children later.'

'Is Dottie okay? The way she rushed off . . .'

'She'll be fine, this just opened up an old wound.' Bessie paused. 'Do you think there's any chance Howard will come back?'

Clem shrugged. 'I don't know, ma'am. It happens. No one saw the Peggy Sue crash because of the thick cloud, but there were no chutes either. She definitely didn't make it home.' He shook his head. 'I hope and pray the whole crew returns. Howard's a good friend of mine . . .' his voice wavered.

'We'll keep hoping and praying too.' Bessie patted Clem's arm. 'Are you sure you won't stay and have some tea with us?'

'No, thank you. I appreciate you asking, but I don't have an appetite for food right now.'

She nodded. 'Please let us know as soon as you hear anything.'

'I will, you can be sure of that.'

174

29

Peter stared at Bessie, not wanting to believe what she'd told him. It couldn't be true. Not about Howard and the Peggy Sue.

'Peter?' Bessie's face was full of concern. 'Are you all right?'

He didn't know what to say, so he just nodded and picked up a flag from the map on the table, twiddling it around in his fingers. Although every single ounce of him wanted to reject what he'd been told, the bitter truth was that the Peggy Sue didn't return from today's mission and was last seen going down. Howard, Walt, Lieutenant Truman and the rest of the crew were missing, along with the Peggy Sue, that wonderful plane which he'd flown in. He'd felt so secure and safe inside her as she'd raced through the air. How could she and all those men be gone?

'Until we know otherwise, we'll keep hoping Howard will come back.' Bessie put her arm around his shoulders.

'Do you think he will? And all the others?'

'I don't know. All we can do is hope and wait.'

The map on the desk blurred as Peter's eyes filled with tears. He'd been around the Rackbridge base long enough to understand the chances of them returning weren't good. So many crews had gone out and never come back again. Why should it be any different with the Peggy Sue and her crew?

'Bessie?' Harry stood in the doorway. 'Marigold's asking for you.'

'I must go to her, Peter, she's upset about Howard, too. I'll be back soon.' She popped a kiss on his head and left.

'It's rough news for you and Marigold to hear.' Harry said, walking over to stand by the table.

'Do you . . .' Peter's voice came out in a croak. 'Do you think he'll come back?'

Harry shrugged. 'I hope he does. I hope all of them do and that's all I can do. They might and they might not.' He sighed. 'It's what happens in wartime, it's not right, but it's the reality of it. People see more of it in this war than the last, what with the planes flying out from here instead of it going on over in France.'

'Were many of your friends killed in France?' Peter asked.

'Too many.' Harry rubbed the back of his neck. 'I was lucky, I came home. Well, most of me did.' He tapped his artificial leg. 'I still think about the ones left behind.'

'What will we do if Howard doesn't return?'

'Remember him as he was and live our lives to the full for him.' Harry put his hand on Peter's shoulder. 'It's what he would want you to do, but don't go down that road till you have to, because there's always hope until we know different.'

Peter nodded. He knew all about hoping. He did it every day, hoping his parents were alive and that he'd see them again. He would do the same for Howard and the crew of the Peggy Sue. Perhaps if he hoped hard enough, it might just work.

* * *

176

'Oh, I . . . can't . . . stop . . . thinking . . . about . . . How-ard.'

Bessie sat on the bed and put her arms around Marigold and gently stroked her back as she sobbed.

'He's in all our thoughts tonight, along with the other young men who were with him.'

Gradually the little girl calmed and relaxed against her, but then she suddenly tensed and turned to look her straight in the eye.

'Do you think he's died like my daddy?'

What should she say? Bessie thought, looking at Marigold's tear-stained face. She'd already suffered from the war, but it was no use lying to her. 'I don't know, I hope not.'

'My daddy said he'd come home, but he didn't.' Marigold leaned back against her again.

'I'm sure he wanted to do, more than anything.'

'That's what Mrs Fox told me. She liked my daddy, he used to help her with jobs around the house. I think you would've liked him, too.'

'What was he like?'

Marigold looked at the framed photograph she'd brought with her from London, which stood on the chest of drawers so she could see it while she lay in bed. 'He was funny, he made me laugh, and he was kind and always singing.'

Bessie listened as Marigold told her about her father and their life in London before war split her family forever.

'What about your father's family? Where did they live?' she asked.

'He didn't have any, he was an orphan and brought up in a children's home. He said that me and Mummy were all the family he ever hoped for.'

Marigold had said nothing about her mother's family, and Bessie couldn't help herself from asking. 'What about your mummy's family? Do you ever see them?'

'No, my mummy's mother died when she was small and her father died just before she went to London.' She stroked the ears of her toy rabbit. 'She hasn't got anyone else.'

Bessie's stomach twisted. Grace had completely cut herself off from the life she'd had in Norfolk, passing only fragments of it on to her daughter. Marigold was unaware there was an enormous gap in her family history because that was how her mother wanted it to be. Bessie desperately hoped that one day, Grace might see fit to change all that. Until then, she must keep her promise, no matter how hard it was and not tell Marigold all the things she'd like to say.

30

August, 1918

Bessie slipped out of the front door and made her way across the lawn towards the large cedar tree, whose wide branches cast a cool shade. On such a warm day, it was the perfect place to take her break and read the letter which had come for her in this morning's post.

She touched the outside of her pocket through the material of her blue VAD dress, feeling the shape of the envelope inside. Getting letters from Harry was like having a part of him with her, helping to ease the ache of missing him. He'd been true to his word and written to her every few days, keeping her up to date with his progress at St Mary's hospital in Roehampton.

Sitting down on the bench, Bessie took out the envelope and opened it, taking out the folded sheet of paper with a joyful sense of anticipation.

My Dearest Bess, she read
I hope this finds you well and happy. I've some good news. I walked ten yards on my own today, with just my two walking sticks ready to catch me if I stumbled. But I didn't. I kept going, and it feels wonderful to walk again. Standing as tall as I was, seeing the world from where I used to. I wish you could have been here to see me.
The fitters here have done a grand job adjusting the leg bucket. They marked the bit giving me trouble and cut the wood away and now it fits like a glove. No more

blisters. It's made all the difference and allowed me to walk again with no pain. I need to keep practising so I can go further and further, and one day soon, I hope, I'll be able to walk up the drive of Marston Hall and see you. Then perhaps we can visit the beck and watch the water swirl under the bridge as we used to.

She stopped reading and looked across the lawn to where patients were sitting in the sunshine, some playing dominoes or cards at the tables. Harry enjoyed being outside in the gardens when he was here, as well as going out in the bath chair, which almost invariably led them to the beck. She hadn't been back there since he left, because it wouldn't feel right to go there without him. Whenever she took a patient out in a bath chair now, she went to other places, never to her and Harry's special place where they'd talked and laughed so much. The next time she went there, it would be with him.

She started to read again.

This afternoon we're off to see another football match at Chelsea. All the men, myself included, enjoy these trips. I'll still be going in my wheelchair for the moment, but before long I'd like to go on my new leg. Walk all the way to the bus, then to the football ground. That will be a grand time. I miss you, Bess, and I tell myself that every day brings me that bit closer to seeing you again. I'll be back as soon as I can. For now, I must keep working hard at learning to walk, and when I've mastered it, I'll be ready to start the rest of my life.
I'm still working on my plans and have nearly sorted it out. The fellows here are a great bunch, and we spend a lot of time talking about our futures. No one's

*sad. These are the most cheerful group of men I've ever
known. We've all been through so much with our lost
limbs, but we're enjoying ourselves. Talking to the others
has been helpful and given me more ideas for my plan. I
can't tell you any more yet — even though you ask me in
your letters. Sorry, but I want to surprise you.
Must sign off now if this is going to catch the post.
Then I'm off to the football.
Take care of yourself, Bess. I know you work so hard
looking after the men.
With my fondest love,
Harry.*

Leaving the letter lying in her lap, Bessie leaned
against the back of the bench and smiled. She was
glad he was happy and getting on better. He'd suffered from blisters on his stump and had had to wait
until they'd healed before he could walk again. But it
sounded as if he was making genuine progress. She
wished she could go there and visit him, but it was
out of the question. For now, she had to be content
with Harry's frequent letters, which she kept tied up
in a ribbon up in her room in the attic.

She still had the bluebell he'd given her, which she'd
pressed in her diary and often took it out to smell;
its faint perfume transporting her to the time in the
bluebell wood when everything had changed between
her and Harry. It was a day she would remember for
the rest of her life.

Bessie knew she had to be patient for now, and wait.
Harry would come back and the day he walked up the
drive to Marston Hall would be one for celebration.
She knew he would do it, and when he did, she'd be
here waiting for him.

31

January, 1945

'Post for you, Mrs Rushbrook.'

Bessie put down the basket of wood she was carrying to the house, as the post boy brought his too-large bicycle to a halt in front of her.

'Hello, Thomas. What have we got today?'

'Just the one.' He rummaged through the bag slung across his shoulder and handed her an envelope.

'Thank you.'

Thomas smiled as he turned his bike around. 'Cheerio then.' He launched himself off with one foot on the lowest pedal, the other scooting him along, and when he'd picked up enough speed, he threw his leg over the bicycle and perching on the high saddle, started pedalling fast to keep upright.

'Mind how you go,' Bessie called after him, watching him sail out of the yard and turn towards the village. He was a likeable lad but had one of the worst jobs as he also delivered telegrams — those unexpected messages which often brought bad news about the fate of loved ones off fighting for the country. Many people dreaded the sight of him coming to their door, but it wasn't fair on him, you shouldn't blame the messenger.

She turned the envelope over to see who it was for, always hoping for a letter from George, but this wasn't from him. It was addressed to her and Harry in writing she recognised — Grace's. It was unusual for her to write to them on their own. Usually, she included a brief note for them in Marigold's letters. Why had she written to them now? Was something wrong?

Bessie tucked the envelope in her coat pocket, picked up the basket of wood and hurried across the yard towards the house. She wanted to know what was in the letter. Did Grace want her daughter to return to London? Surely not, with all those terrible V2 rockets falling? Her stomach twisted at the thought of sending Marigold back while there was still so much danger. It would be foolish, and if that's what Grace was asking in this letter, then she'd fight against it.

Once she'd stoked up the fire, she perched on the edge of an armchair, opened the envelope and took out the single sheet of paper.

January 14, 1945, she read
Dear Bessie and Harry,
I'm writing this separately from a normal letter as I have something which I need to ask you. Please don't feel under any obligation to say yes, if it's not what you'd want to do. I will understand and make other arrangements.
There's no simple way to say this, so I'll just jump straight in. If anything should happen to me, would you please take care of Marigold for me? It is a lot to ask, I know, and that's why you must consider it carefully.
I hope it will never be necessary, but nothing is certain, and especially these days with the V2 rockets aimed at London. Nobody knows where or when they will land next. If I should be unlucky, then I'll go happier knowing Marigold's future is secure.
With love.
Grace.

183

Bessie's hands were shaking by the time she'd finished. She'd never expected this. Moments ago, she had been thinking about fighting to keep Marigold here, when in fact it was Grace herself, who needed to be kept safe. She should leave London, escape all the killing and destruction.

She re-read the letter looking for more clues hidden between the lines, but the message stayed the same. Grace was in fear for her life and wanted to be sure her daughter would be cared for if the worst happened. Bessie was still staring at it when Harry came in, blowing on his hands as he headed straight over to the fire to warm them.

'Whatever's the matter, Bess?' he said when he looked at her.

'Read this.' She handed him the letter.

She watched Harry's face turn pale as he read it.

'That's a bolt from the blue.' He dropped into the armchair opposite her. 'Things must be bad in London to make her think that.'

'She really thinks it could happen.'

'Grace's living with it every day, seeing the results in the hospital.'

'What shall we tell her? Yes?'

'There's no question about it . . . of course we would take care of Marigold.'

Bessie nodded. 'I'll write to her tonight and invite her to come here again. She ought to get out of London, there's plenty of nursing she could do in hospitals around here.'

'You can ask,' Harry said. 'But whether she'll do it is another matter. You know Grace as well as I do. Her stubbornness can get the better of her.'

'I could suggest she do it for Marigold's sake.

184

The child's lost a father, she shouldn't have to lose a mother as well before this war is over. Grace might do it for her daughter.'

Harry took Bessie's hands in his. 'You can try, but don't get your hopes up. It will be up to Grace to decide. All we can do is hope that if she stays in London, none of those damn rockets falls anywhere near her.'

She sighed. 'We mustn't tell Marigold anything about this. If she had any idea that her mother thought she was in such danger it would unsettle her, she worries about her, as it is.'

'The war can't go on much longer now the Allies are breaking through.'

'Hitler's got a lot to answer for,' Bessie said. 'If the wives and mothers of people caught up in this could get their hands on him . . .'

'You'd wring his bloody neck,' Harry finished.

'There'd be an endless queue.' She shook her head. 'Women don't start wars, but they have to cope with the mess they make of innocent lives.'

'You'd never start a war.' Harry got to his feet and pulled Bessie up out of her chair and wrapped his arms around her. 'You were my antidote to war, Bess. If they could bottle your goodness and sprinkle over the Nazis, then it would be over in a trice.'

She kissed his cheek. 'You say the nicest things, Harry Rushbrook, I suppose I should take that as a compliment.'

'You should.' He looked at her seriously for a moment. 'We'll get through this together, Bess. I promise you.'

32

'Prune! For goodness' sake, slow down,' Dottie yelled, as her end of the bow saw rapidly sliced through the air towards her. 'I can't keep up with you, and if you carry on like this, someone's going to get hurt.'

Prune released her end of the saw and it juddered to a halt in Dottie's hand.

'That's it! We're taking a break.' Dottie stood up. 'Come on, let's have a brew up.'

'I'm not thirsty, but you go ahead.'

'I am not asking, I'm telling you.' She put a hand on her hip. 'You can't go on like this, it's not good for you.'

Dottie was worried about her friend who looked unwell; her face pale, with dark smudges under her eyes, and she wasn't sleeping. Whenever Dottie woke up in the night now, Prune was always awake, usually sitting up in bed with the corner of the blackout curtain lifted as she stared out at the darkness. Her friend hadn't slept properly since Clem brought them the dreadful news about Howard ten days ago.

'I know, but . . .' Prune shrugged, her eyes glistening with tears.

'Let's get some tea in us first. It'll help.'

'It's only an hour since we stopped for dinner,' Prune protested.

'So?' Dottie grabbed Prune's hand and led her over to the fire that they kept going just outside the little bivouac shelter where they ate their sandwiches. It provided a welcome warmth when they had a break, and a means of making tea in the billy of water hanging over it. 'There's no one here to tell us what to do, and we always get our work done. We need to have a cuppa and talk for your sake, and the safety of my fingers. I don't like the idea of them being cut off by a runaway saw, thank you very much.'

'All right.'

'Sit yourself down and I'll brew up.'

Dottie busied herself adding tea leaves to the billycan along with a small piece of wood, which she'd learned to do at her training camp. Apparently, it helped to absorb smoke and improved the flavour, and always seemed to work.

A few minutes later, she sat down next to Prune who was sitting hunched up under the bivouac, her long legs pulled up and her elbows resting on her knees.

'Don't let your tea go cold.' Dottie blew on her drink, her breath sending the floating tea leaves skidding across to the far side of the mug.

'I won't. Thank you.'

'My pleasure.' Dottie took a tiny sip of tea. 'Do you want to tell me what's wrong?'

Prune groaned. 'Do I have to spell it out to you?'

'I don't just mean about Howard.' She put her arm around her friend's shoulders. 'But there's something else today. Is it that letter?'

'What letter?'

'Come on, the one that came for you yesterday. I know you whisked it away before I could see it, but Bessie told me about it. Was it from your mother?'

Prune took a gulp of steaming tea and spluttered as the scalding liquid burnt her mouth.

Dottie slapped her on the back. 'It's hot, remember?'

'I'll leave it a while then,' Prune put her mug to the side and hugged her knees. 'The truth is,' she said, staring into the glowing fire, 'I have no idea what it says because I haven't opened it.'

'Aren't you going to?'

'I don't want to. It must be my mother's reply to my last letter asking for her permission to marry Howard. I sent it before he was . . . missing.' She sighed. 'I'm sure whatever she's got to say won't be pleasant.'

'It's taken her a while to write back, I thought she'd do it by return of post.'

'She's been away over Christmas and the New Year, then she visited relatives, so she wasn't returning home until last week. She'd have found my letter waiting for her, and now . . .' Prune's voice faltered as she stared at her mud-caked boots. 'It probably won't matter what she says, because it doesn't look like Howard and I will marry. She'll be happy about that.'

'Don't give up hope. You've got to keep hoping.'

'It didn't work out for you though, did it?' Prune snapped.

Dottie drew in a sharp breath. 'No, it didn't, but there was no chance for my Jim, his plane blew up. But no one saw what happened to the Peggy Sue, so there's always hope.'

Prune looked at her. 'I'm sorry. I shouldn't have said that. I didn't mean it.'

'I know you didn't. But you mustn't give up hope.' She took another sip of tea. 'Are you going to open it then?'

'I suppose I must, sometime.'

'I'll do it for you if you want.'

188

'No, I will.' Prune reached into the pocket of her corduroy breeches and pulled out the envelope. 'Here goes.' She ripped it open and took out a single sheet of thick cream paper.

As Prune read the letter, her face developed a pink spot on each cheek.

'Did she say yes?'

Prune snorted. 'You're a crazy woman sometimes.'

'Seriously, is it what you thought?'

'Read it for yourself.' Prune passed her the letter.

Quickly reading the words written in bold handwriting, there was no doubting Prune's mother's reaction to hearing that her daughter wanted to marry a GI, and not Jeremy. Her answer to the request for her permission was a definite no, and worse, it carried an unmotherly threat of consequences should Prune disobey her.

'No surprise there then.' Dottie passed it back to her.

'None at all.' Prune got up and threw the letter and envelope on the fire, and stood watching them burst into flames, curl, and blacken into ash.

'What now?'

'I wait and hope Howard comes back. If he does, I'll marry him without my mother's permission when I'm twenty-one.'

'But what about her threat to disown and disinherit you?'

'It's my life and I won't marry someone I don't love.' Prune put her hand on her hip. 'If she wants to disown me, that's her business. Her loss.'

'What about if . . . if you never marry Howard?'

'I still won't marry Jeremy. Neither of us wants to. I've moved on and away from all that, Dottie.' Prune took a deep breath. 'If ... Howard doesn't come back, then I'll choose another route for myself. It's my choice and no one else's.'

'Are you going to tell her that Howard's missing?'

'Certainly not! She'd be pleased and I'm not having anyone think that about him, especially my mother.'

33

Late September, 1918

Bessie paced up and down outside the front door of Marston Hall hospital, stopping now and then to peer down the drive. It had taken all her willpower not to go down to the station to meet Harry's train and be with him that bit sooner. She'd only waited here, because she knew how much he wanted to walk up the drive to the hall to see her. His return would be so different from when he'd first arrived here in the back of an ambulance, quiet and withdrawn, filled with turmoil over his future after having the one he'd planned snatched away from him by an exploding shell.

'Any sign of him yet?' Ethel's voice made Bessie jump.

She turned to see her friend, who had poked her head around the front door. 'No, but anytime now.'

'Don't worry, I'm not going to wait with you.' Ethel wiggled her eyebrows. 'Wouldn't want to spoil your reunion. Matron says to remind you about the tea later on. You'll bring him in, won't you?'

'Yes, he wants to come and see everyone, and show off his walking.'

'Enjoy yourself with your beau.' Ethel winked at her before closing the door.

Bessie smiled at her friend's parting words. After Harry had left the hospital, she'd finally been able to talk about her relationship with him, and all the staff knew about his return today. Former patients rarely

191

came back to see them as most of them came from other parts of the country, so Harry's visit was a rare pleasure.

Turning around, she spotted a figure walking up the tree-lined drive towards her. She couldn't make out his face clearly under the dappled shade of the trees, but there was no doubt it was him.

She ran down the short flight of steps and took off towards him, holding up her skirt so she could go quicker. If Matron saw her, she'd tell her not to run, but she wasn't in the hospital and nothing was going to stop her from reaching Harry as soon as she could.

The closer she got, the clearer his face became. He was smiling at her and as she neared him; he opened his arms wide to welcome her. Bessie slowed to a walk just before she reached him, for fear of knocking him off balance. Then she went into his welcoming arms and they hugged each other tightly, standing under the cool shade of the beech trees whose branches met above them.

'It's so good to see you.' She stepped back and held Harry at arm's length, studying his face. 'You look wonderful, so tall and upright.'

He smiled, his blue eyes filled with happiness. 'I've missed you, Bess.' Then he gently kissed her.

'I missed you too. After you left, I kept expecting you to be on the ward, but you weren't there.' Tears suddenly stung her eyes and Bessie looked down at his new leg for a moment to compose herself. 'How's the leg? Did it bear up walking from the station?'

'It's fine. I've been practising and I still walk with a bit of a limp, but that's nothing to worry about.'

'I'm so happy for you. Everyone's looking forward to seeing you, and you're honoured with an invitation to have tea with Matron.'

'It will be good to see her and everybody again.' He gently stroked Bessie's cheek. 'But first I want to be with you. Will you come for a walk with me . . . to the beck?'

She nodded, smiling. 'I'd be delighted to.'

He took hold of her arm, linked it through his, and then laced his fingers through hers as they walked down the drive together.

★ ★ ★

'It's a slightly different view looking at it from up here,' Harry said as they stood on the wooden bridge watching the water flow beneath them. He turned and met Bessie's eyes. 'I've often thought about coming back here with you and what I'd say to you . . .'

'What's that?' Bessie asked. 'Are you finally going to tell me about your plan, or is it still a secret?'

'Well . . .' he teased. 'If you really want to know.'

'I've been waiting for you to tell me for months.' She squeezed his hand.

Harry lifted her hand to his lips and gently kissed it. 'I'm sorry I didn't tell you before, but I had to find out if it was possible. Do you remember that day in the hospital, when I was still in bed and you should have gone off duty?'

'Yes. You were quiet and withdrawn, I knew there must be something upsetting you.'

'You were right, and you told me I should think of another way to follow my dream.'

Bessie nodded.

'Well, I have. Farming's all I ever wanted to do. So, if I can't farm in the fells, then I should do it somewhere else where it's easier for me to get around and where I can manage.'

'You're still going to be a farmer?'

'I am, but on a much smaller scale than on the fells, and no sheep. I'll grow crops to sell, things like fruit and vegetables and keep poultry — things I can achieve.' He took both Bessie's hands in his. 'And I've found the perfect place to do it. I had money put by from the sale of my father's shop, it was enough to buy a small farm. It's here in Norfolk, in a village called Rackbridge.'

'I know it. The train goes through it on the way home.'

'It's small, just twenty acres and includes a bluebell wood.' He smiled at her. 'There are good solid barns and sheds, an orchard and fields. The only thing missing is a house because it was part of a bigger farm that's been carved up and sold in two lots.'

'It sounds good, but where are you going to live if there's no house?'

'I've already sorted that out. I've bought two old railway carriages and I'm turning them into a house. By the time I've finished, it will almost be a perfect home.'

'Almost?'

'There's one more thing . . .' Harry hesitated. 'Would you do me the honour of becoming my wife? I love you, Bess, and if you married me, then my life and home would be perfect.'

Bessie's heart was full as she looked into Harry's eyes, which shone back with love for her. There was only one answer she could give. 'Yes, I would love to be your wife.'

Harry wrapped his arms around her, and she rested

her head against his chest and felt happy. Her life was suddenly turning in a different direction, and she liked the look of it very much.

★ ★ ★

'Engaged?' Matron looked at them, her eyes twinkling. 'Congratulations to you both.'

Bessie inwardly sighed with relief. She'd been worried about telling Matron and had wanted to keep their engagement secret for the time being, but Harry had been bursting with happiness, wanting to tell the entire world straight away.

'Thank you, Matron.' He shook her hand.

'When are you planning on marrying?'

'In the new year,' Bessie said. 'Harry needs to finish the house first.'

Matron nodded. 'I hope the war will be over by then, it can't go on much longer. In the meantime, we've some tea waiting for you. Mrs Taylor's baked a cake, and everyone wants to see you walking, Sergeant Rushbrook. Come along then.' Matron turned and strode off down the hall, expecting them to follow behind.

Bessie squeezed Harry's hand and smiled up at him. 'Come on, we don't want to miss out on Mrs Taylor's cake.'

34

Late January, 1945

Bessie loved this part of the day when everyone was home from school or work, and there was a sense of shutting out the icy darkness and settling down, snug and cosy, inside the house. It was time to eat a good meal and then with the evening stretching ahead of them, a chance to talk or listen to the wireless, sew, knit, play games, or write letters.

She took the lid off the large pan of stew and dumplings and stirred it around, the rich aroma of rabbit and vegetables filling the air.

'Is it ready?' Marigold stood on tiptoes and peered into the pan at the gently bubbling mixture.

'It smells lovely,' Peter said, coming out of his bedroom.

'We can have it as soon as everyone's ready. Not much longer to wait.'

Dottie and Prune were in their room changing out of their dirty work clothes, and when they were ready Bessie would send Peter out to tell Harry to come in.

She'd just put the lid back on the pan when there was a loud knocking on the door. Wiping her hands on her apron, she went out into the porch and opened it to see Thomas, the post boy standing there. Bessie's stomach instantly knotted. He'd already delivered the post today, so coming to Orchard Farm now could only mean one thing . . . and her eyes were drawn to the buff-coloured envelope in his hand. A telegram.

'For you and Mr Rushbrook.' Thomas held it out to her.

Bessie forced herself to speak. 'Thank you.'

He nodded, his eyes full of understanding at what his arrival with a telegram could mean. He quickly retreated down the stairs and slipped away into the darkness.

Closing the door behind her, she stood still in the porch for a few moments and stared down at the telegram in her shaking hands. Was it about George? What had happened to him?

'Bessie?' Peter opened the inner door and looked at her. 'Are you all right?'

She opened her mouth to speak but couldn't seem to get the words out. Swallowing hard, she tried again. 'Could you go and fetch Harry?'

'What shall I tell him?'

'Just say . . . a telegram's come.'

'I won't be long.' Peter hurried out into the darkness.

Alone in the porch, Bessie shivered. A foreboding chill was creeping through her body and she needed to warm herself. Back inside, she saw that thankfully Dottie and Prune were still in their room. Placing the telegram on the table, which was set ready for their meal, she went to the stove and stretched her hands above the hotplate to get some heat back into them.

'Is that a telegram?' Marigold asked from where she sat in an armchair drawing in her diary.

She nodded, unable to speak.

'I don't like telegrams.' She got up and came to stand beside Bessie. 'Mummy got one of them telling her Daddy had been killed.'

She slipped her arm around Marigold's shoulders

and hugged her. She wished Harry would hurry, but at the same time wanted to stay in this moment for as long as possible. Was it better not to know what might be in the telegram, still be living when everything was fine? Once it had been opened, it could change things forever. During wartime, they were usually the harbingers of bad news and nobody wanted to receive one, just in case . . .

How long it was before Harry and Peter arrived, she didn't know; it seemed like forever, and yet it was still too soon when they hurried in, red-cheeked from the cold.

Harry's eyes immediately locked with Bessie's and she knew he was expecting the worst, too.

The door to Dottie and Prune's room opened, and the two young women came out laughing.

'Bessie, you'll never guess . . .' Dottie began but halted and looked around at everyone gathered there. 'What's going on?'

'We've had a . . .' she began, gesturing at the telegram lying on the table.

Dottie put her hand to her mouth.

Prune stepped forward. 'Marigold, why don't you come into our room for a bit. Peter, can you bring something to read to us?'

Peter nodded and with a quick look at her and Harry, dashed into his room, reappearing moments later with a book.

He understands, Bessie thought. He'd told her about boys at school receiving bad news about their fathers in telegrams, so he knew what this one might mean.

'Come on, Marigold,' Peter said. 'I've got a wonderful adventure story to read.'

'You go with the others for a few minutes.' Bessie encouraged her.

'Are you going to open the telegram?' Marigold asked.

She nodded.

'This way.' Dottie took hold of Marigold's hand and led her into her and Prune's bedroom, turning back at the door and giving them a sympathetic smile, before quietly closing it behind her.

The air in the room suddenly seemed charged, like the change in atmosphere just before a storm breaks. The ticking sound of the clock on the mantelpiece became more pronounced and Bessie sank into an armchair, staring at the telegram on the table.

'Can you open it, Harry? I don't . . .'

Without saying anything, he picked it up, checked the address on the front as if to confirm it really was for them, and with one swift movement, slit it open and pulled out the single sheet.

She closed her eyes as he unfolded it. She couldn't bear to watch him read it and see his face when he found out his son . . .

She concentrated on her breathing, trying to steady her heart, which was pounding so hard she could feel her blood pulsing in her temples. In . . . out . . . she told herself. Bessie suddenly felt Harry's hands grab hers and he pulled her on to her feet and into his arms. She didn't have a chance to look at him before he hugged her tightly to his chest. She returned his hug, her throat aching with the effort of holding in tears. To her amazement, Harry was laughing, his body shaking with mirth. She pulled back and stared at him. What was the matter with him? Had the news sent him mad?

'Harry?'

'It's all right, Bess.' He said. 'It's not what you think.'

Pushing herself out of his arms, Bessie rushed across and picked up the telegram from where he'd left it on the table and read it.

COMING TO RACKBRIDGE TONIGHT ON 9PM TRAIN STOP GRACE STOP

A wave of relief surged through Bessie. It wasn't about George; he was safe. Their son was still alive.

Harry shook his head and sighed. 'I never expected it to say that.' He ran a hand through his hair. 'I can't tell you what a relief that is. I thought . . .'

'The worst, like me.' She stopped to let the news sink in. She'd been so scared of what might have happened to their son. She shivered, shaking off the shadow of fear which had wrapped itself around her. 'Grace is arriving here tonight. She never said in her last letter.'

'Perhaps she got some leave at short notice.' Harry took hold of her hand. 'It's good news. Grace's finally coming back. Think how happy Marigold will be.'

'Yes, but . . .' she stopped and smiled. 'It will be strange to see her again after all this time.'

He squeezed her hand. 'Don't fret, it'll be fine.'

'We need to get ready for her.' Bessie's mind raced through all the things they'd needed to do. 'We must sort out where Grace is going to sleep, for a start.'

'The first thing to do is tell Marigold.' Harry nodded towards the window of Dottie and Prune's room, where four faces were peering through a gap in the curtains, anxiously waiting for news.

'Is it time to go?'

Bessie looked up from the sock she was darning. 'No. Another hour, yet.'

Marigold sighed.

'How about a game of draughts with me?' Dottie suggested.

The little girl nodded. 'All right then.'

'Thank you,' Bessie mouthed silently to Dottie while Marigold fetched the board and box of pieces from the dresser cupboard.

Dottie soon had her engrossed in the game, laughing together when they took each other's counters.

Bessie understood how Marigold felt. She wanted to go herself, but there was no point in going too early as the train wasn't due in until nine o'clock. They'd done everything they needed to prepare for Grace, making up a camp bed for Marigold to sleep in on the floor of her room so her mother could have her bed. All they could do now was wait. Darning socks gave her something to do, kept her fingers busy while her mind drifted.

Only a few hours ago, she'd been looking forward to a normal evening, but it had become one of see-sawing emotions. First the shock of the telegram, when fear had turned her blood cold, then the relief and surprise of Grace's coming visit. Now they were waiting, Prune sitting in the opposite armchair reading a book, while Harry and Peter plotted the Allies' latest movements on the map.

On the surface, everything looked calm, but inside, Bessie felt anything but. Only she and Harry knew the significance of Grace's visit. To Marigold, it would bring the joy of seeing her mother again, and the others, Peter, Dottie and Prune, were all looking forward to meeting Grace, whom they'd heard so much about. But for her and Harry, Grace's visit would be a homecoming.

What would Grace be like after all this time? Would she tell Marigold about her past, reveal who they really were? With her visit coming out of the blue, there hadn't been a chance to ask Grace what she planned to tell her daughter when she got here. Would she pretend that she'd never been to Orchard Farm before? Bessie had no idea how she would play it and would have to take her lead from Grace, not daring to hope that this sudden trip here might change things.

Her mind drifted to the last time Grace had been here. She had been so angry and desperate to get away, refusing to listen to them, ignoring their pleas to wait. She had been determined to go . . .

'Do you want some cocoa, Bessie?'

Prune's voice dragged her thoughts back to the present. 'Yes, please, shall I help?'

'You stay there,' Prune said. 'I can manage.'

She glanced at the clock. There were three-quarters of an hour until they needed to leave. Time was dragging tonight.

Prune was watching over a pan of milk on the stove when there was a loud knock at the door. Everyone stopped what they were doing and looked at each other. Then it came again, louder and more insistent. Bessie stood up to answer it, her heart hammering inside her. Who could it be this time? Grace? Had she caught an earlier train?

'I'll get it,' Prune said, already halfway across the room.

She waited, unable to hear what was going on in the porch as Prune had closed the inner door to keep the light in and not break the blackout. Her patience running out, Bessie stood up, ready to see who it was when Dottie cried out.

'The milk!'

Bessie quickly turned to the pan which Prune had been watching over. A froth of bubbles had risen and was about to spill over the sides; she snatched it off the heat, just in time.

'Great reflexes, Bessie.'

She turned at the familiar voice. It was Clem, with his arm around Prune who was both laughing and crying at the same time.

'Prune! What's going on?'

Dottie abandoned her draughts game and rushed over and grabbed hold of her friend's hand.

'It's okay,' Clem said. 'She's had a shock, but it's a good one.'

'For goodness sake, tell us what's happened,' Dottie snapped.

'He's alive,' Prune said through her sobs. 'Howard's alive.'

Bessie looked at Clem. 'Is he?'

He nodded, beaming. 'Yes, ma'am.'

'Is he back at Rackbridge?' Harry asked. The noise had brought him and Peter into the living room.

'Let's get Prune sitting down first, and then you can explain.' Dottie led Prune over to an armchair and pushed her friend down into it. 'Right, tell us everything.' She sat down on the arm of the chair, holding Prune's hand.

'Well, we just received word, so I had to come and tell you,' Clem explained. 'The Peggy Sue was hit and went down, as we thought, but everyone bailed out and parachuted down behind Allied lines.'

'Why's it taken so long to hear about them?'

'Some got injured, and it took time to get back.'

'Have the crew returned to base?' Peter asked.

'Some. Walt's back and some gunners.'

'Where's Howard?' Marigold said. 'Is he there?'

Clem shook his head. 'No. He broke his arm coming down and had it fixed in a hospital, but at least we know he's okay and he'll be back soon.'

'It's such good news.' Bessie sighed with relief, looking at Prune, who despite her red eyes from crying, looked so much happier than she had for weeks. She'd coped bravely with her fiancé being missing in action, but it had taken its toll, her face having a sad look which had never quite left her, even when she'd smiled. Although Prune had kept a stiff upper lip, Bessie had seen how much she'd been hurting inside, but now her hope that Howard had survived had come through.

'Why did the Peggy Sue, go down?' Peter said.

'She was hit by flak, Walt said they had two engines out, no hydraulics or electrics. She couldn't keep flying.'

'Lucky they made it back behind the Allies' lines,' Harry said.

'Yes, sir.' Clem nodded. 'Could have been a whole different story otherwise.'

'We don't want to think about that,' Dottie said. 'It's been quite a night for wonderful surprises.'

Prune stood up and looked around at everyone, her face glowing with happiness. 'Who wants a cup of cocoa to celebrate?'

35

'What's the time?' Marigold was desperate to be there when her mother's train arrived at the station.

'Don't worry, we've got plenty of time,' Bessie said. 'There's a chance the train will be late anyway, but we'll definitely be there at nine o'clock, especially if you keep going as fast as you are.'

Marigold giggled. She'd skipped all the way from Orchard Farm, her body tingling with energy. Normally, she would be in bed and asleep by now, but not tonight. Bessie had let her stay up late to meet her mother.

'I'm glad the moon's so bright.' Marigold gazed up at the big, cream-coloured full moon which cast a milky light down on them. A bombers' moon, they called it, but she hoped there would be no bombers here tonight, just the joy of seeing her mother again.

She'd hardly been able to believe it when Bessie had told her the news. Marigold had wanted her mother to come and visit for ages.

'Do you remember when you met me at the station?' Marigold asked.

'Yes. I was nervous.'

She slipped her gloved hand into Bessie's. 'I was scared and didn't want to come here, but Mummy said I had to.'

'London's not safe for you now.'

'That's what she said. But I'm glad I came, because I love living with you and Harry. And Peter, Dottie and Prune.'

Bessie squeezed her hand. 'We love having you with us.'

Everyone at Orchard Farm had become part of Marigold's family. They were the best people to be with if she couldn't be with her mother. But her life in London seemed far away now.

'Do you think Mummy will like it here?'

'I hope so, though it's very different from London.'

'Much quieter and less busy. I can't wait to show her around. She can help me collect the eggs and feed the chickens. Do you think Harry will let her try milking the cows?'

'Of course, if she'd like to.'

* * *

Nine o'clock had come and gone, but there was still no sign of the train. Marigold's stomach was squirming with excitement; she'd waited so long to see her mother, and every extra minute seemed an eternity. Staring down the line, she strained her ears for the sound of an approaching train, but there was nothing, just the night-time noises of a tawny owl 'kee-wicking' in the trees.

Marigold felt Bessie's hand on her shoulders. 'Don't worry, she'll be here soon. There aren't many trains running on time these days. Do you want to sit in the waiting room for a while, it'll be warmer in there?'

She shook her head.

'All right, but keep moving around so you don't get cold. Why don't you do some more skipping?'

'Can I, on the platform?'

'There's only you and me on here, so it will be fine, just keep away from the edge.'

Marigold felt her blood surge through her as she skipped the entire length of the platform. Her excited energy powered her arms and legs along; it was as if she was flying, her breath billowing out in the cold air, like the smoke out of an engine. Up and down she went, away from Bessie and back again.

She'd just reached the far end and stood for a moment catching her breath when she heard it. Marigold turned and ran full pelt along the length of the platform.

'It's coming!' She skidded to a halt beside Bessie and grabbed hold of her hand. 'The train's coming.'

'Excited?'

Marigold nodded. For some strange reason, now the moment was almost here, she was shy about seeing her mother again. But that was silly because she had been longing for this ever since she'd arrived here. 'I'm nervous,' she whispered.

'Me too,' Bessie said.

She frowned. 'Why are you nervous?'

'Oh, I don't know . . .' Bessie shrugged.

'But why? You knew her before she went to London. She likes you and trusts you, that's why she sent me here.'

'I know, but it's been a long time since I saw her.'

'When did you last see her?'

Bessie didn't answer because with a hissing of steam and squealing of brakes, the train they'd been waiting for pulled into the station.

Marigold's heart was jumping around inside her. Which carriage would her mother be in? She watched as doors flew open and a few passengers stepped out. There were some Americans like Clem and Howard and a few local people, but no sign of her mother.

'Where's Mummy?' Marigold tugged at Bessie's hand. 'Come on, we have to look.'

'Perhaps she fell asleep.'

They walked the length of the train, peering into each carriage looking for a sleeping Grace, but she wasn't in any of them.

'She's not here!' Marigold's voice came out in a squeak. 'Where is she?'

Bessie patted her shoulder. 'Don't worry. I'll ask the guard to help me look again.'

Marigold waited while both Bessie and the guard rechecked the whole train; compartments, corridors, guard's van, everywhere. She was desperate for them to find her mother asleep in a corner somewhere, worn out and unaware the train had arrived at Rackbridge station. But they didn't find her.

'I'm sorry, but she's not on it.' Bessie put her arm around Marigold. 'She probably just missed the train from London and will be here tomorrow instead.'

Marigold's eyes stung with tears, and disappointment flooded through her, quenching her excitement like water on a fire.

'She might be on the next train.'

Bessie shook her head. 'This is the last one today.' She pulled Marigold to her and hugged her tightly. 'I know you're disappointed, but she probably just got delayed. It happens a lot with the war on.'

Marigold couldn't hold back the tears any longer, and they slid hotly down her cheeks as she buried her face in Bessie's coat. She sobbed as the guard blew his whistle, and moments later the train chuffed out of the station.

'We'd better go home.' Bessie held her at arm's length and looked at her. 'Your mother will be here as soon as she can, perhaps on the first train tomorrow.'

Marigold nodded and tried to smile, but her face wouldn't quite do it. She didn't feel happy and couldn't pretend.

As Bessie led them out of the station, she turned her head to check the platform one last time, just in case her mother was there and somehow, they had missed her. But it was empty.

★ ★ ★

'Are you asleep?' Bessie whispered.

Harry turned over and faced her. 'No. Can't you sleep?'

'I keep going over and over tonight in my mind.' Bessie sighed. 'It doesn't make sense, Grace sending the telegram and not coming.'

'There's probably a good reason for it. You said yourself she might have missed the train from London, or they cancelled it at the last minute.'

'I know, but . . . I've got a bad feeling about this. I don't know why, but it seems odd she should telegram out of the blue, then not turn up.'

He took hold of her hand. 'Grace got leave at short notice, thought she'd visit, then the train was cancelled, or she missed it, simple as that. She'll probably turn up tomorrow.'

'Do you think she suddenly changed her mind? Decided she couldn't come back after all?'

'Grace wouldn't let her daughter think she was coming and then change her mind. She'd have known how much Marigold was looking forward to seeing her.'

'Marigold was so disappointed.'

'You know what trains are like these days. We'll

probably get another telegram in the morning saying she's arriving tomorrow afternoon.'

'I hope so, Harry. I really do. When she didn't turn up, it made me realise how much I want to see her. I've wanted that for a long time . . . but tonight when it looked like she was finally returning after all this time . . . I was scared of seeing her again.' Bessie's voice cracked with emotion. 'When she wasn't on the train, I wanted to cry along with Marigold.'

'You've never stopped caring for her, have you?'

Bessie shook her head. 'Have you?'

'No. But it runs far deeper with you.'

'I made that promise about Grace a long time ago, and I meant it. Nothing's changed about that, even after what happened . . . and it never will.'

Harry put his arms around her and held her. 'You're a fine woman. When you give your word, you stick to it, through thick and thin.'

She hugged him back. Whenever she'd made a promise, it was, as far as she was concerned, forever. Bessie didn't take them on lightly, but when she did, then she carried them out to the best of her ability. It was what her parents had taught her to do as a child.

Bessie had given her word to Grace, and to Peter's parents that she'd care for their children. With her wedding vows, she'd given her promise to Harry when they married. Her promise about Grace still stood strong, and she'd willingly given it. She'd kept them all.

But there was another promise. One which had been forced upon her, and it grieved her. She had honoured it, but it haunted her. Bessie wished that she'd never been forced to make it . . . It was her promise, her secret, and she had to bear it on her own. She couldn't even share it with Harry.

36

Bessie took a bite of toast and sighed happily as the flavours burst on her tongue. Creamy butter and strawberry jam on Mrs Taylor's freshly baked bread; it was the best thing she'd ever tasted.

'How's that?' Ethel asked.

'Wonderful. You wouldn't believe how delicious it is.'

She took another bite and again the flavours and textures of the simple food entranced her. Bessie had eaten nothing for the past two days. While she'd been so ill, all she could manage were sips of water which had soothed her burning throat for an instant, before it had throbbed once more, matching the ache in her head and limbs.

'I'm glad to see you eating.' Her friend perched on the chair beside Bessie's bed. 'We were all worried about you. You even had Matron sitting with you during the night.'

'Matron, really?'

'You don't remember?'

'I vaguely remember someone like Matron being here when I woke up once. But I thought I'd dreamed it.'

'I'm not surprised with the high fever you had. Still, you're on the mend now.' Ethel patted Bessie's arm. 'We must build you up again and get some strength back into you. This Spanish flu's bad, it's had people

211

dropping like flies.'

'How many more have it?'

'There's you, Agnes in the kitchen, and four of the men. Thankfully, no one's . . .' Ethel hesitated. 'Everyone's on the mend now.'

Bessie knew what she'd been about to say. No one's died. This influenza was proving to be a killer, and she'd been fortunate to survive it. Now she had to concentrate on getting stronger, because she and Harry were to be married in the new year.

'When you've finished your toast, I'll help you have a wash and change into a clean nightgown. There's someone waiting to visit you.'

'Who?'

'Harry.'

'I was going to see him . . .' Bessie recalled how she was getting ready to go out when she'd been taken ill. It had come on so quickly, she hadn't been able to send him word that she couldn't meet him.

'You had him worried when you didn't turn up. He came looking for you and has been coming in everyday to check how you are. Matron even let him sit with you for a short while when you were asleep.'

Bessie stared at Ethel. 'Matron allowed him here, in my room?'

'Just for a few minutes, while she stood guard over you. She could see how worried he was and took pity on him.'

'I didn't know he'd been.' The thought of Harry sitting by her bedside made her heart swell with love for him.

'Eat up, then we can get you ready for your visitor. You're still too weak to get up, so Matron's allowing him to come in here for a few minutes. I'm to be your chaperone.' Ethel raised her eyebrows. 'Matron's orders.'

A short while later, Bessie lay propped up on a pile of pillows, waiting. Washing, changing her nightgown, brushing and re-plaiting her long hair, had made her feel so much fresher and better, and she was ready to see Harry. Ethel's news that he'd been in and sat by her, had surprised her. Not that he wouldn't have wanted to see her, but the fact that Matron had allowed him to. For all her gruff exterior, Matron's heart was pure gold, and she would thank her for her kindness.

There was a light tapping on the door, and before she could call out, Ethel opened it and stuck her head in.

'Are you ready?' Her friend beamed at her. 'I've brought your visitor.'

Bessie straightened the shawl around her shoulders and nodded, her heart quickening.

Ethel opened the door wide and stepped aside to reveal Harry. 'In you go, you've only got five minutes, so don't waste it. I'll wait here, just outside.'

Harry limped over to her bedside as fast as he could and sat down on the chair.

'Bess.' His blue eyes met hers as he took her hand. 'It's wonderful to see you looking so much better.'

'Hello.' She smiled happily at him. 'I'm so glad you're here. I heard you came to visit me, but I had no idea you'd been.'

'It was just for five minutes, Matron's orders, but she's been good to me, letting me see you.'

'I'm sorry I didn't come to meet you the other day . . . I was getting ready and then the influenza stopped me.'

213

'It doesn't matter, the important thing is you're getting better. Though I wondered if you'd suddenly decided I wasn't the man for you, and perhaps were having second thoughts about marrying me.' He teased her.

Bessie grabbed hold of Harry's other hand, so she held both of his in hers. 'Never! I want to marry you and nothing, and no one's going to stop me from being your wife and spending the rest of my life with you.'

Harry laughed, the corners of his twinkling eyes creasing up. 'I love you, Bess.' His voice was gentle. 'Marrying you will make me the happiest man alive.'

★ ★ ★

Wrapped up warmly in her greatcoat, scarf, gloves and hat, Bessie strolled around the hospital's garden. Having time like this, to wander at will, was alien to her, and she was itching to get back on the ward and be useful. She'd been up and out of bed for over a week, but Matron wouldn't yet pronounce her fit for work, not even for the easiest of jobs. 'A day or two more of rest, nutritious food and fresh air,' Matron had said that morning. Then, and only then, Bessie could start work again. The war might be over now, but they still had men to care for, so she planned to carry on nursing until she and Harry married.

Deciding to walk down the drive to the gate and back before going indoors, she'd just turned onto the treelined drive, when she saw the telegram boy come peddling from the Hall. Had he brought news of another convoy on its way? Bessie wondered. Perhaps she should return straight away, because if more

214

patients were expected, then Matron would be glad of any help, even from her.

Walking in through the front door, Bessie ran into Ethel who was hurrying towards the ward.

'There you are! Matron's looking for you.'

'For me?' Bessie smiled. 'Does she need more help with the convoy?'

Ethel looked puzzled. 'What convoy? We're not expecting one.'

'Oh, I just saw the telegram boy and assumed that's what he'd brought news of.'

Ethel shrugged. 'If there's one coming, I don't know where we're going to put any new patients - all the beds are full.'

'I'll find Matron. Perhaps she's changed her mind about me starting work.'

Bessie was happy about the thought of getting back to being useful again, when she tapped quietly on Matron's office door a few minutes later, after taking off her outdoor clothes.

'Come in.' Matron's voice was loud and clear.

She opened the door and stepped inside. 'I heard you wanted to see me, Matron.'

'Yes, please sit down.' She waited until Bessie was seated on the chair opposite her desk. 'A telegram has come for you, my dear.'

The bubbles of happiness which had filled her instantly popped as her stomach clenched tight. Why would anyone send her a telegram? Telegrams usually brought bad news.

'I . . .' Bessie began.

'Would you like me to open it for you?' Matron asked.

She shook her head. Whatever it was, she had to

215

see it for herself. She took the offered telegram and tore it open with shaking hands. Taking out the folded sheet of paper, she opened it and read the words on the printed strip.

MOTHER ILL STOP COME HOME AT ONCE STOP

Her mother was ill? But she was as strong as an ox. Bessie could never recall her being sick before, nothing ever laid her low. What could be wrong with her?

'Is it, bad news?' Matron's voice was kind.

Bessie nodded, and handed her the telegram to read for herself.

'You're not quite fit yourself yet . . .' Matron sighed. 'But you must go home. Pack a few things and I'll get one of the orderlies to take you to the station in the trap. It will be quicker and will help to conserve your strength for when you get home.'

★ ★ ★

Bessie was worried. For her father to send a telegram and want her home at once, something must be seriously wrong. She still wasn't fully fit after her illness and in no way prepared for this, but there was no question that she wouldn't go and look after her mother.

Opening the front door of her parent's house, it was unnaturally quiet. There was no sign of anyone, neither her parents, nor little Grace.

Putting down her bag, she called out. 'Father? Mother?'

There was movement above, and she heard the

clump of feet coming down the stairs. The stair door opened, and her father stepped down into the kitchen.

'Bessie.' He smiled wanly at her. 'You've come.'

'What's happened? What's wrong with Mother?'

'Influenza.' He sighed. 'She's in a bad way. The doctor's not hopeful.'

The doctor. Her father had called the doctor. She'd never known that happen before; her mother must be extremely ill. Quickly shrugging off her coat and hat, she made her way upstairs, her heart thumping hard at the prospect of what she'd find.

Opening the door at the top of the stairs, Bessie crept into the room and up to the high double bed where her mother lay. Martha Carter's face had a pale sickly hue; her skin stretched over her skull and her sunken eyes ringed with dark smudges. Bessie had to stop herself from gasping. Her mother's normal appearance was strong and ruddy looking, she'd never seen her like this.

'Bessie.' Her mother's voice was little more than a whisper, and the effort of saying one word brought on a coughing fit.

'I'm here.' She gently took hold of her mother's hand, which was icy cold, cradling it in both of hers, trying to warm it.

'Promise me . . .' Her mother halted to catch her breath. She took several gasps. Each one made her chest rise and fall sharply, as she battled to suck in enough air. 'Promise . . . me . . . you'll . . . look . . . after . . . Grace.'

'Of course, I will. I'll stay here until you're well and strong again.'

Martha's blue eyes bore into Bessie's. 'When . . . I'm . . . gone. Dead. Promise . . . me.' She gasped to catch her breath and then started coughing.

'But you will get better. It's a bad flu I know, but you'll soon recover. I know you will.'

Her mother shook her head slowly, and with a great effort levered herself up onto her elbows and looked at Bessie. 'Promise . . . me.' Then she collapsed back against her pillow.

Bessie looked up at her father, who stood silently by his wife's side, his hand resting gently on her shoulder. He didn't say anything, but she could read the pleading look in his eyes as they met hers. He gave one brief nod.

A rising panic welled in Bessie's chest, and she had to struggle hard to calm it. How could her mother die when she was such a strong woman? She couldn't die. She mustn't.

'Bessie?' Her father broke his silence, and she knew what he wanted her to say.

'Yes, of course, I'll look after Grace.' If it would help her mother, then she would tell her what she needed to hear. She meant it too if anything happened to her mother, but it wasn't going to. She would get better, like Bessie had done herself. It might take her a while to get back her full strength, but she would.

'Thank . . . you.' Her mother's voice was faint, and she struggled to catch her breath as it rattled in her chest.

'Where's Grace, Father?' Bessie asked.

He turned to glance at her. 'She's with Mrs Williams, next door.' Then he returned his gaze to his wife.

He looked scared, Bessie thought, and it sent an icy trickle sliding down her spine. He was a man who seldom showed emotion, but from the look on his face, it was as if he'd already given up and believed his wife was going to die. A flame of anger flickered into life inside her. She would not give up without a fight — she'd do everything possible to help her mother fight the influenza, use every ounce of her nursing knowledge.

Bessie laid her hand on her mother's brow. It was burning up and needed to be cooled down.

'I'm going to get a cloth and some water. I won't be long, Mother. I'll be right back.'

Her mother nodded and smiled at her. 'Thank . . . you.'

Bessie returned her smile. 'I've got plenty of nursing practice, I can look after you.'

'And . . . Grace,' her mother whispered and then gasped for breath.

'And Grace. I promise.' She left the room, rushing down the stairs leading to the kitchen.

Bessie quickly found a cloth, filled a bowl with tepid water and went straight back upstairs to her parents' room. But as soon as she entered, she knew something was wrong. Her father sat hunched forward in the chair beside the bed, his hands clasping her mother's, who from the look of her had fallen into a deep peaceful sleep. She was no longer labouring to breathe, gasping for each breath. The room was deathly quiet.

Bile rose in Bessie's throat; she was going to be sick. Swallowing hard, she rushed over to the bed, put the bowl and cloth down on the bedside chest, and reached for her mother's wrist to check her pulse. But there was nothing. Her mother had gone, sleeping, the sleep from which no one awoke.

She held on tight to her mother's hand, struggling to keep a hold on the surge of emotion rushing through her. She could hardly believe her mother was dead. Yet her mother had known she was going to die and had accepted it, while Bessie had tried to fight against it. But there'd been no chance. The influenza had claimed another victim.

'Father?'

He raised his head slowly and the sight of silent tears rolling down his cheeks stunned her. She'd never seen him cry before, not even when Robert was killed. He'd always had a quiet strength about him, but now it had crumbled. Bessie knew she had to be strong — for her father and little Grace — to help them get through this.

'I'll see to her.' Bessie laid a hand on her father's shoulder. 'When you're ready.'

He nodded and bowed his head again. She went out of the bedroom, closing the door quietly behind her to give him time alone with his wife. When he was ready, she'd take care of her mother, wash her and lay her out. Usually, people in the village called Mrs Neal to do that for them, but Bessie didn't want that for her mother. She knew what to do from helping Sister at Marston Hall when a patient had died.

★ ★ ★

Bessie gently brushed her mother's hair, then plaited it into a long honey-blonde rope, laying it across her shoulder and down her chest. She was ready. Washed and changed into a clean nightgown, and looking at peace, as if she were just asleep.

Her work done, Bessie dropped onto the chair beside the bed, her eyes stinging with tears. Her mother was too young to die, only forty-two years old.

She should have had years of life ahead of her, not cut off so cruelly by influenza. Bessie had survived it, so why hadn't her mother? It wasn't fair.

She shuddered; it was no use thinking like that. This Spanish flu wasn't taking the old and infirm as any normal influenza might. This one was worse, even killing young men who'd survived the trenches and deserved to come home and live in peace.

There was going to be a vast hole in the family without her mother. She'd been the sun around which the rest of them had orbited, the centre of their universe. She had held the family together, and her mother had known that. During her last living minutes, she'd sought someone to fill her shoes, asking Bessie to take over from her and look after Grace, and, naturally, she'd care for her father, too. It was her duty, her responsibility. Bessie would move back home and never return to Marston Hall to nurse the soldiers.

She began to sob. Not only had she just lost her mother, but the future she'd planned. Fulfilling her promise would mean not only the end of her VAD work, but the chance of a life with Harry. She couldn't marry him now. Her duty to her family must come first — the future she'd been so happy about was gone.

Bessie's hands shook as she pulled out her handkerchief and dabbed away the tears running down her cheeks.

37

January, 1945

'I don't want to go to school. Please let me stay at home.'

'You've got to go, Marigold. You mustn't miss your lessons and being there will help the time pass.' Bessie put her arm around the little girl's shoulders. 'Your mummy wouldn't like you missing out on your education.'

'But what if she comes and I'm not here?' The little girl's bottom lip wobbled.

'Then perhaps she can meet you after school if she's here by then. But we don't even know if she'll come today.'

'I hope she does.'

'We all do, but we must wait and see.' Bessie picked up Marigold's coat from where it was warming in front of the stove. 'Come on, get this on, or you'll be late.'

When Marigold had finally left for school, Bessie poured herself a cup of tea and sat down in the armchair to drink it. She'd nearly let the child stay at home as she looked pale and had dark smudges under her eyes from too little rest, but keeping her off school wouldn't have helped. It was best for her to carry on as normal and hopefully, Grace would arrive sometime today, and they'd finally be reunited.

Bessie took a sip of tea and leaned back into the chair. All she wanted to do was sleep, a deep, dreamless sleep to escape the worry that gnawed inside her. Harry had reasoned it all out with her last night, and she knew what he said made sense. But she still couldn't shake off the feeling there was something wrong, and that's why Grace hadn't been on the train.

It wasn't like her to feel this way. She was usually a straight, down-to-earth sort of person, not one who tended to have strange feelings of foreboding. This was odd, and it worried her, but there was nothing she could do except wait, hoping that Grace would either arrive sometime today, or at least send word.

Bessie focused her thoughts on yesterday's joyful news about Howard. It had been lovely to witness the change in Prune. All the sadness which had weighed her down over the past few weeks had lifted. Now they could start looking forward to a wedding once he was back and well again — that was something good to come out of the war.

★ ★ ★

It was late morning and Bessie had just taken the last loaf out of the oven, the room smelling of freshly baked bread, when Harry came bursting into the house.

'Look what's arrived, Bess.' He waved a buff-coloured envelope in the air. Another telegram. 'I told you Grace would probably send one today.'

Bessie's stomach knotted. It might be from Grace telling them when she was arriving, but the sight of it still sent a chill finger down her spine.

'Do you want to open it?' Harry offered her the telegram.

She shook her head. 'No, you do it.'

'She'll probably be here this afternoon.' He slit the

223

envelope open.

Bessie watched him take out the sheet, unfold it and read. The look on his face said it all. It hadn't brought good news.

A swell of panic rushed through her. What did it say? Not George. Please, not George. She snatched the telegram from him before he could tell her and read it for herself.

GRACE INJURED STOP IN ST THOMAS HOSPITAL STOP MRS FOX

She stared at the words, not wanting to believe them, but it was there in front of her, printed in black and white. Grace didn't arrive last night because she'd been injured. How and when? How badly hurt was she? Serious enough for her to be in hospital, and for her landlady to send word instead of Grace herself.

'I've got to go to her,' Bessie said.

'Hold on.' Harry took hold of her hand. 'Slow down, we don't know what's happened.'

'She's injured and in hospital, that's sufficient!' Bessie's voice broke. 'I knew something was wrong, I could feel it here.' She put her hand to her chest. 'But I thought I was being . . .' She shook her head and took a deep breath. 'I don't know what's gone on, Harry, but I must see her.'

'You've never been to London before. How will you find your way? Where are you going to stay?'

'I've got a tongue in my head; I will ask the way. London's full of strangers these days and they get around fine, so will I.'

'Do you want me to come with you?'

Bessie shook her head. 'Thank you, but they'll need

224

you here.'

'What do we tell Marigold?'

'Nothing. Not until we know what's happened, there's no point upsetting her.'

'What about the others, they'll wonder where you've gone?'

'You'll have to think of something.' Bessie undid her apron and flung it over the back of a chair. 'I need to get ready.'

Inside their bedroom, she leaned against the wooden bedstead for a few moments. She was on the verge of breaking down and weeping, but she must not. She needed to be strong and keep a grip on her emotions. Grace was injured, and she had to go to her. How bad those injuries were and what had caused them, they didn't know. There was no clue in the telegram.

Bessie swallowed against the ache in her throat. She'd sensed something was wrong. Her instinct, her . . . she took a sharp breath, don't even think about it, it wouldn't do any good, she told herself. She had to be sensible about this if she was going to get to London and Grace.

Taking the small leather suitcase down from the top of the wardrobe, she began to pack. How long she'd be away Bessie didn't know, but she couldn't take much. A change of underwear and a clean night-gown, a dress, her hairbrush, washing things. The case was almost full when Bessie's eyes were drawn to her old diary lying on the chest of drawers. Without stopping to think why, she put it in and closed the lid.

★ ★ ★

'Bess, are you sure about this?' Harry asked as they stood waiting on the platform at Rackbridge station.

'I am. I need to go.'

He nodded. 'I hope it's nothing more than a broken ankle, but at least you can find out and see Grace.'

'I'll send word as soon as I know what's happened. Dottie and Prune will help out until I get back.'

'What about those rockets?' Harry's eyes held hers. 'I'm worried about you going there.'

Bessie took both his hands in hers. 'I'll be all right. You told me not so long ago, that sometimes you have to take risks in life.'

'I remember.'

'I'll be careful, I promise. I have every intention of coming home again.'

When the train arrived, Harry hugged her tightly. 'Take care.'

Bessie swallowed back tears as she climbed into a compartment, and turned to look back out at Harry, whose face betrayed his anxiety. This war had a lot to answer for, she thought.

38

'Is she here?' Marigold burst into the house, her cheeks glowing pink. 'I ran all the way back.'

'No, I'm afraid not.' Harry had been waiting indoors for her to come home from school, along with Prune and Dottie. After Bessie had left on the train, he'd sent a telegram to London, then driven the pony and trap over to the wood where the two Timber Jills were working to ask them for their help. 'We haven't heard from her.'

The little girl's shoulders drooped, and her eyes filled with tears. 'I thought . . . she'd be here. I've been thinking about her all day.'

Dottie put an arm around Marigold and hugged her. 'I know you're disappointed, my lovely. Let's get this off, and we'll make you something to eat and drink. Put some milk on to warm please, Prune.' Dottie helped Marigold off with her coat.

'I'll hang it up for you.' Harry was glad to escape out into the porch for a moment. It had gone well so far. Having the two young women here made it much easier. When he'd told them what had happened, they'd immediately wanted to help, coming home early to be here when Marigold returned from school, and to cook the tea.

Stepping back into the room he heard Marigold ask, 'Where's Bessie?'

It was the question he'd been dreading, but it wasn't fair to let Dottie and Prune answer.

'Bessie's not here. She's gone to visit someone

who's not well.' Which was partly true. Harry wasn't comfortable with not telling her the whole truth, even if it was to protect her. But it was for the best.

'Who has she gone to see?' Marigold asked.

'Someone she used to know in the Great War,' he said, thinking fast. 'Bessie went on the Norwich train.' More facts. 'And will be back in a day or two.'

Marigold nodded.

'So, we're on chef's duties tonight,' Prune said. 'You haven't tasted our cooking before, have you?'

'You're in for a treat.' Dottie handed the little girl a plate of bread and jam. 'Do you want to help us when you've finished this?'

'Can I?' Marigold looked pleased.

'Absolutely! You'll be a great help.' Dottie ruffled Marigold's hair and cast a look over at Harry.

He nodded back at her, relieved. Marigold seemed happy, and with Dottie and Prune's help, they'd get through this without upsetting her. All they had to do was wait until they heard from Bessie, hopefully with news that Grace had nothing worse than a broken ankle. Then he could explain to Marigold exactly why her mother hadn't arrived.

'I'll get on with the milking . . . unless you want me to help cook the tea too?' Harry said.

Marigold giggled. 'I've never seen you cook.'

'I don't know if you can,' Dottie said. 'Can you?'

'Well, I can make toast, boil an egg, bake potatoes and make porridge — just simple things.'

'We'll manage fine between us.' Prune said, putting on an apron. 'Won't we, ladies?'

★ ★ ★

Harry was in the woodshed, filling up the baskets with logs for the fire.

'Tea's ready,' Prune called, coming into the shed. 'We'll eat as soon as Peter's home, he shouldn't be long now.'

He threw the last piece of wood into the basket and brushed the sawdust off his work-roughened hands. 'Thank you. I don't know what I'd have done without yours and Dottie's help.'

She nodded; her features shadowed in the low light of the tilly lamp. 'We're glad to help and will do it for as long as you need us to. Did Bessie know how long she'd be away for?'

'No. It depends on what she finds when she gets there. If Grace is badly injured, she'll probably want to stay longer. I . . .' Harry paused as the shed door opened, and Peter stepped forward into the dim light.

'I thought I heard someone in here.' The boy was wearing his school uniform, his satchel slung over one shoulder. 'What's happened? Has Marigold's mother arrived?'

Harry and Prune glanced at each other.

'No, she's not here,' Prune said.

'Why didn't she come?' Peter asked. 'Have you heard from her?'

'No,' Harry said. 'We haven't, but . . .'

'What is it?' Peter's eyes searched his face. 'What's wrong?'

Harry looked at the boy, who often seemed older than his years, as circumstances had forced him to confront some harsh things in his short life, moulding him into an understanding and thoughtful person.

'Peter . . .' Harry hesitated, wondering what to say — he didn't want to lie to him. 'We heard this morning that Marigold's mother has been injured and is in hospital. That's why she didn't come. We don't know how badly hurt she is, Bessie's gone to London to see her.'

'What about Marigold?' Peter asked. 'Has she gone, too?'

'No, she's still here, but she doesn't know about her mother yet. I've told her that Bessie's gone to see a friend who's ill.'

A look of anger passed over the boy's face. 'But it's not the whole truth.'

Prune put her hand on Peter's arm. 'It's part of it. We don't want to worry Marigold until we know exactly what's happened.'

'What we told her isn't a lie, we've just been selective with the facts.' Harry sighed. 'Telling her enough, but not scaring her.'

'You *must* tell her.' Peter's face had become blotched with red. 'You need to tell her the truth. If her mother's injured, she should be told. If it was me, I'd want to know straight away, nothing held back.'

Harry shook his head. 'But you're older than her.'

'Yes, but Marigold's tougher than you think. She survived the Blitz; her father being killed and then being sent to live with strangers. She coped with all of it.' Peter drew in a sharp breath. 'Holding back the truth might make it worse when you do tell her, because everyone else would have known except her.'

Harry shrugged his shoulders. 'I honestly don't know what's the best thing to do.'

'Then tell her.' Peter folded his arms.

'I think if Marigold is told about her mother she'll be terribly upset and worried,' Prune said. 'We only want to protect her.'

'It's hard enough being away from your parents and home, without important things being kept from you. If I was her, I'd want to know the truth, even if it hurt.'

Harry rubbed the back of his neck. 'I must think about it. I understand what you're saying, but I must be sure first. So, please, say nothing to Marigold about it.'

'I won't. I'd better go in and get changed.'

'Tell the others we'll be in soon,' Prune called after him as he left.

'What do you think?' Harry asked.

'I can see his point. Children have suffered in this war, as much as anyone else. Marigold's been through a great deal already, and that makes us want to protect her more. But I can't help wondering how I'd feel if I was her. She's only got her mother left now, and she thinks the world of her.'

'Exactly.' Harry sighed. 'Bessie's not here to talk it through with, she always knows what to do for the best.'

'Didn't she tell you what you should do?'

He shook his head. 'She was in a hurry to get away and her mind was on Grace. She said I'd think of something.'

'I've not seen Peter like that before. He didn't agree with the idea of anything being held back about parents.'

'It's especially hard for him not knowing where his parents are. Us holding the truth from Marigold struck a raw nerve in him.' Harry picked up a basket of wood. 'It makes me think we should be completely honest with her. Perhaps I'll talk to her after tea.'

'Are you sure?' Prune picked up the other basket.

231

'No, but I'll go with Peter on this one, and hope it's the right thing to do.'

* * *

Marigold's throat hurt, and Harry looked blurry through the tears in her eyes. He'd explained that the reason her mother hadn't arrived last night, was because she'd been injured and was in hospital, and that's who Bessie had gone to visit.

'We don't know how your mother's hurt,' he said gently. 'Hopefully, she's just got a broken ankle and will soon be up and about, then she can come and visit you.'

'I . . .' Marigold croaked. She swallowed and tried again. 'I want to see her.'

Dottie sat down beside her and put her arm around her shoulders. 'Of course, you do, my lovely, but we need to wait until we hear from Bessie.'

'How . . . did it happen?' she asked.

'We don't know,' Harry said. 'She might have fallen over or . . .'

Different ways her mother might have been injured jumped through her mind. She could've tripped and fallen on the stairs going down the underground. But there were worse ways to be hurt in London these days. Marigold shivered at the thought of the horrible rockets which had made her mother send her away; it might have been one of them that injured her.

'What . . . if . . . she . . . dies...?' Marigold sobbed. 'I'll be an orphan like my daddy was and have to live in an orphanage.'

'No, you wouldn't,' Harry said kindly. 'Whatever happens, you will always have a home here with me

232

and Bessie. But don't think about that now.'

Dottie pulled her into her arms and hugged her tightly. 'Your mother will be fine, and she'll come and visit you here as soon as she can.'

Marigold wished with all her might that her mother was all right. Bessie had gone to London and would see that she got better. She was good, kind, and would take care of her mother, just like she'd cared for Marigold since she came to Norfolk. If she couldn't go to London, then Bessie was the next best thing. Her mother would be glad to see her, wouldn't she?

39

London

The damage the Luftwaffe had inflicted on the city had shocked Bessie. Although she'd heard reports about it on the wireless and read articles in newspapers, none of them had prepared her for the reality of seeing such destruction. The sight of so many gaps where buildings once stood, empty now, like missing teeth, or the piles of rubble, where wooden beams lay splintered into matchsticks, had brought tears to her eyes. Yet life carried on around the devastation, Londoners went about their business, battered but not defeated.

Now standing outside St Thomas', staring up at the hospital, which was bathed in moonlight, she could see that even this hadn't escaped the Germans' bombs. Hospitals, with their sick and wounded, were as much a target as the rest of London.

Somewhere inside, Grace was lying injured. How badly and in what manner, Bessie had no idea. Her mind had run through many different scenarios on the long journey here. From Grace already back home with only a few scratches and bruises, to her fatally injured. There was only one way to know exactly how she was, Bessie had to go inside and find her.

Picking up her case, she took a calming breath, and marched into the hospital. As Bessie went through the doors, the familiar smell of carbolic hit her, clean and comforting. If Grace was hurt, then this was the best place to be, with doctors and nurses to treat her physical injuries, and perhaps while she was here, they could heal the deep wound between them, too.

★ ★ ★

The nurse had warned her, but Bessie couldn't help gasping at the sight of Grace. She lay still, her hair and face grey with dust, and her clothes torn and filthy. A hospital, to Bessie, conjured up images of pristine white sheets and immaculate cleanliness. Not this.

'It looks bad,' the nurse whispered to her. 'But it's for the best, as it helps to minimise the shock.'

She nodded, unable to tear her eyes away from Grace, whose stillness, combined with the grey dusty pallor of her face and hair, gave her the appearance of a statue. The nurse had explained that Grace had been buried under a fallen building, and brought in unconscious, with two broken legs. Her legs had been seen to, cleaned up and plastered, and were now hidden in the bed under a cage. The rest of her would be tidied up later, once she'd recovered from the shock of what had happened to her.

'Can I stay with her?'

The nurse nodded. 'Just for five minutes.'

'Thank you.'

Standing beside the bed, she was glad of the surrounding screens providing some privacy, as her tears spilled over and ran down her face. She'd never imagined her next meeting with Grace to be like this. That should have been in Norfolk, with her arriving on the train and now be enjoying her stay at Orchard Farm. Not lying in a bed after being pulled out from a ruined building brought down by a rocket. Damn the war, she thought. How many more lives was it going to hurt before the end?

She gently took hold of one of Grace's hands. It felt cool beneath the layer of gritty dust. Bessie had held that hand so many times, starting on the day Grace had been born.

'Grace,' she whispered. 'It's me, Bessie. I've come to see you.' She knew the young woman probably couldn't hear her in her sleep, but had to tell her she was here in case somewhere deep inside her brain it might register. 'I'll be back again tomorrow. I promise.'

She squeezed Grace's hand gently, then laid it carefully on top of the bedclothes. With a last glance at her, Bessie parted the screens and walked towards the door.

'Mrs Rushbrook?'

She looked at the older woman who'd stepped forward as she left the ward.

'Yes.'

'I'm Ada Fox, Grace's landlady, and her friend.' She held out her hand and smiled.

Bessie stared at her, not quite registering at first. 'Oh, Mrs Fox . . . it was you who sent us the telegram.' She shook her hand. 'Thank you, we didn't know why Grace didn't come.'

'I thought you'd be worried. How is she?'

'She's sleeping now.'

'Sleep's the best thing for her after what she's been through.' Mrs Fox sighed. 'Grace was so excited about seeing Marigold again. She was on her way to the station when the rocket hit; had only left the house ten minutes before. I ran out to see what was going on, if I could help. I didn't know Grace had been caught in it

236

at first, I thought she'd got away.' Her eyes filled with tears, and she took a deep breath and gathered herself together. 'When they started digging out where the shops had come down, there she was. She'd been saving her sweet ration for Marigold and must have gone in to buy her some sweets . . .'

Bessie touched Mrs Fox's arm.

The older woman pulled a clean handkerchief out of her handbag and dabbed at her eyes, taking a moment to compose herself. 'Well, I'm glad you came. Now where are you staying tonight?'

'To be honest, I hadn't thought about it.' Bessie frowned. 'I just wanted to get here to see Grace. I suppose I'll . . .'

'You must come home and stay with me. Grace would want that.'

'Thank you. It's very kind of you, but . . .'

'I'd be glad of your company at a time like this. You'd be helping me out, too.'

'Perhaps I should wait here at the hospital, to be near her.' Bessie waved her hand helplessly. 'Then I'll be here when she wakes up . . .'

'You won't get much sleep sitting on a chair in a corridor, and you'll be no good to Grace tomorrow if you're tired. My house isn't far away, so it won't take you long to get back here in the morning.'

Bessie sighed. She was exhausted. The horror of the telegram, the long journey, seeing Grace like this, it had all taken its toll. She felt weary to the bone. 'You're right, Mrs Fox, I know, it's just that . . .'

'Please, call me Ada.' She linked her arm through Bessie's. 'I understand how you feel, honestly, I do, but she's in the best place and they'll take good care of her.'

She glanced towards the ward where Grace lay and then back at Mrs Fox. 'Thank you, I'll be glad to come and stay with you.'

★ ★ ★

'I don't know about you, but I could do with a nice hot cuppa.' Ada shrugged off her coat and hung it on a hook in the hallway.

'Yes, please, that would be lovely,' Bessie agreed.

'Leave your case here for now, and let me take your coat, then I'll put the kettle on.'

Bessie took off her coat and handed it to Ada, who hung it up, then led the way down the hall to the door at the far end. Following behind, she thought how strange it was to be here in Grace and Marigold's home.

'I live in the downstairs half,' Ada explained, as she placed the kettle on the stove. 'Grace lives upstairs. Marigold and poor John lived there too, before . . .' She sighed. 'After Marigold went to stay with you, Grace and I started having our meals together, it made sense to combine our rations, and I like someone to cook for. Are you hungry?'

'I had some sandwiches on the train,' Bessie said.

'That was hours ago. How about some toast?'

'Thanks, but honestly, I'm fine. A cup of tea's all I need.'

Ada looked at her. 'If you're sure? Tea will do you good, anyway.'

A few minutes later they were settled at the kitchen table, warming their hands around their cups.

'It's time to spill the beans, Bessie,' Ada said.

'What do you mean?'

238

'I was expecting you at the hospital tonight. Harry sent me a telegram saying you were on your way and asking me to look out for you.'

Sudden tears filled Bessie's eyes. 'He was worried about me coming here on my own.'

'He's a caring man.' Ada took a sip of tea. 'I was glad to come and find you. I'd been there earlier, and it gave me a good reason to go back, I didn't want the nurses thinking I was a nuisance and throwing me out.'

'Harry would have come with me, but he needed to stay at home and look after everything.'

'Does Marigold know her mother's been hurt?'

'No. At least she didn't when I left. It upset her when Grace didn't arrive last night, but we thought she'd just missed the train, or they had cancelled it. We'd hoped Grace would come today or at least send word.' Bessie frowned. 'Marigold was at school when your telegram arrived, and I set off before she came home. It's up to Harry to decide what to tell her, though I think he'll probably wait until he hears from me. There's no point in upsetting her unless we have to.'

'You can let them know how she is tomorrow.'

'I'll send a telegram home after I've been to see Grace.'

★ ★ ★

Bessie was wide awake. She was tired but couldn't stop herself from worrying, while images of Grace lying in the hospital bed played through her mind. Then there were thoughts of what was happening back at Orchard Farm. How was Harry managing? Was Marigold all right?

She turned onto her side, trying to get comfortable in the unfamiliar bed. Bessie wasn't used to sleeping without Harry, his presence beside her reassuring and comforting; now, when she could have done with some of that, he was miles away from here.

It was no good. Sleep wouldn't come, so Bessie flung back the covers, got up and padded over to the light switch near the door, and flicked it on. Opening her suitcase, she took out her diary and climbed into bed again. If she couldn't sleep, then she'd read.

40

3rd December, 1918
Harry's coming tomorrow. I'm meeting him at the station and will talk to him there, then he can go straight back on the next train. It must end.

★ ★ ★

It was still dark outside when Bessie made her way downstairs. She banked up the embers of the fire and soon had a warm blaze going, which threw out a welcome heat. Glancing at the clock on the mantelpiece, she saw it was just past five o'clock; too early for her father and Grace to be stirring. But she was wide awake and had been for a while. She had tried to fall asleep again, but there was too much on her mind for her to settle. Instead, Bessie had decided to get up, do something to pass the time and distract herself from what lay ahead today.

Crouching on the rag rug in front of the stove, she held out her hands to the heat. Bessie wished she could warm up her heart as easily, but since her life had suddenly changed, it was as if it had been frozen, like a fallen leaf encased in an icy winter puddle.

Bessie shivered. She must forget the future she'd planned, because events had now shunted her down another path. She was trying to accept it, but it wasn't easy, and the hardest thing would be telling Harry that everything had changed.

She could have told him in a letter, but it wouldn't

241

have been fair to the man she loved. Bessie owed it to him to tell him face to face, and had waited until after her mother's funeral, then written to him explaining what had happened and asking him to visit her.

He'd be expecting to come to the house and meet her father and Grace, but Bessie wouldn't be bringing him back here. To make it easier, she would tell him at the station, make the split short and swift. It would be better for him in the long run, she reasoned. Then he could go home, and she would return to her new life caring for her father and Grace. That was the plan. Bessie had spent hours agonising over it, although carrying it out would be far harder.

In the meantime, she had jobs to do. Standing up, Bessie smoothed her skirt down and pushed the kettle onto the hot plate. It would be coming up to the boil by the time her father came downstairs wanting a cup of tea.

★ ★ ★

Bessie's stomach clenched into a tight knot as the train chuffed into the station. She wanted to be here, and yet a hundred miles away. How she was going to tell Harry that he must make a life without her, she didn't know. It wasn't what she wanted for either of them, but it had to be done. Bessie had no choice. The promise she'd given her mother had changed her future. And Harry's, too.

The train halted, and she glanced up and down the carriages looking for him. There he was, stepping carefully down from a compartment near the far end of the train. He waved, then limped along the platform towards her as fast as he could, weaving in and out of the other passengers, a beaming smile on his face.

Bessie felt frozen to the spot, and suddenly started to cry, fumbling in her coat pocket for a handkerchief. But before she could wipe away her tears, Harry was beside her.

'Bess.' He spoke tenderly, taking the handkerchief from her hands and dabbing at her wet cheeks. Then he bent down and kissed her.

'Oh, Harry...' Her voice was hoarse.

'Come on.' He linked one arm through hers and drew her towards the exit. 'Let's get you home.'

Bessie allowed him to lead her out through the station yard, relieved to be with him again.

'Which way?' he asked as they reached the road. 'Left, or right?'

She needed to put a stop to this, she realised, coming to her senses. 'Neither!'

He looked at her, his eyes full of concern. 'What's wrong, Bess?'

'I need to talk to you.'

'We can do that at your father's.'

'No, not there.' Bessie's mind rapidly worked out where they could go. Not back into the station as there were too many people about, they needed a quiet place where they wouldn't be disturbed. The church. They could sit in the porch and she'd tell him there. 'This way.'

'Where are you taking me?'

'Somewhere private where we can talk.'

Bessie led Harry to the church and in through the lychgate, under which her mother's coffin was carried two days before. Glancing over to the right, she could see the brown earth piled on top of her fresh grave.

Pushing all thoughts of that aside for now, she walked into the church porch, sat down on the bench running along the side, and motioned for Harry to do the same.

'What's wrong?' He sat beside her, taking hold of her hand. 'I can see from your face that something's the matter.'

Bessie curled her free hand into a fist inside her coat pocket, the nails digging into her palm. Now the time had come, she didn't want to tell him, say words she truly didn't mean. But she must, there was no other choice.

'I'm . . .' Bessie croaked. She cleared her throat, looked him straight in the eye and started again. 'I'm sorry, but I can't marry you now.' She pulled her hand out of his.

It was done. She wanted to break down and weep, express how her heart was cracking inside its icy prison.

He stared at her, frowning. 'Why not? Don't you love me anymore?'

'I do love you.'

'Then why? I don't understand.'

'It's because I *can't* marry you now.' She bit her lip to stop herself from crying.

'What's changed? The last time I saw you, you were so happy, and talking about us getting married in the new year.'

Bessie looked down at her hands, which were twisting the handkerchief she'd fished out of her pocket. 'I want to marry you, but I just can't. Not anymore.'

Harry stood up and paced around the porch. 'Let me get this straight, you say you can't marry me, but it's not because you don't want to. So why?' He rubbed the back of his neck. 'What's happening here? Tell me.'

Tears stung Bessie's eyes again, but she was determined not to cry. She must be strong. 'Just before my mother died, she asked me to promise to take care of Grace and I did. I gave her my word.' She hesitated for a moment. 'My life has changed. I've got to take over from mother, I'm not free to marry you anymore.'

'So, the reason you can't marry me, is because you promised your mother you'd look after Grace, that's it?'

She nodded and looked up at him. His blue eyes held hers and then to her surprise he smiled.

Harry sat back on the bench beside her and took her hands in his. 'Looking after Grace shouldn't stop you marrying me. You can be my wife, and care for her. She can come and live at the farm, too.'

Bessie stared at him for a moment as his words sank in. 'You'd be happy to have my sister living with us?'

'Yes.'

The thought that he would still want to marry her and have Grace live with them, hadn't occurred to her. Most young men wouldn't want their wives to come with added responsibilities and more mouths to feed, but Harry wasn't like that. He was lovely, caring and sweet-natured, and she loved him with all her heart. Relief flooded through her. She could marry him.

'Thank you.' Bessie smiled happily at him.

'Your father could live with us, if he wanted to.'

Bessie's heart dropped like a stone to the bottom of a pond. Her father . . . would he allow Grace to live with her and Harry? If he didn't, then she still couldn't marry because she needed to be wherever Grace was.

'He might not want to, or even allow her to live with us. If he won't let Grace leave, then I can't.'

Harry put his arm around Bessie, hugging her to him. 'One step at a time. We need to ask him what he thinks first. There are lots of ifs and we can't plan until we know how he feels for sure.' He pulled back and looked deep into her eyes. 'Remember this, Bess Carter. I love you and you love me. Right?'

She nodded.

'One way or another, we're getting married and you'll still be able to keep your promise to look after Grace. We'll sort it out . . . together.'

* * *

Grace lay snuggled in Bessie's arms, slowly drifting off to sleep with the gentle motion of the rocking chair. Bessie pressed down softy with her feet on each fall forward, sending them backwards again. To and fro, back and forth. She found the rhythm soothing while she waited to find out in which direction her future lay. The one certainty was wherever it was, it would be with Grace.

The little girl stirred slightly in her sleep and snuggled in closer against her. This small movement stirred something in Bessie's chest, which she'd never allowed herself to acknowledge before.

She plopped a kiss on Grace's blonde head and closed her eyes, trying to focus on the gentle rocking. But her mind wouldn't be distracted, because out in the forge her future was being discussed as Harry talked to her father. Bessie would have gone with him, but he'd insisted he should go alone. Part of her wanted to protest that she should be there to

246

have her say, while another part was glad to be out of it.

Bessie's wishes were clear. She wanted to marry Harry but would only do so if Grace went with her. He was happy for Grace to live with them. All that was agreed upon but depended on one thing — her father's permission. He must agree to Grace leaving the forge and moving to the farm. Bessie sighed. Her entire future hung in the balance, depending on whether her father said yes. Or no . . .

'Bess?'

She struggled to surface from the foggy depths of sleep, having dropped off, her lack of sleep from the previous night catching up with her.

'Bess.' Harry's voice came again.

She forced her eyes open and saw him standing in front of her. Her heart leapt. What had her father said? She anxiously scanned his face for any clue.

'What did he say?' Bessie sat forward in the rocking chair, her arms tight around the still sleeping Grace.

'Your father said yes.' Harry's face broke into a wide smile. 'Grace can live with us after we're married.'

She could hardly believe it. 'Really?'

He nodded. 'Really and truly.' He reached out and gently stroked her cheek. 'We'll be married in the new year, and then Grace will come and live at the farm. Your father thinks it's a good idea as long as he gets to see her often.'

Relief and happiness flooded through Bessie. They were going to get married and spend the rest of their lives together.

★ ★ ★

Bessie halted on the bottom step of the stairs and looked across the kitchen at her father, who sat quietly by the fire. He was staring into the open door of the stove, where the orange flames flickered brightly. Her chest tightened at the thought of him living here on his own after she and Grace left. Would he be all right? She needed to talk to him about the future, check he really was happy they were doing the right thing. There hadn't been time before, and it was something she must ask now it was just the two of them.

'She's asleep.' Bessie sat down opposite him. 'Drifted off as soon as her head hit the pillow.'

Her father nodded. 'She's a busy little thing, it's no wonder she tires herself out.'

'I need to ask you something.'

He turned to face her. 'Go on.'

'Are you sure about Grace coming to live with Harry and me?' She frowned. 'I'm worried about you being left on your own. How are you going to manage the house and the forge?'

He leaned back in his chair, his elbows resting on the sides, his work-roughened hands clasped in front of him like a roof. 'I'm certain it's the right thing to do, because Harry's a fine man and will be a good husband to you, and for Grace, because she needs you to look after her. I'm sure your mother would approve.'

'But what about you?'

'Don't you worry, I'll be fine. I will miss Grace, but I hope I can see her often. You'll make sure that that happens, won't you?'

'Of course.' She reached out and touched his arm. 'You could come and live with us too. Harry told you that, didn't he?'

'He did, but my life and work are here. This . . .' he waved one hand around, 'is where I belong. It's my home and I don't want to go anywhere else.'

'What about the house and your meals?'

'I've been thinking about that. I'm sure I can cook a little, not in the way your mother could, but if you'll teach me a few things before you leave, I will be fine. I thought I might get Mrs Williams from next door, to come in and look after the place for me. Do a bit of housekeeping and cooking for me.'

It sounded as if he'd got it all worked out. Bessie's heart lifted. 'I would have been happy to stay and take care of you.'

'I know you would, and I thank you for it, but you're doing what your mother asked you to . . . looking after Grace . . .' He leaned forward and added another bit of wood to the fire. 'It shouldn't stop you from following your wishes and marrying Harry. Your mother was as pleased as punch about you getting wed.'

Bessie's eyes stung with tears. 'I'm lucky Harry is happy to have Grace with us.'

Her father nodded. 'He's a good man.'

He is, Bessie thought. Harry Rushbrook was the best of men. Only that morning, she'd believed her future with him was over, but Harry hadn't wanted to let her go and had made it possible for them to be married — him and her father. The two most important men in her life.

41

January, 1945

The plinking of jets of milk hitting the bottom of the metal pail usually made Harry feel contented and happy. No matter how often he'd heard it before, he still loved the sound, but not on this Saturday morning. He'd slept fitfully because Bessie wasn't there beside him; the bed had been so empty without her. Nothing was right, and the entire house felt wrong. The worry about what was going on in London had kept him awake long after he was normally asleep. Then there was Marigold to think about . . .

Buttercup raised a back leg and took a well-aimed kick at the bucket, sending it clattering across the floor, and a puddle of creamy milk spread over the stones, running down into the cracks like tiny rivers.

'Whoa, girl!' Harry stood up from the milking stool and righted the rolling pail, then went around to the usually placid Buttercup's head, where she was tethered to the wall while she ate from the trough. 'You can feel it too, can't you?' He rubbed under the cow's chin which she always loved, and she stretched her head up, exposing more of her neck for him to stroke.

He should have been concentrating on the milking and not fretting about what was happening, he thought. There was nothing he could do but wait until they'd heard from Bessie. Worrying wouldn't get them anywhere, all it did was upset the milk. And as his granny used to say, there's no point crying over spilt milk, literally in this case. He just had to get on with it.

Giving Buttercup's chin a final rub, he sat back down on the three-legged stool and started to milk again. This time he hummed gently, which helped to concentrate his thoughts on the job in hand. Buttercup seemed to approve, letting her milk flow free and the pail quickly filled with the creamy liquid.

When Harry had finished milking, he led the cows out to the meadow and stood leaning on the gate looking at them for a few moments, thinking about the day ahead. The best thing to do was to keep everything going as normal, and there was plenty of work to get on with. With Dottie and Prune doing the cooking, they would manage while they waited to hear about Grace.

* * *

London

Bessie's heart was fluttering like a bird trapped in a cage, as she approached the screen surrounding Grace's bed. The nurse had told her she was awake and waiting to see her.

Pull yourself together, Bessie told herself. How many times had she longed to see Grace since she'd left all those years ago? Their reunion wasn't happening the way she would have wanted, but it was as it was, and she had to make the best of it. She took a few steadying breaths, plastered a smile on her face, then pulled the screen aside and stepped through.

'Hello.' Grace lay propped up on some pillows and held out her hand to Bessie.

She strode across and took hold of her offered hand. 'Hello, Grace.' She smiled at the young woman who looked so different from the previous evening. The dust and dirt had gone, and she now wore a hospital gown. Her face was pale and marked with bruises and scratches, but the real Grace was back, from her blonde hair to her blue eyes.

'They told me you were here last night.'

Bessie nodded. 'You were asleep, but they let me stay for a few minutes. Ada came and took me home.'

'She's kind like that.' Grace looked her straight in the eye. 'I had a dream about you. You were saying you'd come back. You promised.'

Bessie's breath caught in her throat. 'That's what I said to you before I left. Maybe you heard.'

'Perhaps I did.'

They fell into silence for a few moments.

'How are you feeling? You look much better than last night.'

'Much cleaner, you mean. It was lovely to have a wash and get rid of the dust . . .' She bit her bottom lip. 'I'm lucky to be here. If I'd gone any further down the road, I would have been a goner. I stopped to buy Marigold some sweets . . . then there was this almighty bang and a roar . . . and it all fell in around us.'

'They had to dig you out.'

A look of horror passed over Grace's face and she looked older than her years for a moment. 'I don't remember.'

'Ada sent us a telegram saying that you'd been injured, and I came straight away.'

Grace's eyes glistened, and she managed a wobbly smile. 'I'm glad you're here.'

'I wanted to see you. I had to come.' Bessie swallowed

252

hard against the tightness squeezing her throat.

'Where's Marigold?'

'At home. She was at school when Ada's telegram came, and we thought it best that I come alone . . . we didn't know what to expect, and I couldn't risk bringing her here while the rockets are still dropping.'

'I want to see her so much . . .' Grace's voice wavered. 'But I'd rather she was safe.'

'She's desperate to see you, too.'

'They're moving me out of London this afternoon. They need to get the beds empty for the next wave of casualties.'

'Where are they taking you?'

'I'm not sure yet, but it should be safer than here. I'll come and visit Marigold as soon as I can.' She nodded towards the cage that surrounded her broken legs. 'I need to talk to you before I go. I . . .'

A nurse popped her head around the side of a screen. 'Everything all right in here?'

It was Helen MacDonald who'd brought Marigold to Norfolk last summer.

'Hello, Bessie. It's lovely to see you again. How's wee Marigold?'

'Oh, hello. Marigold's fine, thank you.'

'That's good to hear. Grace has cleaned up nicely, don't you think? What a difference a wash and brush up makes.' Helen winked at her friend. 'Would you like a chair, Bessie?'

'Yes, thank you, I'll come and get it.'

'No need. Be back in two ticks.'

Helen's head disappeared, and Bessie and Grace looked at each other.

'I never thought I'd end up being a patient on Helen's ward.'

'I didn't see her here last night.'

'She wasn't on duty then.'

'Is this the ward where you work?'

Grace shook her head. 'No. I'm on the next floor up.'

The screen parted and Helen came in with a chair. 'There you go.'

Bessie smiled at her. 'That's kind of you, thank you.'

'My pleasure. I'll leave you two to talk.' Helen turned to go, then twirled back again. 'I nearly forgot. We've had word that you're leaving earlier than expected, Grace. We're just waiting for the ambulances to be organised and then you'll be off. It shouldn't be too long.' She went out, pulling the screens closed behind her.

'Please, sit down,' Grace said. 'We haven't got much time.' She waited until Bessie had settled herself on the chair, then looked her straight in the eye. 'I need to say something before I go . . . I'm sorry for what I did. I was wrong.' She fiddled with the edge of the sheet covering her. 'I should have listened to you and Harry . . . but I thought I knew better. When I got to London, it was a complete mess. The address he'd given me didn't exist, and I never saw him again.'

Bessie put her hand over Grace's and squeezed it gently. 'We all make mistakes and want to go our own way in the world.' She paused. 'But why didn't you come home again?'

'I was too ashamed and stubborn. I was scared you might not want me back after what I did, and . . . I dare not risk that, so I stayed and built a life for myself here.'

'We would've welcomed you back.' Bessie's voice caught in her throat.

'I missed you both so much.' Grace's eyes filled with tears. 'I wanted to come home, but I thought cutting myself off completely would make it easier to bear. I'd made my bed, so I had to lie in it. Get on with life in London and forget about my home with you and Harry.'

'We missed you. There hasn't been a day gone by when I haven't thought of you, wondered where you were and what you were doing.' Bessie's voice wobbled. 'I hoped that wherever you were, you were happy. We were so pleased when you wrote and trusted us to have Marigold.'

Grace nodded. 'If she couldn't be with me, then you and Harry were the two people I'd trust to look after her. You both cared for me, took me in when I was small and looked after me. You've been the best sister to me, Bessie, and . . .' She halted as tears slid down her cheeks. 'I let you down.'

'You didn't.' She stroked Grace's hand. 'We were happy to look after you and both loved having you with us.'

'You promised our mother, didn't you? Promised her you'd care for me, and you kept your word.'

'It was a promise I was glad to make and keep.' Bessie's heart was hammering inside her. Now was the time to do what she'd wanted to do for years.

'Are you all right?' Grace looked worried.

She met Grace's eyes. 'I was brought up to believe that when you made a promise, you kept it. Mother was very strict about that; it didn't matter whether it was standing your boots tidy or something far bigger. Your word was your bond.' Bessie sighed, heavily. 'But she once made me make a promise that I didn't want to . . . every bit of me screamed and raged against it, but I had to make it . . . and I've stuck to it ever since . . . It was not long after you were born.'

Grace frowned. 'I don't understand. Mother didn't die until I was three . . . she asked you to look after me just before she died, didn't she?'

'Yes, that's right. But the promise I'm talking about was given on the day you were born . . .' Bessie's mouth went dry and she stopped to swallow. 'She made me promise I would never tell you who I really am.' She bowed her head for a few moments before fixing her eyes on Grace's again. 'I am . . .' The words seemed to stick in her throat. 'Your *mother*, not your sister.'

Grace gasped. 'My mother?'

'Yes.'

'But how?'

'I was engaged to William, your father, and we'd planned to marry on his next leave from the Front, only he was killed before he could come home. I found out I was expecting you after he died; he never knew.'

'What happened?'

'Mother arranged that I should leave my work as a VAD for a while, and go home to look after her because she was supposedly ill. They kept me out of the way once it was obvious that I was having a child, while mother pretended she was having one. The plan was to pass my baby off as hers. After it was born, I'd go back to working as a VAD again, and they would bring my baby up as my brother or sister.'

'Is that what you wanted?'

'No! But I didn't have a choice...' She shrugged. 'Mother threatened to disown me if I didn't do as she said. I'd have been an unmarried mother, with no support and all the shame such a position gave, and probably ended up in the workhouse with my baby.

With you.'

Grace frowned. 'What about our father . . . I mean, your father?'

'He went along with it. My mother was in charge, and he did what she said for a quiet life. I suppose he thought it was for the best. At least my child would be cared for in a family, and not cursed with the stigma of having an unmarried mother.' Tears rolled down Bessie's cheeks. 'I didn't have a choice. If I wanted my baby to have a chance, I had to accept it. I gave mother my word and I've stuck to it all these years . . . but when I saw you lying here last night . . .' Her voice wavered. 'I knew I couldn't do it anymore. You are my *daughter* and I had to tell you the truth.'

'I'm so glad you did.' Grace's voice caught, and she swallowed down a sob. 'You've always been like a mother to me, anyway. It makes sense that you truly are my mother. I'm happy to know who you really are.' She smiled and took hold of Bessie's hand. 'So, George is my actual brother too. That's good. We were more like brother and sister than aunt and nephew, anyway.'

'I think George will be pleased, too.'

'What about Harry? I bet he wasn't happy with your mother making you do that.'

Bessie's chest tightened. 'He . . . Harry doesn't know about it. As far as he's concerned, you're my sister.'

Grace's eyes widened. 'When you say you'll keep your word, you really mean it, don't you?'

'I will tell him when I get home. I've had enough of secrets . . . though I'm not sure how he'll take it, he's always said I'm the most honest person he knows, but all along I have been hiding the truth . . .'

Grace squeezed her hand. 'You don't have to tell him about it; this can stay between me and you. No one else has to know.'

Bessie sighed. 'Thank you for saying that. But I need to be honest with him. Now I've broken my word to my mother and told you, I owe it to him. When he married me, he became not only responsible for me but for you too, and he was happy to do that. He's always loved you like a daughter. It's only fair he knows, but . . . I don't know what he'll say, or if he will ever forgive and trust me again.'

'Harry loves you. He's a good man.'

'I've wanted to tell him so many times, but I couldn't.' Bessie fished in her handbag and brought out a white handkerchief and dabbed at her face. 'I hope he'll understand and forgive me for what I've done.'

42

Norfolk

'Do you think Marigold's mother will be all right?' Peter pulled on his end of the bow saw, sending another shower of sawdust spurting onto the dark ground, peppering it like snow.

'I hope so.' Harry glanced at him, thinking he didn't look his usual self today. 'Are you all right?'

'I'm fine.'

Harry didn't believe him, something was wrong with the lad, but he clearly wasn't willing to talk about it. He'd speak about what was bothering him when he was ready. Peter was a pleasure to spend time with when they worked together on the farm. His natural way with animals had given him an advantage, turning a city boy from Vienna into one completely at home in the countryside.

'What will happen to Marigold if her mother dies?' Peter blurted out.

The little girl had asked Harry that same thing last night, and his answer had been simple.

'She'd stay here with Bessie and me, this would carry on being her home,' he said. It would be what her mother wanted, what she'd asked for. Although he hoped they'd never need to do it, because for that to happen it would mean Grace would have died.

'She's lucky. I really hope her mother will be fine, but if she doesn't make it, then at least Marigold will have you and Bessie to look after her.'

'Don't say anything about that to her, will you? We don't know yet how badly Grace has been injured.'

'I won't,' Peter said. 'I don't want to upset her.'

They carried on sawing in silence; just the rough sound of the sawblade biting its way through the wood. Harry stole a few glances at the lad and could tell from his face there was something else bothering him.

'Harry?' Prune called, walking across the yard towards them.

He brought the saw to a juddering halt. 'Is everything all right?'

'Yes, it's fine. Dottie and I are going to take Marigold for a walk.'

'Good idea. Perhaps we'll have heard something from Bessie by the time you get back.'

'Would you like to come with us, Peter?' Prune asked.

'No thanks, I'll stay here. We need to get this wood finished.' He gestured towards the pile of branches yet to be sawn into smaller pieces for the stove.

'We'll see you both later.' Prune headed off towards the gate where Dottie and Marigold were waiting for her.

'I can manage this on my own, if you'd like to go with them.' Harry took hold of his end of the saw again.

'No. I'd rather stay.' Peter pulled on his end of the saw and they fell into an easy rhythm, back and forth, as the metal blade bit into the wood. Down and down it went until only a sliver connected the two pieces. They stopped sawing as the weight of the unsupported piece snapped the join, and the log tumbled onto the pile they'd already cut.

Harry moved the branch along the sawhorse, made the first few cuts to form a groove and was ready to start again, but instead of taking hold of his end of the saw, Peter stood staring down at his feet.

'Are you all right?' Harry asked.

Peter jerked his head up, and for a split second, Harry would have sworn the boy's eyes were glittering with tears, but then he blinked, and they were gone.

'We can have a rest for five minutes.'

'No, I'm ready.' Peter took hold of the saw and once more they fell into the sawing rhythm, working in silence and adding to the pile of logs, piece by piece.

They were on the last branch when Peter suddenly asked, 'do you think my parents are still alive?'

Harry stopped sawing. So that was what he'd been thinking about. What should he say? he wondered. The truth.

'I hope they are.'

'But do you think they are?' Peter's face wore a pinched, haunted look which Harry had never seen on him before.

He sighed. 'I honestly don't know. These are difficult times so all I can say is, I hope they are. I know that's not what you wish to hear, but you'd prefer me to be truthful.'

What had happened to his parents or where they were now, Harry had no idea. When Peter had first come to Orchard Farm, they'd written to him regularly, but then the letters had stopped. Why Harry didn't know, but with the danger Jewish people were facing from the Nazis, it was likely they had ceased writing because they couldn't anymore, not because they didn't want to.

'If . . .' Peter began, then halted. He took a deep

breath and tried again. 'If they've died, what will happen to me when the war's over? Where will I go?'

'Nowhere, not if you don't want to.' Harry leaned across the sawhorse and laid a hand on Peter's shoulder. 'Whatever happens, you will always have a home here with Bessie and me. I hope you'll be reunited with your parents, but if that can't happen, then you know you can stay here.'

Peter's eyes were bright with tears. 'Thank you.'

'Has what's happened with Marigold's mother made you think of your future?'

Peter nodded.

'War's a nasty business, and it doesn't just affect adults, children get caught up in it too. But you're not to worry about never having a home.' Harry took hold of the saw. 'Let's finish this last one, then we'll go in and have a cup of tea.'

43

'Marigold's quiet today.' Prune watched the little girl skipping along in front of them.

'It's not surprising.' Dottie sighed. 'Her father killed, and now her mother's been injured by this blasted war.'

'It could be a broken ankle or . . .'

'Or much worse. We don't know anything for sure until we hear from Bessie.'

'Come on, let's catch her up. Race you.' Prune started to run, her long legs eating up the road.

Dottie took off behind her, her later start preventing her from catching up.

'Watch out, Marigold!' Prune shouted, waving her arms. 'We're coming!'

The little girl spun round. 'Are you two having a race?'

Prune reached her first and stood hands on hips, laughing as Dottie came in close behind.

'Unfair start, you went off before me.' Dottie's breath plumed in the cold air.

'You could have another race and I'll say go,' Marigold suggested.

Dottie shook her head. 'Let's do something together to help us keep warm.' She put her arm through Marigold's and nodded for Prune to do the same on the other side. 'Have you seen The Wizard of Oz film at the pictures?'

Marigold nodded. 'My dad took me.'

'Well, do you remember when Dorothy, the Lion,

263

the Scarecrow and the Tin Man go along the yellow brick road? They linked their arms like us, and they danced along. Like this.' Dottie demonstrated the movement. 'Do you think we could do that?'

'Easy,' Marigold said. 'I love skipping.'

Prune caught Dottie's eye over Marigold's head and nodded her approval. Taking the girl's mind off her worries was the best thing to do. Good old Dottie, coming up with something like The Wizard of Oz. It was perfect.

'If we skip to the right, and then to the left,' Dottie said, encouraging them to match her movements. 'That's good. Now a bit quicker.'

The three of them progressed along the road, almost spanning the width of it as they moved from side to side.

'Can we sing as well?' Marigold asked.

'I don't see why not? Prune, are you up for a sing-song?'

'Absolutely.'

'Ready then, keep your legs going, one . . . two . . . one . . . two . . . three . . .' Dottie counted them in. 'We're off to see the Wizard . . .'

Any words they didn't know, they hummed, then started all over again.

They'd warmed up and had almost reached the turning leading down to Rackbridge base, when a man riding a bicycle rounded the bend and headed straight towards them.

Dottie quickly pulled Marigold's arm, dragging her and Prune out of the way as he careered past them, coming to a screeching halt a few yards down the road.

'It's Clem,' Prune said as he jumped off his bicycle and pushed it back to meet them.

'Was that me riding on the wrong side again, or were you guys all over the place?' He grinned. 'I know I've got it wrong before, but I was sure I was on your British side.'

'We were going down the middle,' Dottie said.

'Skipping from left to right. Like they do in The Wizard of Oz,' Marigold added.

Prune nodded. 'We were over on your side, Clem, and our side, and in the middle!' She laughed, and the others joined in.

'I'm sorry, if we scared you, Clem.' Dottie managed to say a few moments later.

'That's okay. I was on my way to see you. I've got some good news.' He beamed. 'Howard's back.'

Prune's heart jumped. She stared at him as the news sank in.

'Really?'

'Yes, ma'am, and he's desperate to see you.'

Prune could second that. There wasn't anything she wanted more in the world than to see Howard again. 'I'll come straight away.'

'It's not as simple as that. He's confined to base for a few days for debriefing. He can't come out, and you can't come in,' Clem explained. 'But there's no reason why you shouldn't meet through the fence. Not if we're careful.'

Prune nodded. 'Anything. When? Where?'

'Eleven hundred hours. At the perimeter fence where it meets the corner of the wood off Bright's Lane. No one should see us there. Do you know where it is?'

'I do,' Marigold said. 'Peter and I have been around there. I can show you.'

Clem glanced at his watch. 'I've got to get back.

265

Remember, eleven hundred hours.'

'I'll be there,' Prune promised. 'Tell Howard, I can't wait.'

'I will.' He climbed onto his bicycle and pedalled off fast in the direction of the base's main gate.

'When's eleven hundred hours?' Marigold asked.

'Eleven o'clock.' Dottie glanced at her watch. 'That's in half an hour.'

'We'd better get a move on then, I don't want to be late,' Prune said. 'Marigold, are you sure you know where to go?'

The little girl nodded. 'I know where he means. Don't worry, I'll take you there.' She held out her hand. 'Come on.'

Prune took Marigold's hand. 'Lead the way.'

'You take my other hand, Dottie,' Marigold said.

Dottie hesitated. 'I think it would be better if Prune went with you on her own. She hasn't seen Howard for a while, and they've got a lot of catching up to do. I'm sure she doesn't want lots of people there.'

'But I'll be there,' Marigold said.

'I'm not going without you.' Prune touched Dottie's arm. 'Howard's your friend, too.'

'All right, then. We can say hello, then Marigold and I can go off for a bit and leave you two to talk?'

'That's a good idea.' Prune smiled at her friend. 'Thank you. Come on, no more talking, I've got a date to keep.'

* * *

Prune stood under a large oak tree at the edge of the wood, while Dottie kept Marigold occupied scuffling through fallen leaves farther in. Her stomach was

266

turning somersaults as the seconds slowly ticked by. Glancing at her watch again, she saw it was almost five past eleven; they were late. Perhaps they weren't coming.

Her doubts disappeared with the sound of an approaching jeep coming along the perimeter track. It was them. The sight of Howard sent her heart racing.

'Prune! They're coming.' Marigold shot past her towards the fence.

'Wait!' Dottie ran after her, calling to Prune, 'I'll let her say a quick hello, then we'll disappear for a bit.'

'Thanks.' Prune stood rooted to the spot, watching as Clem stopped the jeep close to where Marigold waited. As Howard climbed out, she saw that his right arm was in a sling, but otherwise he looked well.

'Hello, Howard,' Marigold called.' I'm glad you came back.'

'So am I, honey,' he replied.

'It's lovely to see you,' Dottie said. 'Welcome back.'

He smiled at her. 'Thanks.'

'If you'll excuse us, we have some leaf scuffing to finish.' Dottie put her arm around Marigold's shoulders and steered her towards the wood.

'Sure.' Howard looked past them, his eyes locking with Prune's.

They stood staring at each other for a few seconds before Prune launched herself across the few yards to the fence. The bones in her legs seemed to have turned into jelly, but somehow, she managed to propel herself along and rushed headlong into the wire, bouncing into Howard who waited on the other side of the fence, as close to her as he could get.

'Hello, sweetheart.' He pushed the fingers of his

267

left hand through the honeycomb of gaps to reach out to her.

'Oh, Howard . . .' Prune entwined her fingers with his, savouring the sensation of his touch on her skin, something she'd feared would never happen again. 'I . . .' she began, but Howard silenced her with a kiss, their lips meeting in a gap between the wires.

'I've been thinking about doing that all the way home.' He drew back and studied her face. 'I've missed you so much.'

'I've missed you, too. You can do that again if you like.'

He laughed. 'I do like.' He kissed her again.

A cough made them pull apart, looking to where Clem stood a little way behind Howard, holding a bulky parcel. 'I hate to break you up, but we've only got a couple of minutes here. We mustn't risk being caught.'

Howard groaned. 'I know. We've got a lot of time to make up for, and we will. Soon.'

'I'll throw this over for you, I don't think you'd do it with one arm. Here you go.' Clem sent the parcel sailing over the fence and Prune caught it in both hands. 'Great catch! I'll be in the jeep. One minute, okay?'

Howard nodded as his friend smiled at them both and returned to the jeep.

'What's this?' she asked.

'A present for you. It's my chute, I thought you could make your wedding dress from it. It saved my life, so I reckon it's perfect to dress the woman I love in when she marries me.'

Prune's eyes filled with tears. 'Thank you.'

'Now I'm back, we'll get our wedding in motion.'

'Come on, Howard,' Clem called. 'Time's up.'

'Okay.'

'When will I see you again?'

'As soon as they'll let me out.' He leaned towards the fence once more and kissed her. 'I love you, Prune, and can't wait for you to be my wife.'

44

'Mr Rushbrook!'

Harry turned to see Thomas striding across the yard towards him, and quickly plonked down the pail of milk before he dropped it.

'Another telegram for you.' Thomas pulled one of the familiar envelopes out of his bag and held it out.

Harry's heart raced at the sight of it. After the ones they'd received in the past few days, he didn't know what sort of news it brought. Good or bad.

He smiled at the young lad who had the hard job of delivering them. 'Thank you.'

Thomas nodded and quickly turned on his heel, heading back to where he'd left his bicycle leaning on the gate.

Harry stared at the envelope which was addressed only to him. Was it from Bessie? There was only one way to find out, so he tore it open and unfolded the single sheet of paper.

GRACE BROKEN LEGS NOW MOVED OUT OF LONDON STOP COMING HOME TONIGHT STOP

'Thank God.' He took a steadying breath. Broken legs would mend, and better still, Grace was no longer in London. It was good news to tell Marigold. And Bessie was coming home tonight. He'd be there to meet her, although she hadn't said which train she would be arriving on, so he'd meet each one until she

270

returned. Harry couldn't wait to see her again, she'd only been gone since yesterday, but it had felt like an age.

★ ★ ★

London

IS YOUR JOURNEY REALLY NECESSARY? The words on the poster caught Bessie's eye as she walked across Liverpool Street station's crowded forecourt. Yes, it was, she thought to herself as she headed towards the entrance to platform ten from where the train for Norwich was due to leave. She'd always minded the messages on the government's posters and did her bit for the war effort, but this trip to London had absolutely been necessary. Probably the most important one she had ever made. Now she was here, well she had to make another journey to get back home again.

There was no sign of the train on platform ten. The tracks stood empty, dirty and dusty. It was likely to be delayed like they all were these days. Picking her way along the platform, Bessie received and returned smiles from the waiting passengers, many of whom were in uniform, armed with a kitbag and on route to who knows where.

She found a space and put her small suitcase down, standing it upright to sit on until the train arrived. Perched on top of her case, Bessie sat and watched people coming and going for a while. She felt restless, worrying about what was to come, and in need of some distraction. Rummaging inside her handbag, she took out her diary and opened it at the place marked with

271

a piece of ribbon. It was the last entry. She hadn't felt the need to write in it any more after that.

2nd January, 1919, Bessie read
Our wedding day! Harry and I are getting married this afternoon at two o'clock. I shall become Bessie Rush-brook instead of Bessie Carter. How strange that sounds, but I like it. I'm so happy and not at all nervous. Not a bit. I know it's the right thing for me to do. It's what I want — to be married to Harry for the rest of my life.

That hadn't changed, and it never would as far as she was concerned, but what she was going to tell him could destroy their marriage. How he would react, Bessie wasn't sure, but it was time for him to know the truth about her. She would have to accept the consequences, whatever they might be.

Bessie closed the diary and ran a finger over its soft cloth cover, before putting it away in her bag. She had finished looking into the past; it was the future that counted now.

*

Norfolk

Bessie was now on the final leg of her journey home. It had taken hours to get back, and she'd been fortunate to catch the last train from Norwich. The thought of being home again filled her with joy . . . but the feeling was short-lived, the tight knot in her stomach reminding her of what she had to do. Revealing her secret to Harry, after all these years, could destroy her happy marriage and crumble their home life to dust.

She was scared. How would Harry react to her secret? Telling him the truth would make everything he had known about her false. Worthless. Worse still was the fact that she'd lied to him. Her secret had haunted her for years, but it wasn't going to anymore. Bessie had had enough of it and needed to be free to acknowledge her daughter. Nearly losing Grace in the rocket blast had made that crystal clear to her.

Promises were only for keeping if you meant them and they came from your own free will. But not those pressed upon you by others. Facing the consequences of breaking hers was the price she was prepared to pay. Bessie owed it to herself, and to her daughter, to finally be true.

The train slowed, and Bessie gathered her things together as Rackbridge was the next stop. Standing up, she pulled her case down from the overhead rack, then sat back down on the springy seat with it balanced on her lap.

'Your stop next?' an elderly lady in the opposite corner asked.

Bessie nodded. 'It's been a long journey and I'll be glad to get home.'

'There's no place like it,' the woman said. 'That and your family are what's important in life, especially these days.'

'That's very true, I've just been to see my daughter.' The words spilled out before she had time to think about them, and a spark of joy leapt in her heart. Being able to call Grace her daughter felt wonderful.

'Goodnight,' the woman said, as the train pulled into the station.

'Goodnight.' Bessie turned the handle on the door and climbed down onto the platform.

The cool, clean air hit her like a shower of water on a hot summer's day. It refreshed her and sloughed off the tiredness as she breathed in deeply, taking in the familiar scent of the countryside, which was so different from London.

'Bess!'

She spun round and saw her husband limping towards her, the broad smile on his face clear in the moonlight. Her heart leapt at the sight of him and she rushed to meet him, throwing her arms around him, nearly knocking him off balance.

'Harry.' Bessie spoke into his chest as he hugged her tightly.

He pulled back and looked at her. 'I missed you.' Then he kissed her tenderly.

Bessie's eyes filled with tears. 'I missed you, too. I'm so glad to be back.'

'Let's get you home.'

'I didn't expect you to be here to meet me,' she said, as Harry helped her up into the trap. 'How did you know which train I'd be on?'

'I didn't.' He climbed into the trap and took up the reins. 'I met the earlier one and came back again for this train.'

'Oh, Harry . . .' Bessie leaned across and squeezed his hand. 'I'm so glad you were here to meet me.'

He smiled at her. 'I wanted to see you again as soon as I could. And I thought you'd be tired and appreciate a ride home.'

She nodded. 'It's lovely to be met and driven home. Thank you.'

'How's Grace?'

'Apart from two broken legs, cuts and bruises, she seems all right. She's lucky to be alive. Now they've sent her out of London to convalesce, Grace is much safer, too. She'll write and let us know where she is.'

'It could have been a lot worse. How did it happen?'

'She was caught in a V2 blast and was . . .' Bessie's voice wavered. 'They found her buried under a fallen building and had to dig her out.'

'Buried alive . . .' Harry shuddered. 'The thought of that used to scare men at the Front.'

'Thankfully she was unconscious when they dug her out, she doesn't remember much about it.'

They fell into silence for a few moments with only the sound of the pony's hooves clip-clopping on the road, and the twitting and kee-wicking of a pair of tawny owls calling in the trees further down the lane.

'I don't think we should tell Marigold about her mother being buried,' Harry said. 'It would be best coming from Grace herself, if she ever decides to tell her. Broken legs are enough.'

'I agree. How is she?'

'She's fine now she knows her mother's going to be all right, although she wants to visit her in hospital. I told her we'd have to wait and see.'

'It all depends where Grace has been sent to. She said she'll come here as soon as she's able to.'

'It will be good to see her again. It's been far too long.' He paused. 'How was it with her? Was she . . . did she say anything about what happened after she left here?'

'Yes, and it was a sham. The fellow she chased after wasn't where he said he'd be, and she never saw him again. Grace apologised for how she behaved.' Bessie reached over and took hold of his hand. 'We talked about it and straightened it out, everything's out in the open now. I'll tell you about it properly tomorrow.'

'That's good.' Harry leaned over and kissed her cheek. 'The family's back together again.'

An icy hand gripped Bessie's heart. Would he still think so tomorrow after she'd told him the truth? She needed to tell him, but not now while she was so tired. Tomorrow was soon enough. She would have one last precious night as the wife Harry thought he knew.

45

Bessie sat on the bed staring at the words written for her so long ago.

Whatever you are — be that.
Whatever you say — be true.
Straightforwardly act.
Be honest in fact.
Be nobody else but you.
Be nobody else but you.
All that is best for thee.
That best I wish for thee.

Would Sergeant Harmer have chosen that poem if he had known what secret she carried? *Whatever you are — be that.* But she hadn't, at least not in name, so that everyone knew who she really was. When Grace came to live with her and Harry, Bessie had loved and cared for her like a daughter, but never openly acknowledged that she really was her daughter.

She snapped her diary shut. Reading it had whisked her back to life during the last war, when she'd looked after the wounded soldiers. Those days had been hard, but there'd been many moments of joy and laughter, too. Best of all, was Harry's arrival at Marston Hall. He'd brought part of her to life again. Dear, sweet, loving Harry . . .

Bessie pulled open a drawer, laid the diary inside and quickly shut it away. The past was the past; it was the future she must focus on now.

The farm was quiet. Prune and Dottie had taken the children out on a bicycle ride, with the promise of a picnic and a campfire. Harry was still indoors after their meal, reading the newspaper by the fire. With no one else around to disturb them, it was the perfect moment to tell him. She stood up and steeled herself — it was time to be honest with him.

'All unpacked?' He looked over the top of the newspaper as Bessie settled down in the opposite chair.

'Yes, there wasn't much.' She stared down at her lap.

'Are you all right, Bess?'

Her mouth was dry and her heart pounding. This was it.

'I need to talk to you about Grace.' She hesitated . . . then pushed herself to tell him before she lost her nerve. 'You see . . . I've not been honest with you about who she really is. Grace isn't my sister . . . she's my . . . *daughter.*'

There, her secret was out. Bessie watched Harry's face, biting her bottom lip, her hands firmly clasped together to stop them shaking. He'd put the newspaper down and was regarding her with an unfathomable look on his face. Was he angry? She willed him to say something . . . anything . . . but he didn't. He merely nodded at her, encouraging her to go on.

'I'm so . . .' Her voice caught in her throat, and she paused to gather herself together. 'I'm sorry I lied to you. I didn't want to, but I had no choice. I had to keep my promise.'

She waited for Harry to speak, but he still remained silent. His face was calm and betrayed no hint of what he was thinking or feeling.

'Aren't you going to say something?' Bessie blurted

278

out. It was agonising waiting for his reaction.

'Finish your story first, then I will.'

She hadn't expected him to react this way. Whenever Bessie had imagined herself telling him, she thought he'd be upset, angry, at least show some emotion, but his calmness was unnerving. Was this a case of the calm before the storm?

'I'd better start at the beginning. I was engaged to William, and we were . . .' She told him the same story as she'd told Grace the day before, and he listened without interrupting her. 'I wanted to tell you about Grace and be honest with you, but I couldn't. Please understand I had no choice.' She stopped for a moment, sighing heavily, her shoulders slumped, then went on. 'When she came to live with us after we were married, it was as if I'd finally been given a chance to be her mother. Care for her like any mother would, only I could never tell her who I really was. But I could cope with that. I had to.' Bessie blinked away threatening tears. 'I hated knowing I'd deceived you. I'm sorry, but I haven't been the person you thought I was.'

It was done. Harry now knew the truth about her. She hung her head, waiting, the room quiet except for the ticking clock.

'Bess?' He took hold of her hand and leaned forward, gently stroking her cheek. She looked up at him, her eyes meeting his.

'I've always known what sort of person you are. Good, kind and caring, the woman who I wanted to be my wife. Still want for the rest of my life.' He smiled warmly at her. 'You haven't told me anything I didn't already know.'

Bessie stared at him, lost for words for a few

moments. 'What do you mean?'

'It's nothing new to me. I've known for a long time that she's your daughter.'

Her stomach lurched. 'How?'

'Your father told me when we talked about Grace coming to live with us before we were married. He thought I should know the truth, and told me he wasn't happy about your mother forcing you to make that promise when Grace was born. He was frightened for you, worried she'd disown you, and you'd both end up in the workhouse if he didn't go along with it.'

Bessie shook her head . . . all this was hard to take in. Harry had known all these years. 'Why didn't you tell me you knew?'

'It wasn't my secret to tell. I thought you'd let me know one day.' His blue eyes were full of love. 'And you have.'

'But . . . what must you think of me for lying to you?'

'I've never thought of it as a lie, more a keeping to your promise. I admire you for sticking to your word, even though it hurt you.'

She frowned. 'But aren't you angry that I deceived you about such an important thing?'

'No, not at all. I saw things in France which made me appreciate how fortunate I was to come through it. Grace's father didn't. I was lucky to meet you, and luckier still that you wanted to take up with me. I wasn't going to judge you for something forced upon you.' He stood up and gently pulled her to her feet. 'I never have, and never will.'

Bessie nodded, unable to speak as he put his arms around her and hugged her.

'You were a wonderful mother to Grace, and it saddened me she didn't know who you really were.'

'She does now.' She pulled back a little and looked up into his face. 'I told her yesterday. I hadn't planned to, but when I saw Grace lying in that hospital bed, I knew I had to tell her. Promise or not. I broke it.'

Harry nodded, approvingly. 'It should have dissolved when your mother died. You could have taken Grace as your daughter then; she was young enough to have accepted it.'

'Easier said than done. You didn't know my mother. She'd probably have come back and haunted me.'

'From what you've told me, and your father, I've a good idea what sort of woman she was.' He touched her face. 'But you're free of it now.'

She sighed. 'But it's not finished yet, there's Marigold.'

'Your granddaughter! And you a grandmother. When are you going to tell her?'

'I'm not. Grace wants to be the one to talk to her about it, and it must wait until she sees her. What Marigold will say when she finds out, I don't know?'

'She'll be delighted! She loves you, Bess. She was lost when you weren't here and has been following you around like a sheep since you got home. She'd be right beside you now if Dottie hadn't taken her out.'

'I hope she doesn't think badly of me for lying to Grace all these years.'

Harry drew her back into his arms. 'You have nothing to worry about. Nothing at all.'

46

'Do you think she'll change her mind?'

Prune pulled a face. 'No, she won't. I'm sorry.'

'Hey, it's not your fault.' Howard wrapped his good arm around her, hugging her to him. 'We'll wait until you're twenty-one, it's only a few weeks away now.'

'I know, I wish . . .' she shrugged. Her mother's attitude hadn't softened, she was adamant that she'd never give her permission for them to marry. This saddened Prune deeply, especially as they wouldn't need it soon anyway. It would have been so much easier, kinder, and loving for her mother to have given her blessing.

'Maybe your mother will come around when she realises that we are getting married, with or without her approval.'

'I doubt it.'

Howard took hold of Prune's hand as they headed towards Orchard Farm.

'I'll get the paperwork sorted out, and as soon as you're twenty-one, you can sign it yourself and then we're on our way to being married. By my reckoning, we'll be able to marry around the twelfth of May. How does that sound?'

'Wonderful.' Prune smiled happily at him. 'Bessie will make my dress and ones for Marigold and Dottie too. There's enough parachute silk to do all of them and still have plenty to spare.'

'You can relax about me flying on any more missions for a while. The doc says this arm will take a couple of months to heal and get back to full working order again, and because it's my right hand, it needs to be fully functional before I'm fit to fly. I'm on ground-based duties till then.'

'Good. I hated you going on missions.'

'I know, honey. At least the Peggy Sue didn't let us down, even when she was done for, we all got out.'

When they reached the farm gate, Prune stopped and warned him, 'Peter wants to hear what happened. He's desperate to find out about the Peggy Sue.'

'It's okay. He flew in her too. I'm happy to talk about it, and grateful no one died.'

'Thank goodness.'

'Hey, I told you I'd always come back. And I did.'

Prune kissed him gently. 'I'm delighted you did.'

'Same here.' Howard looked at her, his eyes warm with love.

★ ★ ★

'The flak knocked out two engines. We had no hydraulics or electrical systems and no controls, so we knew the Peggy Sue wouldn't make it home again. Walt ordered us to bail out.'

Prune watched as Howard told his tale. Everyone at Orchard Farm was gathered in the house to hear him; Harry, Bessie, Dottie, Peter and Marigold — all delighted he was back and listening to what had happened to him. As he spoke about failed engines, no controls, and the order to parachute out, an icy finger trailed down Prune's spine because it could've turned out so differently with the entire crew going down with the plane. They'd been fortunate they'd all had time to get out. She and Howard had been given another

283

chance at a life together, and she wasn't going to miss out on that for anyone. Certainly not for her mother and her odious threats.

'What happened to the Peggy Sue?' Peter asked.

'She went down in the ocean, off the coast of Belgium.' Howard paused. 'You know, I kinda like the thought of her being buried at sea, rather than smashed and burnt on the ground. She was a fine plane and deserved a good resting place.'

'You make her sound like a person,' Dottie said.

'She was as important as any of the crew. She carried us safely there and back on all our missions, except the last one . . . we were fond of her.'

Peter leaned forward in his chair. 'What happened when you bailed out?'

'Thankfully, my chute opened, and I could see some of the other guys coming down. It was windy, so we were blown about a bit. I had a bumpy landing and ended up with this.' He held up his plastered arm. 'Luckily, we came down behind Allied lines, so it was safe.'

'Why did you save your parachute?' Marigold asked.

'I thought it would make a good wedding dress for Prune. It would've been a waste to leave it there with material in short supply.'

Bessie laughed. 'It's enough for several wedding dresses.'

'I'm only planning on getting married the once.' Howard winked at Prune.

'What happened next?' Peter looked eager for more of Howard's story.

'I gathered up my parachute as best I could and walked to the nearest farmhouse. They gave me something to eat and drink, then took me to a United States

Army post. From there, they sent me to an army hospital for an operation on my arm; that's why it took longer to get back than the others. I'm sure glad to be here.'

'It's good to have you home,' Harry said. 'Will you have to fly again?'

'No, sir. Not for a while until I'm properly healed.'

'Thank goodness for that,' Bessie said.

'Will Walt and the crew fly again?' Peter asked.

'Yep. They're being given another plane. Walt told me he's gonna name her the Peggy Sue Two.'

Peter nodded, smiling. 'I like that.'

47

April, 1945

'Ow!' Marigold yelped. 'You pricked me.'

Bessie sighed. 'I'm sorry, but you keep jiggling about. It's hard to pin the material when you're moving so much.'

'I can't help it.' Marigold had never felt so excited in all her life. It was like all her Christmases and birthdays rolled into one. 'Is it time to go yet?'

Prune laughed. 'Marigold! That's the fourth time you've asked in the past half hour. Anyone would think something exciting's happening today from the way you're carrying on.'

'It is!' She looked hard at Prune and then giggled. 'You're teasing me.'

'Take no notice of her.' Dottie stood on tiptoes and planted a kiss on Marigold's cheek. 'It's only natural to be excited about seeing your mother again.'

'But we need to get this pinning finished first,' Bessie said firmly. 'I won't be going to the station until it's done.'

From her elevated viewpoint standing on the chair, Marigold looked at Bessie kneeling on the floor, who had a serious, no-nonsense look on her face, which she got when she meant business. She knew Bessie would stick to her word, and Marigold didn't want to risk not being at the station when her mother's train arrived, so she nodded meekly and stood still. She must be patient and wait while Bessie pinned and tucked the material, turning her this way and that. But it was hard.

'That's better.' Bessie's voice was muffled as she spoke with her lips clenched around some pins. 'Good girl.'

'You're doing great,' Prune said. 'You'll soon be done, then it will be my turn.'

Prune had changed out of her usual clothes and, like Marigold, was wearing a dress made from parachute silk — her wedding dress. It wasn't finished yet, but already it looked lovely. The material was smooth and hung to the floor in long drapes, which swished when she walked.

Marigold usually loved the dressmaking sessions with the others. Since Howard had given Prune his parachute, they'd spent hours working on the dresses. It was always a fun time, with lots of laughing and telling of stories. It was only because her mother was coming and she was so desperate to see her again, that she was so jumpy today.

She'd watched Bessie and Prune work out the designs for the dresses first. Bessie had drawn patterns on paper, pinned them onto the material and cut out the pieces, and then sewn them together. Gradually the dresses had grown from drawings into real things they could wear. Marigold had never seen it happen before as her mother bought all her clothes, saying she couldn't sew. It had been wonderful to watch the entire process, and she had asked Bessie to teach her to make clothes. Bessie promised that she would teach her how, but not until after the wedding when there'd be more time.

'All done.' Bessie's voice interrupted her thoughts.

'Really?' Marigold glanced down at the bottom of

her dress, which was bristling with pins.

Bessie nodded. 'All pinned and ready to hem. Dottie, can you help Marigold take it off, so she doesn't get pricked again?'

'Come on, then.' Dottie held out her hand to help her off the chair. 'Hold up your dress and step down gently.'

Wary of the sharp pins, Marigold took care to hold it away from her bare legs as she stepped down.

'Before you ask, we've got to leave here in half an hour,' Bessie said. 'Harry's getting Jenny and the trap ready. So, when you've taken off your dress, put your best clothes on and brush your hair, then we'll be able to go.'

Marigold didn't need to be told twice. 'Thank you.'

'You're welcome. Right, Prune, your turn, let's see if you can stand as still as Marigold did.' Bessie winked at her then turned her attention to the hem at the bottom of the wedding dress.

★ ★ ★

'They'll be out in five minutes.' Peter stroked the pony's velvety nose while Harry held onto her bridle. They'd harnessed her up to the small trap which Bessie would drive to the station, and he'd been into the house to tell them it was ready.

Harry took his watch out of his waistcoat pocket and checked the time. 'If they don't leave soon, they'll be late.'

'Bessie was working on Prune's dress.'

'I reckon it'll be the best wedding dress for miles around, going by the amount of time they've spent on it.'

288

'Will Prune live in America with Howard after they're married?' Peter asked.

'I expect so. Although not till the war's over. It will be strange for her living in a foreign country. Though America sounds a great place from what Howard and Clem have told us. I expect she'll do fine there.'

'Do you think I've done well since I came to live in a new country?'

'You have, lad.' Harry smiled at him. 'The way you've settled in and become one of us, I often forget you weren't born here.'

Peter recalled the day he'd arrived on the boat from Holland, not knowing anyone here. He had been so scared. How things had changed since then. 'At least I can speak English now.'

'You soon learned how to. You knew more English than we did German.'

'Now I know English better than German.' He frowned. 'I've forgotten a lot of German words.'

'Do you remember much about your home in Austria?'

'Living there seems a long time ago, like another life. My memories of it are misty. I can't remember it all, just bits.' He closed his eyes to help him focus. 'I remember our home, the smell of Mama's cooking. My best friend, Otto.' A picture of his friend's face grew in his mind. 'His parents tried to get him a place on the train I was on, but they couldn't.' He had no idea what had happened to him. Had he left on a later train and was living somewhere else in England? He hoped so.

He opened his eyes and met Harry's. 'I remember some nasty things too. Things we weren't allowed to do anymore, like going to school.' He sighed. 'I never thought I'd come to England on my own.'

'You were very brave.'

Peter poked at a stone with the toe of his boot. 'I'm not sure if I was brave, because it felt like an adventure at first. I didn't really know what was happening until we got to England.'

'Would you like to return to Austria when the war's over?'

'I don't know, it depends on where my parents are. I couldn't go back without them. My home's here for now.'

'And for as long as you want and need it to be.' Harry put his hand on Peter's shoulder. 'The war won't last much longer. They've almost reached Berlin, so it must soon end.'

'What will happen then?'

'The fighting will stop, and our soldiers can come home. Life will return to normal.'

'What about the Americans?'

'They'll go back to America. It'll be a lot quieter around here without them,' Harry said. 'We'll miss them.'

It was hard to imagine life without the war. It had been going on for so long now, they'd lived with it day after day. It would seem strange when it finally ended, even though it's what everyone wanted. But after the war . . . Peter didn't know what would happen, where he'd be or who with. He wouldn't know where his future lay until he found out where his parents were and what had happened to them. When the news came, would it be good? He desperately hoped it would be . . . But what if it wasn't?

'Here they come.' Harry nodded towards the house where Bessie and Marigold were hurrying down the steps.

'It's time to go.' Marigold's voice was high with excitement as she rushed across the yard.

'Let me help you up.' Peter offered his hand and helped her into the trap. He was pleased for her. She hadn't been able to visit her mother in the convalescent home as it was too far away, but now the day had finally arrived when they'd be reunited. Who wouldn't feel happy about that?

48

It still looked the same, Grace thought, watching the Norfolk countryside passing by outside the train window. There were plenty of signs of wartime, the crisscrossed paper on windows, sandbags piled up at stations, servicemen and women on the trains and platforms, but deep down it was the same familiar landscape that she'd known so well.

Grace eased out her legs, stretching them as far as she could, as hours of sitting on trains were making them ache.

'Are you all right?' the WAAF servicewoman who sat opposite her across the compartment asked. 'I'll move along so you can stretch your legs out properly.'

'No, I'm fine, thank you. They're at full stretch now.' Grace smiled. 'It's just they were both broken recently and ache a bit if I sit for too long.'

'Breaking both legs is hard,' the WAAF said. 'If it's only one, the other can take the strain. How did it happen?'

'V2 rocket blast, in London. But I'm lucky, I survived. I'll soon be able to walk again without those.' She nodded towards her walking sticks propped in the corner by the window. 'I'm glad to be out of hospital and on my way home.'

'It's great you're heading home again,' the WAAF said, sympathetically.

Home, Grace thought; that had slipped out without her thinking. Her home for the last ten years had been London, but thinking of Orchard Farm in that

292

way again after all this time gave her a warm glow.

Over the weeks while she'd been convalescing, Grace had had a lot of time to think about how the foundations of her life had shifted after Bessie's revelation. It was taking a while to change the habit of a lifetime, and now think of the woman whom she'd believed was her mother, as her grandmother, and Bessie as her mother instead. But she was gradually growing used to it, and it felt right because Bessie had been like a mother to her in everything but name.

The other thing that had been concerning Grace was what she wanted for her and Marigold's future. She'd come to a decision which she hoped Marigold would also feel happy with, because it would completely change their lives.

The train slowed and from the sight of familiar landmarks, the square tower of St Andrew's church, the tall elms outside the village, Grace knew where she was. They were coming into Rackbridge. A wave of excitement surged through her — she was about to see her daughter again.

As they pulled in alongside the platform, Grace caught sight of Marigold and Bessie waiting for her and waved to them, hoping they'd spot her as the carriage slid past them and came to a halt.

Grabbing her sticks, she stood up.

'Let me help you with your things,' the WAAF offered. 'Is that yours?' She pointed to Grace's brown leather case in the overhead luggage rack.

'Yes. Thank you.'

Grace reached out to open the door but was beaten to it as it was pulled open from the outside by her daughter.

'Mummy!' Marigold shrieked.

Her throat tightened. 'Hello, darling.'

'Hello, Grace.' Bessie greeted her warmly. 'Step back a moment, Marigold. I need to help your mummy out, then you can give her a hug.'

With the help of Bessie and the WAAF, Grace carefully lowered herself onto the platform. Then Marigold gently and lovingly, put her arms around her and hugged her tightly. Leaning on one stick, Grace wrapped her free arm around her daughter and dropped a kiss on Marigold's hair, delighted to be reunited.

'Thank you for your help,' Grace heard Bessie say. She glanced up to see the WAAF passing her case out to Bessie.

'That's some welcome home.' The WAAF smiled at them. 'Lucky you.'

She nodded. 'Yes, I am lucky. Thank you for your help.'

'My pleasure. Goodbye then.' The WAAF pulled the door closed and with a wave settled back in her seat.

Grace looked over Marigold's head at Bessie, whose face was warm with love as she watched them, her daughter and granddaughter together.

'It's good to see you.' Bessie leaned over and kissed Grace's cheek.

Marigold loosened her hold around Grace's middle and looked up at her. 'We came in the trap, so you don't have to walk back. It's this way.' She held out her hand for Grace to take.

'I'm sorry, I can't hold your hand while I'm using these sticks. But you could hold on to my elbow instead?'

Her daughter frowned as she regarded the walking

sticks. 'Why have you got them, I thought your legs were better?'

'They are, but I still walk a little stiffly and they help me balance. The doctor told me I won't need them for much longer.'

'It's this way.' Marigold gently took hold of Grace's elbow. 'When we get home, I'll show you where everything is. Don't worry, you'll soon learn your way around.'

Grace caught Bessie's eye, and they smiled at each other, clearly thinking the same thing. Marigold had no idea that she didn't need to be shown where anything was because she already knew, but her daughter didn't know that. Not yet.

★　★　★

'Here's Orchard Farm,' Marigold proudly announced as the pony automatically turned in at the gateway.

Grace had dreamed about this place so many times over the years, and now she was finally back. It looked the same, the barn and sheds, the gate leading to the orchard, and the house which was so different from their terraced home in London. She couldn't take her eyes off it. It was just as she remembered, except for the paper strips that crisscrossed the windows. It was still painted the same deep green.

Marigold noticed her staring. 'That's the house where we live. Remember, I told you about it in a letter, it's made from two railway carriages.'

Before she could reply, a familiar voice called out. 'Grace!'

It was Harry. The sight of him limping across the yard towards the trap jolted her. When she'd last seen him, his thick hair had been a dark brown, now it was streaked with silver — but then, that had been ten years ago. The evidence of the passing time on him sent a dart of anguish through her. She should have returned long ago. But there was no turning the clock back, it was what she did now, and in the future, which was important.

Grace smiled warmly at him. 'Hello, Harry.'

Walking close behind him was a boy who must be Peter, going from the description Marigold had written in one of her letters. He smiled shyly, taking hold of the pony's bridle to steady her while they got out of the trap.

'Mummy walks with sticks,' Marigold informed Harry as he opened the trap's little door, ready to help them out.

Grace noticed Harry's eyes dart to the walking sticks propped up by her case.

'Like I did when I got my new leg, they're good for helping you get moving again.' He winked at Grace.

'The doctor says Mummy won't need them for much longer,' her daughter added taking his hand and climbing down the steps, jumping to the ground from the final one. Turning back to her, she added, 'You mustn't jump the last bit, Mummy.'

Grace laughed. 'I'm not going to.'

Marigold watched, eagle-eyed, as she slid herself along the bench seat and took Harry's offered hand, her eyes meeting his. 'It's good to see you.'

He nodded. 'You, too.' He held onto her hand as she carefully climbed down and stepped gently to the ground.

Bessie passed her the walking sticks, and with them in place to keep her balanced, Grace took her first steps back at Orchard Farm. As she did so, a warm rush of contentment radiated through her. She'd finally come home.

Looking around, she was eager to go everywhere and see everything, take part in life on the farm again. But she couldn't do it all, not yet. There would be plenty of time and no need to hurry. She was going to enjoy being here with Marigold.

49

'That's enough story for tonight.' Grace closed the book and put it on the chest of drawers beside the bed.

'A bit more, Mummy, please.'

'No. I'll read you some more tomorrow.' She took hold of Marigold's hand. 'I need to talk to you.'

'What about?'

'Something important.' Grace hesitated; was this the right moment to tell her? But if not now, then when? Tomorrow? Was there ever a good time to explain to someone that you hadn't been completely honest with them?

'Mummy?' Marigold's voice broke into her thoughts. 'Do you enjoy living here?'

'Yes, I love it.'

'What do you especially like about it?'

'Everything, everybody, the people and the animals. I enjoy helping on the farm and being in the countryside.' Marigold frowned. 'Why are you asking me, I thought you were going to tell me something important?'

'I am.' She smoothed the eiderdown with her hand. 'I wanted to ask what you thought first.' Her mouth had gone dry and her heart raced. Grace met her daughter's eyes. 'I'm glad you like it here . . . because I did when I was a child.'

'Did you come and visit?'

'Not exactly . . .' She paused, biting her lip. 'You see, I grew up here.'

298

Marigold looked confused. 'I don't understand.'

'I haven't told you everything about my life, only bits of it. I hid important things from you and I'm sorry. I thought I was doing the right thing at the time. But now I realise it wasn't the best thing for you. Or me.' The words tumbled out of her.

'What are you talking about, Mummy?'

'It's a long story.' Grace stopped and stretched out her legs.

'Are they hurting?' Marigold's face was full of concern.

'They're aching a bit. I need to stand up and stretch them out.' She grabbed her sticks and eased herself off the bed to standing, then walked around the room, up and down for a couple of minutes. Once the ache had faded, she sat down on the bed.

'Lie down beside me.' Marigold threw back her covers and motioned for Grace to come in. 'You can stretch your legs out while you tell me your story. You'll be comfortable and warm at the same time.'

'Good idea.' She carefully lowered herself down beside her daughter, who threw the blankets over them both.

'Comfy?'

'Yes, thank you.' Grace smiled at Marigold, who lay on her side facing her, her head propped up with her elbow. 'Right. My long story. Well . . . I suppose the best place to start is at the beginning.' If she'd told Marigold this a few months ago, before Bessie had revealed who she was, then it would have been a slightly different tale. The one she was now about to tell was the truth; what had gone before didn't count anymore and would only be confusing. Perhaps she would tell her, eventually. Or she might not. The true story from the past and what effect it had on the future was what was important here.

'Mummy!'

'I'm sorry, I was gathering my thoughts and getting everything straight in my mind. Right, from the beginning . . . I was born in a village about fifteen miles north of here in 1915. My father was a soldier, and my mother was a VAD nurse . . .'

'Like Bessie.' Marigold interrupted. 'She was a VAD nurse, too.'

'Yes, she was . . . you see . . .' Grace's voice wavered. 'Bessie is my mother.'

Grace watched the colour drain from Marigold's face, her blue eyes wide as she stared at her. She could see her daughter's mind working furiously, trying to make sense of what she'd been told. Then, to her relief, a smile curved at the corners of her mouth.

'If Bessie's your mother, then that means she's my grandmother and Harry's my grandfather.'

'You're half right. There's a lot more of my story,' Grace said. 'Harry isn't my actual father. Though he brought me up as good as any father could. My real father died in France during the Great War. He and Bessie were going to be married on his next leave, but it never happened. Bessie found out she was expecting me.' She paused for a moment and then went on. 'For a woman to have a baby when she's not married, well . . . lots of people didn't approve of it, they still don't even now. After she had me, her mother, my grandmother and your great-grandmother looked after me. When I was a few weeks old, Bessie returned to working as a VAD. She met Harry a few years later.'

'And they got married,' Marigold said.

'Yes, they married after the war was over, and I came

to live with them here when I was three. My grandmother had died from Spanish flu not long before I
moved here.'

Marigold's forehead creased in a frown. 'Why didn't
you tell me who Bessie and Harry really were before
I came here? You always said your parents were dead.'

Grace's stomach knotted. Marigold had asked the
obvious question, and if she was going to tell her the
truth, then it had to be all of it. She hoped she would
understand.

She turned so that she was lying on her side, looking directly at her daughter. 'Because I thought they'd
both died. I only found out a little while ago, that who
I believed was my mother, was actually my grandmother. You see, I didn't know Bessie was really my
mother, I'd always been told she was my sister.'

'Your sister? Why?'

'Remember how people think badly of unmarried
mothers and their children. Well, my grandmother
offered to raise me as her daughter because she wanted
to protect me and Bessie, and thought that was the
best way to do it. Otherwise, Bessie and I could have
ended up in the workhouse.' Grace stroked Marigold's
hair. 'My grandmother insisted Bessie promise never
to tell me who she really was. And she didn't. Not
even after my grandmother died, and I came to live
here with her and Harry. Bessie hated not telling me,
but she kept her promise, even though it hurt her.'

Marigold pulled a face. 'That's sad, poor Bessie.
How did you find out she's your mother?'

'She told me when she visited me in St Thomas'.
I'm glad she did because it was the right thing to do.
Bessie had been forced to make that promise when
she didn't want to and had kept it for too long.'

Marigold nodded and lay silently, absorbing everything she'd been told, cuddling her toy rabbit. Grace was grateful that she was taking the news calmly and seemed happy that Bessie was her grandmother, and Harry as good as any grandfather.

'Mummy, why didn't you tell me about Bessie and Harry and growing up here?'

'Because I was foolish.' She sighed. 'I did something I wasn't proud of, and I was too stubborn to go back and say sorry. I tried to forget about my life here and stayed in London. I never lied to you, Marigold, but I didn't tell you everything. I'm sorry, it was wrong of me.'

'What did you do?'

'When I was eighteen, I met a young man from London while I was working for Bessie's cousin who had a guesthouse in Sheringham, down on the coast. He was staying there, and I thought myself in love with him, and he with me. He wanted me to move to London and spun a yarn, tempting me with a tale of bright lights and fancy living.' She had been such a gullible fool, and it had cost her dearly. 'Bessie and Harry advised me not to go, not straight away. You see, I hardly knew him and yet I was prepared to leave everything and go to London to be near him. I foolishly believed I might even marry him one day. I wouldn't listen to anyone's advice and . . . I ran away on my own.'

Marigold gasped. 'What happened? Was that Daddy?'

Grace shook her head. 'No. He was a far better man than the one I left my home for. When I got to London, I discovered that he'd given me a false address, and I never saw him again. I'd made a massive

302

mistake.'

'What did you do?'

'I got a job in service for a while. Then I trained as a nurse and met your daddy. After we got married you came along.'

Marigold looked thoughtful. 'But why didn't you come back here?'

'Because I was young and foolish.' Grace shrugged. 'And far too stubborn for my own good, and I was afraid they wouldn't want me here after I ran off.' She blinked against threatening tears.

'Bessie and Harry wouldn't have turned you away.'

'I know that now. I wanted to return so many times, but the longer I left it, the harder it became.'

'Why didn't you tell me?' Marigold asked.

'Because it was simpler to tell you the bare facts. It made it easier for me to forget.' She took a deep breath. 'But then the war came, and your . . .' Grace's voice wavered. 'Your daddy was killed . . .' She paused to compose herself. 'Then when the rockets started falling with no warning, I had to get you out of London. This was the best place to send you, I knew you'd be safe here, well cared for and with people I trusted.' Her tears spilled over, running down her cheeks.

'Don't cry, Mummy.' Marigold put her arms around Grace and hugged her.

'Aren't you angry with me for not telling you the truth?'

The little girl shook her head. 'No. Though I think you were silly not to come back straight away. I'm glad you sent me here. I love it. And I love Bessie and Harry as well.'

'How would you feel if we didn't return to London after the war?'

'You mean not go back and live in Mrs Fox's house?'

Grace nodded. 'We could stay here in Norfolk, rent a house somewhere near here, and I could get some nursing work again as soon as I'm fit. Would you like that?'

Marigold's face broke into a beaming smile. 'I'd love it. I'd still be able to see Bessie and Harry, and Mrs Fox could come and stay with us for a holiday. I want to stay here.'

Grace laughed and hugged her daughter tightly. What a lovely, thoughtful child she'd grown into. Taking the chance to send her to live away from her had been worth every minute of missing her. Marigold was safe and, at last, she knew where and who she came from. They both did.

* * *

'Mummy told me about your secret promise.'

Bessie stopped stirring the porridge and pushed the saucepan off the heat, her stomach suddenly leaden. She turned to face Marigold, who sat in the armchair near the stove watching her, relieved that it was only the two of them in here. Harry and Peter were out doing the milking, and everyone else was still in bed. This was something Bessie needed to talk with the child about on their own.

'What did she tell you?' Her voice wobbled, betraying the turmoil inside her.

'That you're my grandmother!' Marigold jumped off the chair and flung her arms around her. 'What shall I call you?'

Bessie's throat tightened as she hugged the little girl. Was it going to be this simple? she wondered;

304

Marigold, accepting the truth so well. But then, Bessie wasn't a stranger being thrust upon the child and told that she was her grandmother. The child had got to know her properly, after living with her, day after day.

Marigold loosened her hold and stepped back, looking up at her. 'Should I call you Granny?'

'If you want to.' Bessie's voice caught in her throat. 'What do you think of me being your . . . granny? And your mummy being my daughter?'

'I think it's wonderful, Bessie. I mean . . . Granny.' Marigold giggled. 'If I had to choose someone to be my granny, then I'd pick you.' She looked thoughtful. 'But I think it's sad you weren't allowed to tell Mummy who you really were.'

'There were good reasons for it.' She tucked a loose strand of Marigold's blonde hair back behind her ear. 'But at least Grace knows who I am now, and so do you.'

'Mummy said you and her could have ended up in the workhouse.'

She nodded. 'Perhaps. It happened to some unmarried mothers and their babies. I was lucky my parents helped me.'

'Will she call you Mother now instead of Bessie?'

'I'm not sure. Grace has called me Bessie all her life, so it might be hard to change now. I don't mind if she doesn't. It's enough that she knows who I am.'

'Can I call Harry Grandad?'

Bessie smiled. 'I think he'd like that.' He would, she knew it. 'I'd better get on with the porridge or it won't be ready for breakfast.' She moved to the stove and pulled the saucepan back onto the heat and started stirring again.

'Wait, I've got something else to tell you. It's important.' Marigold took a deep breath. 'We're not going to go back to London after the war. We want to live here in Norfolk.'

Bessie dropped the wooden spoon in the porridge, staring at Marigold, who hopped from foot to foot with excitement, a smile on her face. 'Are you sure?'

'It's true.' Grace stood in the door of her bedroom, leaning on her sticks.

'I had a lot of time to think about what I wanted to do while I was in hospital, and I've decided I'd like to come back and live here. I'll rent somewhere and get a job nursing again. Be a district nurse, I've always fancied that.'

Bessie opened her mouth to speak, but no words came out. She swallowed and tried again. 'That's wonderful news.' She rushed over and threw her arms around her daughter, hugging her close.

'You're pleased?' Grace's eyes were glistening when Bessie released her.

'I'm delighted! You're welcome to live here with Harry and me for as long as you need. This is your home if you want it to be.'

The smell of something burning reached Bessie's nose. 'The porridge!' She hurried across the room and grabbed the saucepan off the stove. Stirring the spoon around, she revealed a thick black layer sticking to the bottom of the pan.

The door opened, and Harry came in carrying a jug of milk. 'What's that smell?'

'Burnt porridge,' Bessie said. 'But it doesn't matter.' She pushed the saucepan to the back of the stove. 'We've got something much more important to tell you.'

'Can I tell Grandad?' Marigold asked.

She watched Harry as what the little girl had called him sank in. The look on his face spoke a thousand words.

'Marigold, you'd better tell . . .' Bessie caught his eye and winked at him, 'your grandad, what's going on.'

307

50

Bessie glanced at the clock on the mantelpiece. It was one minute to three. Harry, who stood behind her chair, laid a hand on her shoulder and she grasped it, glad of his support.

Everyone was waiting. Grace sat in the opposite armchair with Marigold on her lap. While Dottie, Peter and Prune stood in a row, their arms linked. The room was silent except for the hum from the wireless and the clock ticking down the seconds until the sound of Big Ben's chimes rang out. Bessie stiffened. One, two, three, she counted as the rich, resonating tone of the bell filled the air.

'This is London, the prime minister Winston Churchill . . .' the announcer declared.

Then Churchill's deep tones spoke out through the wireless and she closed her eyes, focusing on his words announcing the Germans' surrender. The war in Europe was over. Bessie sighed with relief. They'd known this was coming, but she hadn't been able to believe it until she heard it from Churchill himself. Her throat tightened and tears smarted behind her eyelids. It was finally over.

'Have we won?' Marigold asked.

'Shhh!' Grace said.

Bessie opened her eyes and smiled at her grand-daughter, listening as Churchill reminded them that there was still work to be done. The war against Japan wasn't yet won, but it would be, she thought. It was only a matter of time, and then the world would be at peace again.

'It's over!' Dottie said as Harry turned off the wireless at the end of Churchill's speech. 'It's really over.'

The two young women hugged Peter between them. Bessie stood up and walked into Harry's open arms. Resting her head on his chest, her mind drifted back to the last time she'd heard that a war was over — Armistice Day, 1918. She'd never dreamed they would be in the same position again. Once was enough, twice was too much. Bessie never wanted to go through a war ever again as long as she lived.

'Listen!' Peter said. 'They're ringing the church bells.'

Everyone paused, listening as the sound of pealing bells floated in from St Andrew's down in the village.

* * *

'It's a shame they're all confined to base,' Prune said. 'I'd love to have celebrated with Howard tonight.'

She and Dottie were sitting on the farm gate watching the light show over Rackbridge base. Bessie, Harry, Grace and the children had been out there with them enjoying the spectacle, but had just gone inside as it was late.

'It's probably for their own good,' Dottie said. 'Going by what they're getting up to on the base tonight, can you imagine if they'd been let loose in the village in such high spirits? The constable would have had forty fits.'

Prune laughed. 'I suppose you're right.'

'You can't blame them though. They must be so

relieved and happy now they never have to face flying over Germany again. No more never knowing whether they'll come back from a mission or not. It's over for them, and they can go home soon.'

Another burst of flares exploded upwards in arcs over the base, lighting up the darkness with red and green glows, like a beautiful firework display.

Dottie sighed happily. 'It's good to see the sky lit up again after years of hiding away in the darkness. Life's going to get back to normal, although it's been so long, I'm not sure I can remember what that is anymore. And you . . .' she nudged Prune, 'will soon be married. Only three more days to go. Are you getting nervous?'

'No, not at all. I've never been so certain about anything in all my life.'

'Do you think your mother will turn up?'

'I'm not expecting her to.' Prune's mother had maintained a deathly silence, not replying to her last letter in which she'd told her where and when, her wedding would be and inviting her to come. 'It's entirely up to her. I've invited her, and she knows the time and place. I am going to marry Howard and if that means she cuts me out of her life, then it's her loss. I'm not the one closing the door.'

Dottie linked her arm through Prune's. 'Perhaps she'll have a change of heart and turn up on the day to surprise you. You're her only child and you'll be off to live in America soon, and it'll be much harder to come and see you there.'

Prune pulled a face. 'I know that, you know that, and so would any sensible person, but I'm afraid my mother's stubborn and opinionated, and her ridiculous views hold her back.'

310

'You never know, she might come round.'

'That's up to her . . . I'm not going to let it spoil my wedding day.'

Whoosh! More flares zoomed skywards and exploded over the base in an arc of light.

Dottie gasped. 'Look at that! It's so pretty. Looking on the bright side, at least Howard's parents are happy about the wedding.'

Prune nodded. 'They've been so kind, writing to me and welcoming me into their family already. His mother seems warm and friendly, nothing like mine.'

51

12th May, 1945

Bessie stepped back and surveyed the dress. 'Lovely . . . it fits you like a glove.' She smiled at Prune. 'You look beautiful. Howard's going to . . .'

'Hardly recognise you.' Dottie grabbed hold of Prune's hand. 'Only kidding! Bessie's right though, you look wonderful. You've scrubbed up well for a Timber Jill.'

'You've turned out nicely yourself,' Prune said, looking at her friend in her parachute-silk matron of honour dress. 'Shame you're not walking out with some nice GI too. Perhaps one of Howard's friends might take your fancy today?'

'You know I'm going to be a career girl.' Dottie put a hand on her hip. 'I am perfectly happy the way I am.'

'Shame. We could've had a double wedding . . .' Prune teased, her eyes sparkling, and her cheeks slightly flushed.

'One bride is enough to cope with,' Bessie said. 'How long have we got, Dottie? Can you check the time for me?'

Dottie put her head around the bedroom door and looked at the clock on the mantelpiece. 'It's one o'clock.'

Bessie nodded. 'Half an hour until we need to leave. I'll check how Grace is getting on with Marigold.' She paused in the doorway. 'Try to keep her calm, Dottie.'

Popping into Marigold and Grace's room, Bessie saw

everything was under control. Marigold was already wearing her bridesmaid dress and Grace was doing her hair, taking out the rags and carefully shaping the curls around her fingers.

'You look lovely, Marigold,' Bessie said. 'Can I do anything to help?

Grace shook her head. 'You sit down for five minutes, you've been busy all morning.'

'I won't argue with that.' A sit down was much needed, Bessie thought; it would be a chance to rest and gather her thoughts before the wedding started.

Settling down in the armchair by the stove, she stretched out her legs and pushed herself back into the chair. She'd only closed her eyes for a few minutes when Harry's voice made her jump.

'Bessie.'

She looked at him standing in front of her, smart in his suit. He rarely wore it, which was a pity because he looked so handsome in it. From the expression on his face, she knew something was wrong. 'This has just come for Peter in the post.' He held out a white envelope bearing a French stamp, with Peter's name and address typed on the front.

Bessie's heart plummeted. He hadn't received a letter from anyone for ages, not since his parents' last one. She took the envelope, examining it carefully, but there was no clue who it was from.

'Should we give it to him?' Harry asked.

'Does he know about it?'

'No. I took it from the postboy.'

'I'm not sure.' Bessie sighed. 'For it to arrive today, of all days . . . with Prune's wedding . . .' Her eyes met his. 'It could be bad news.'

'That's what I thought.'

'If it is . . . then it would spoil the day for him and everyone else.' Bessie frowned. 'I think we should give it to him tomorrow. One more day won't make a difference.'

'It's addressed to the lad and I think he should have it. He's waited long enough, and I know he'd prefer to get it today.'

'How do you know what he'd want?' She asked. This was the last thing they needed on Prune's wedding day. Bessie didn't want to risk the young woman's special day being blighted, not after all she'd been through with Howard going missing.

'Because he told me. When Grace was injured, he was adamant Marigold should know. It upset him deeply that she was being kept in the dark, and he said if it was him, then he'd want to be told. Straight away.'

'I don't know.' Bessie bit her bottom lip.

'How would you feel if it was you?'

'I'd want to know, of course, but I'm an adult. He's a child.'

'Not such a child as some. I think we should give it to him. If it's bad news, then we must deal with it.' Harry encouraged her. 'But it might not be.'

'You decide, I can't....' She glanced at the clock; it was ten past one. 'We need to leave for the church in twenty minutes.'

Harry stooped to kiss her cheek and went back outside.

Bessie sighed. Of all the days for a letter to come, this had to be the worst. What would they do if it was bad news? They'd have to try to keep it from everyone.

She was about to get up when Peter burst in through

the door, the white envelope clutched in his hand. He rushed past her without saying a word and straight into his room, Bessie's old sewing room, which he'd swapped with Marigold now Grace was staying here.

★ ★ ★

He stared at the front of the envelope where his name was printed in black type. Peter Rosenfeld, then Orchard Farm's address, with the word Angleterre, added at the bottom and a French stamp in the corner. From France. Who did he know in France? No one. What was this about? Why were they writing to him? He never had any post, not since his parents stopped writing. There was only one way to find out. Open it.

His hands were shaking so much, he could hardly open the envelope. He grabbed a pencil, thrust it into the top and slit it open. Inside was a single sheet of paper. With his heart racing, he pulled the letter out, unfolded it and stared down at the words, which misted and twisted out of focus as his eyes filled with tears.

Peter wiped his eyes with the back of his hand and read the once familiar writing. His father's.

Dear Peter, he read, glad it was written in English.

We are so happy to be able to write to you again. Both of us are alive and well. We have spent three years hiding here in France. Hidden by a wonderful woman who risked her life for us, and we have been fortunate to survive. All those years in hiding, we thought of you

315

every day and hoped you were well and happy. Not being able to tell you of our plan to go into hiding was difficult, but essential. We could not reveal it for fear the letter would fall into the wrong hands and our secret be exposed. Now the war is over, and we are free again. We will come and find you as soon as we can.

We send you our fondest love.

Papa & Mama

They were alive. Gulping sobs surged up, making his body shake as he cried. All the worries he'd been carrying dissolved away, replaced by a huge sense of relief. He had been so scared that his parents had been taken to a concentration camp and become victims of the Nazis' wicked regime. But miraculously they had survived, hidden by a kind person, and now his family would be together again.

Breathing steadier and feeling calmer, he lay back and stared at the letter. Re-reading it, word by word, searching for every meaning, every ounce of information.

'Peter?' Bessie's voice called from the other side of the curtain. 'Can I come in?'

'Yes.'

Bessie pulled the curtain aside, and he saw the colour drain from her face as she looked at him.

'It's all right,' Peter said. 'They're alive.' He held the letter up. 'My parents are alive.' His voice broke, and he started to cry again.

'Thank God.' Bessie swooped down and wrapped her arms around him, sitting on the bed and cradling him to her.

Peter closed his eyes and let Bessie's warm arms comfort him. His tears soon stopped, and a sense of peace and contentment filled him. When he heard someone else come quietly into the room, he opened his eyes. It was Harry. He stood looking down at him, his face full of concern.

'They're alive. My parents are alive.'

Harry let out a sigh and put his hand on Peter's shoulder. 'That's the best news. I'm so pleased for you, lad. Where are they?'

'In France.' He looked at the address at the top of the letter. 'Near a place called Orange. They've been in hiding and will come and find me as soon as they can.'

'We'll welcome them here,' Bessie said. 'I look forward to meeting them.'

'Where is everyone?' Dottie's voice called from the main room. 'It's nearly time to go or we'll be . . .' Her words dried up when she looked around the curtain and saw Peter, Bessie and Harry.

'Peter's had some good news,' Bessie said.

'I've had a letter from my parents, they're in France.'

Dottie squealed and rushed over to hug him. 'That's wonderful, Peter. I'm so happy for you.' Straightening up she said, 'I know it's traditional for the bride to be late, but we don't want to get Howard too worried, do we?'

'The wedding!' Bessie gasped. 'I almost forgot. Come on everyone, we've got a wedding to go to.'

52

'Are they ready?' Bessie whispered to Dottie, who was peering through the church door.

Dottie nodded, stepping back. 'Howard looks nervous.'

'That's normal. Though our bride . . .' Bessie smiled at Harry, Prune and Marigold as they walked towards them, 'is quite calm and serene looking.'

'You look beautiful.' Dottie adjusted Prune's dress so that the skirt fell as it should.

'Howard's going to be thrilled . . .' Bessie halted, her attention drawn to the soldier who'd walked in through the church gate and was striding up the path towards them, a beaming smile on his face. 'It can't be . . . Harry, look!'

'Hello, Mum.'

Bessie rushed into his open arms and George picked her off her feet and hugged her tightly.

'What are you doing here?' She asked as he put her back on the ground.

'I came over with some POWs on a transport plane. I've got a seventy-two-hour pass, so I thought I'd come home. Hello, Dad.'

She watched her husband and son embrace, blinking away tears. How wonderful to have George arrive today. It truly was a day of celebration.

The parson appeared in the doorway, signalling it was time for the wedding to begin.

'We'll see you inside.' Bessie smiled at the bridal party and linked her arm through George's and led him into the church.

'How did you know we'd be here?' she whispered as they took their places in the pew beside Grace, who'd thrown her arms around George as he sat down next to her.

'When I got off the train, our vigilant stationmaster told me where you'd all be,' George said, softly.

The first few notes of the music blasted out of the organ and Bessie rose to her feet along with the rest of the congregation, a mix of British and Americans. Each one of them here to see Prune and Howard make their vows to each other, and to wish them well for their future life together.

* * *

Bessie thought Orchard Farm had never looked more beautiful. The apple trees were full of pink blossom, its gentle perfume filling the air and attracting a humming orchestra of bees. Arching high above them, the perfect blue sky was dotted with chattering swallows.

'Penny for them?' She smiled at Harry as he slipped his arm around her waist.

She let out a contented sigh. 'I was thinking how lovely everything looks. And . . .' she gestured with her arm, 'how wonderful it is to have everyone here together.'

He nodded. 'And George home.'

'That's a bonus.' Her heart was full to bursting with happiness. 'It's as if we've come out the other end of the tunnel. We made it through and have a lot to be thankful for. Now we can get on with our lives again without the war hanging over us. We're free.'

George took another Norfolk shortcake from the delicious spread of food and drink set up on a table beneath the boughs of an apple tree, and bit into it.

'Hey, that's the second one of them you've had in a couple of minutes,' Dottie said, watching him eat it. 'Don't they feed you in the army?'

'Not on delicious food like this.' He waved the last piece of shortcake before popping it into his mouth. 'Ma's cooking is the best.'

'I agree with you.'

'Anyway, how do you know it was my second one?' George raised his eyebrows. 'Are you keeping an eye on me?'

Dottie's cheeks grew warm. 'Well, I er . . .' What should she say? She had been watching him but wasn't going to admit it. 'Bessie asked me to look after the food and make sure everyone has something to eat. I happened to notice that you seemed to be fond of those shortcakes, that's all.'

George grinned at her. 'Would you like some?' He took another shortcake from the pile on the plate and broke it in half. 'Share one with me?'

Dottie smiled, looking into his eyes, which were a beautiful clear blue, full of light like the sky soaring above them. 'All right, then. Thank you.'

★ ★ ★

'Your parents are in France then?' Clem asked.

'Yes, they were hiding there all this time, and I never knew.' Peter could still hardly believe it. He'd read their letter so many times now that he could recite it

320

by heart.

'I'm real happy for you.' Clem patted his shoulder. 'You must've been worried about them.'

'I was.' He had done his best to get on with life in England, and worked hard at school, but all the time there'd been the nagging worry about his parents. What was happening to them? And lately, were they even alive? He'd been so fortunate they had survived and one day, they'd come here to find him and then they could rebuild their lives together. 'I can't wait to see them again. And you'll be going back to America soon.'

Clem took a sip of his ginger beer. 'Yep, we'll be shipping out as soon as we can. Everyone's eager to get back to their families. It's a long time since I was there and I'm ready to go home.'

'You've liked England though, haven't you?' Peter asked.

'I sure have. Meeting all you folks, who made us so welcome, and visiting old buildings. I love the old churches and castles; we have nothing like that back home.'

★ ★ ★

'How are you feeling, Mrs Peterson?'

Prune beamed at her husband. 'Extremely happy.'

'I'm glad to hear it,' Howard said. 'You're not upset your mom didn't show up?'

'No, not really. I honestly didn't think she'd come, though I suppose deep down, part of me hoped she would.'

He pulled her into his arms. 'It's a shame, and I'm sorry she feels that way. We could visit her if you like,

321

she might change her mind if she saw us together, especially now we're married.'

'No, we could get there, and she won't even see us. It's better to wait for her to change her mind . . . if she ever does.' She sighed. 'Your parents are completely different though; they've been so welcoming to me.'

'They're looking forward to meeting you.'

'I hope you've only told them good things.'

Howard smiled at Prune, his eyes holding hers. 'There are only good things to say about you. I am a lucky guy. I got through the war and now I'm taking a fabulous wife home with me to keep.'

★ ★ ★

'Ready?' Grace asked.

Marigold nodded and picked up the basket with a red and white gingham cloth draped over the top.

'Let's go, take it nice and steady so we don't drop anything.' She followed her daughter out of the house carrying the wedding cake which Bessie had made for Prune and Howard. It had no traditional white icing because of the rationing, but instead was decorated with delicate violets and primroses dipped in precious sugar, which sparkled in the sunshine.

'Are you all right, Mummy?' Marigold walked beside her across the farmyard, towards the orchard where the reception was in full swing.

She smiled at her daughter, who looked lovely in her parachute-silk bridesmaid dress. 'Yes, I'm fine.' Marigold had been like a mother hen, fussing over her ever since she'd arrived here. She still kept a careful check on Grace, even though she was finally free of her walking sticks. It was good to be back with her daughter and here on the farm with Bessie and Harry. She felt like she'd truly come home and returned to her family again.

'Do you think Prune's going to like her surprise? We've done ever so well keeping the secret.' Marigold beamed, showing her missing front tooth. 'We have. She doesn't suspect a thing.'

★ ★ ★

Bessie watched as Prune's eyes filled with tears as she lifted the cloth off the basket, and read the label tied onto the neck of one of the three bottles.

'Are you okay, honey?' Howard slipped his arm around her waist.

Prune nodded. 'It's from my mother.'

'Your mom?'

'It's the champagne my father put away for when I got married. She's been saving them for years.'

'And she sent them here last week with strict instructions not to give them to you until after the wedding,' Bessie explained.

'It was a surprise for you,' Marigold said. 'Do you like it?'

'Yes, very much. I'd forgotten about them . . . but my mother remembered.' Her voice wavered. 'It was kind of her to send them.'

'We should go visit your mom,' Howard said.

Prune nodded and smiled at him, her eyes glittering with unshed tears. 'Soon, before you get shipped back to America.'

'I'm sure she'll be pleased to see you,' Bessie said. 'It will give her a chance to get to know Howard, see what a lovely young man you are.'

323

Howard laughed. 'Whoa, Bessie! You'll have me blushing if you carry on.'

'Let's open them.' Prune took a bottle of champagne out of the basket.

Bessie shook her head. 'You keep them to have on your honeymoon.'

'I want to share them with you all,' Prune said, looking round at everyone. 'You've all been like a family to me and I'd like you to have some.'

'Can I have some too?' Marigold asked.

Prune laughed. 'If it's all right with your mother.'

'You can have a taste of mine,' Grace said.

A few minutes later, after Howard had popped the corks from the bottles, and the champagne poured into an assortment of glasses and cups, and shared around between everyone, Prune raised her glass.

'To my lovely new husband and my dear friends.'

'And to Prune's mom,' Howard added, smiling at his wife.

'And to all mothers,' Grace said, raising her cup and meeting Bessie's eyes.

Bessie looked back at her daughter and smiled happily. 'To all mothers, everywhere.'

Dear Reader,

I hope you've enjoyed reading *Secrets and Promises* as much as I loved writing it. It was my first full-length book, starting off as a plan for a would-be serial in *The People's Friend* magazine, but ending up as a novel! The following year it was published in two linked *People's Friend* pocket novels, and then in 2013, I published it as an ebook under a different name.

Fast forward a few years, and having written my *East End Angels* series, and the start of the new *Women on the Home Front* books, it's been a delight to revisit, re-edit and polish *Secrets and Promises*, and relaunch it so new readers can enjoy it.

It's a book that's dear to my heart, including parts of my family history and upbringing in rural Norfolk. I was fortunate to grow up on a smallholding where things like milking a cow, teaching a calf to drink from a bucket and making butter were part of my life. I didn't realise it at the time, but those experiences would be perfect for my stories one day!

If you're interested in keeping in touch and being the first to know about new books, cover reveals, hearing more about my writing life and behind-the-scenes chat, as well as exclusive competitions, then do sign up to join my Readers Club and get my newsletter delivered to your inbox.

I love to hear from readers — it's one of the greatest joys of being a writer — so please get in touch. You can contact me via my website www.rosiehendry.com or my Facebook page Rosie Hendry Books, follow me on Twitter @hendry_rosie or on Instagram at rosiehendryauthor

If you have time and would like to share your

thoughts about *Secrets and Promises*, please leave a review. I read and appreciate each one and it's wonderful to hear what you think of the story. It helps me with my writing, knowing what readers enjoy and think, and also encourages other readers to try my books. Thank you!

With my warmest wishes,
Rosie

Acknowledgements

Many people helped me with this novel, from researching historical facts to giving their support during its writing and editing.

The research, which was such a great pleasure to do, gave me an insight into the lives of others during the First and Second World Wars. Grateful thanks to the Imperial War Museum in London, the 2nd Air Division Memorial Library in Norwich, and Neil Storey, who answered my questions about VAD's in Norfolk during WWI. The Poppy Line also allowed me to spend time in their wonderful Railway Cottage. Sheila Everett told me how her family sent eggs by post during the war, and Katherine Ball shared what it was like to live in a house made from old railway carriages. Finally, thank you to my parents for answering my many queries about life in wartime Norfolk.

Thank you to Melanie Underwood for her careful editing, and to Stuart Bache for the wonderful cover.

My many dear writing friends have been a tremendous support and have provided much fun and laughter too. You are all amazing and I am fortunate to have you in my life.

Lastly, thank you to my husband, David, for his understanding and loyalty, and to Isobel, too.

We do hope that you have enjoyed
reading this large print book.

Did you know that all of our titles
are available for purchase?

We publish a wide range of high
quality large print books including:
Romances, Mysteries, Classics
General Fiction
Non Fiction and Westerns

Special interest titles available in
large print are:
The Little Oxford Dictionary
Music Book, Song Book
Hymn Book, Service Book

Also available from us courtesy of
Oxford University Press:
Young Readers' Dictionary
(large print edition)
Young Readers' Thesaurus
(large print edition)

For further information or a free
brochure, please contact us at:
Ulverscroft Large Print Books Ltd.,
The Green, Bradgate Road, Anstey,
Leicester, LE7 7FU, England.
Tel: (00 44) **0116 236 4325**
Fax: (00 44) **0116 234 0205**

THE MOTHER'S DAY VICTORY

Rosie Hendry

Norfolk, 1940. As war rages on, the residents of Great Plumstead are doing all they can to help the war effort, from running the mobile canteen for the Women's Voluntary Service to organising clothing drives and collecting salvage. When a young German girl seeks refuge at the local hall, many welcome her with open arms, while others treat her with suspicion. But when the government try to send her back, it'll take the whole community to keep her safe from war.